STANDING

SIDEWAYS

STANDING SIDEWAYS

J. Lynn Bailey

For Jason and Michael.
Separated by heartbeats, bonded by eternity.

And,
For Mr. Joe

"To be gravely affected, one does not necessarily have to drink a long time nor take the quantities some of us have. This is particularly true of women. Potential female alcoholics often turn into the real thing and are gone beyond recall in a few years."

—*The Big Book of Alcoholics Anonymous*

Tracy and Poppy are worried about me.

It isn't because I haven't said more than ten words in the last thirty-three days to Tracy. And it isn't because my food consumption, according to Poppy, is like a rare sighting of the nene bird on the island of Maui. Of course, some would beg to differ that the nene bird is quite common to the locals and Maui visitors. Though, if you ask my dad or any immediate member of the Stone family, it's unusual, almost extinct and elusive, as we have yet to see the nene bird on Maui in the month of March during the last eight trips we've taken.

It's about Jasper's shirt.

"Liv, you haven't taken...*his*"—she can't bear to say his name—"shirt off in weeks."

Last week, it was two weeks. Tracy, my mother, pointed this out then, too.

With my earbuds balled at my side, I look at Tracy, unsure of what she expects me to do because, at this point, I'll do anything to shut her up.

I'll go see Dr. Elizabeth again, I want to say even though I kicked her out of the Jasper Grief Recovery Plan—unbeknownst to Tracy.

I'll pretend to burn his AC/DC shirt. Because this shirt is the only shirt that still has his scent.

"Liv, I'm worried." Tracy sits down on the couch next to me. The grooves, the tracks that represented a smile at one time, are deeper, more pronounced, making her face look long and heavy.

The dark circles under her eyes reflect sleepless days. Tracy is on night shift, a nurse, at Redwood Memorial Hospital. In my defense, it's a faded AC/DC shirt I found in Jasper's hamper the day he flew down to Los Angeles to visit our dad. I was about to wash it.

Biting whatever's left of my thumbnail, I look at my phone to see if there's a return text from Simon, but Tracy's hands catch my eye. I want to say, *You could use some food, Mom. You're shaking.* But I don't.

Poppy is staring out the front window of our old Victorian, her dyed flaming-red hair and tight curls perfect. She turns to face Tracy and me. "She's right, you know. You really ought to take Jasper's shirt off. And eat something, for God's sake, child." Poppy looks back at her daughter, her eyebrows furrow. Tracy's bottom lip starts to quiver, and I roll my eyes—maybe partly because I'm annoyed, but also because I don't know how to fix this. This is the third time I've seen Tracy's tears.

"Mom." But the word comes out rushed, hurried. As if she's the last person I want to be with right now. And maybe this is true, too.

Tracy shakes her head, as if trying to free us from our tragedy, placing her fingertips to her lips. Poppy glides across the room to Tracy, and she places her hands on her daughter's shoulders, kissing the top of her head. "Your mother's worried, Liv." Poppy's voice is calm, quiet. She continues to tell me my promiscuity with Simon James isn't the right way to get through this and how sex won't heal my heart. She tells me I've never acted like this and that this isn't me.

Things I already know.

I want to argue with her. Tell her she doesn't know what she's talking about because she's never been a twin. But I don't for two reasons.

1. You never argue with the matriarch of the family.

2. I don't want to freak Tracy out.

The last time I answered Poppy in front of her, she called the psychiatrist she works with at her home at ten o'clock at night.

Poppy, my grandmother, has been dead for nearly five years.

The pain is coming back again, this time from my chest. Not a hurt pain, but an ache, like my chest is about to crack open and explode with tears because I'm too prideful to allow them to leak from my eyes. I know it's time to take the white pill that's in my pocket.

Jasper used to fix things between Tracy and me. He used to be our words. The words we couldn't speak to each other.

I take my earbuds and push them into my ears as the ache deepens. I turn my music up, praying the bass will push me to Jupiter or Pluto—a solar system visit involving three hundred sixty-five days of stars and planets.

Anywhere but here.

Away from this couch.

Away from Tracy.

Leaving Belle's Hollow for good.

Maybe I can live in space where gravity is a pastime and my tears won't be able to fall.

Jasper used to say our mom and I were too much alike, and that was why we couldn't communicate.

I look to Tracy to see if she's allowing the tears or if she's pushing them back, like me. She's catching each one with her fingers. She's been working a lot of overtime since Jasper passed. I guess she does it for the same reason I do what I do—to forget our new reality for just a moment.

My phone chimes and it stops my music. It's a text from Simon. Transitory relief meets my chest and the pain subsides because I know relief is coming soon.

Simon: Meet u in 5. R spot?

"Got to go." I stand, sliding my phone into my pocket, praying Tracy doesn't say something like, *Please don't go. I need you.* Because I have to go. I have to leave her here in her pain because I can't handle life on life's terms right now.

Thank God she doesn't say anything.

I pause at the door, wanting to turn around and stare back at her, but I can't. Instead, I listen to the silence, her world and mine, and turn to face the outside. I bet she's stroking her coffee mug, her eyes transfixed on Jasper's chipped mug that reads, *Jasper Stone, Grand Teton National Park,* that Poppy bought both of us when she and Grandpa vacationed in the Grand Tetons. Tracy's nails, the chipped red paint reflecting great patient care and maybe lack of love for herself—wrap around the *S* and the *E* of Jasper's name on the mug.

Between us, the silence grows, making me feel more invisible than I have since Jasper and I were kids. Jasper was always her favorite. And it was all right for a long time. Besides, I was closest with Ned, my dad, until he decided one day, three years ago, that he found his twenty-four-year-old transplant secretary from Los Angeles more alluring than his family. *Transplant* in our area means, not born and raised in Belle's Hollow. Ned told us he was moving to Los Angeles. Who does that? Walks away from his legal practice and leaves his family behind to pick up the pieces? A dick. I used to call him a douche until I found out that *douche* was defined as a shower of water.

That, he is not.

Maybe that's why I'm still mad at Jasper for leaving for Los Angeles. He was trying to right our dad's mistakes, trying to see his point of view. If Jasper had never left for Los Angeles, this wouldn't have happened. This thought alone makes my insides run hollow, my throat grows cold, and the emptiness stick to my insides like black tar.

I make my way through town on foot and casually shove the white pill in my mouth. I walk up toward the green belt that surrounds Belle's Hollow. Our town was built inside a redwood forest on a hillside that slowly meanders down toward the ocean. Population: 5,000.

Jasper and I were raised here, explored every inch of Belle's with curiosity and love for the gentle giants. You couldn't do anything in Belle's without the entire world knowing. Just like when my dad was caught with his girlfriend in Breck's Tavern's restroom. Gloria Randall was there with her friends, Nancy Boeing and Stacy Lynch, who witnessed the whole thing.

My mom was pulling a double for Macy Landry who'd just had twins.

Nice guy, huh?

I hit Stop on the music as I approach the wall of trees and peer into darkness. It's just past four thirty p.m., but in the redwoods, it's always dark at their trunks.

"Hey."

I hear his voice and feel his hands come around my sides from behind. His nose nudges between my earlobe and my neck. The way he does this isn't soft. I know this has nothing to do with the sex we're about to have; it has everything to do with two people grieving for the same person.

"Nice shirt." He turns me around, pushing my waist-length, light-blonde hair to the side. A "dancer's figure" is how Tracy has always referred to my body. Where my breasts just barely fill an A cup and my hips are nothing but bone. I think it was her softer way of saying, *Shaped like a boy.*

Simon was Jasper's best friend.

After Tracy and I returned from Los Angeles, Simon and I ran into each other at Green's Pharmacy. He didn't look good, and I know I resembled something of a well-spun piece of blonde cloth with snakes for hair and flames of fire in my eyes, like some sort of Greek goddess, though an ugly one—whoever she is.

Somehow though, I feel closer to Simon than to anyone. Not that he and I are friends. In fact, I've loathed him at some points in my life. His sarcasm I want to smack right out of his head, and I'm pretty sure I did when we were ten.

He's the bad boy who lives disguised under sheets of armor—lanky, simple brown hair, blue eyes, and a few freckles on his nose. Nothing glaringly obvious indicates that his parents are almost nonexistent. That they might or might not work under the table as trimmers for the Steins and that they might or might not be using a white substance that keeps them up for days at a time to get their *work* done.

Tracy would have adopted Simon long ago if he had agreed. He's the boy who is always on the brink of a good decision, but in the last minute, he never pulls through. Like his body should be littered with ink, maybe a teardrop from his eye—though I don't think he's ever murdered anyone. No, I take that back. I know he's never murdered anyone. He's the boy who should smoke cigarettes behind Bob's at lunch and break. But he's never gone that path.

Simon James is your normal-looking boy with moments of clarity, which, I think, has kept him in a good position not to go to prison. And I think Jasper helped him stay on the right path—until now.

Every time we touch, I feel like he needs this as much as I do.

First, in the beginning, it was just our tongues that became entangled. It was simple and easy. And comforting. But, for some reason, we just needed more. Then, things progressed quite quickly.

5

Fingers pushing.

Arms squeezing.

Tongues everywhere.

And, now, we meet here four times a week to have sex.

I feel him harden against my stomach, and I look into his eyes. He's been crying. Since Jasper died, I've never seen the evidence that Simon James, resident bad boy/not bad boy, cry, but I've seen the aftermath. I don't ask if he's all right because I know he isn't.

I'd gladly give up my therapy appointment for Simon. I'd give up my therapy appointment with Dr. Elizabeth for him if I knew he would go. If I knew it would help. I'm not even sure his parents have come out of their drug-induced coma long enough to know that Jasper is dead.

His dull blue eyes, plagued with bad memories, prove the bright blue is sitting back, hidden behind the bruises that he carries underneath his clothes. The ones I see. And the dull blue tells a different story than what comes from his mouth. The darker story. The one he pretends Jasper and I don't know, the one he doesn't want us to know.

Simon would have an excuse.

I fell down the stairs.

I burned myself.

I ran into the wall.

Unbeknownst to me, he's already laid a blanket down. Part of this whole song and dance makes my stomach creep up into my throat. Simon has never done something like this in the two whole weeks we've been sleeping together. Like he's trying to make this a romantic thing. But it isn't. Not to me. It's an existential need. And sex seems to be the momentary cure, even at the risk of losing Simon as a friend. Even if it is at the risk of his girlfriend, Whitney Patmore, finding out. Even if it is at the risk of losing my dignity, my self-respect, or anything logical that goes along with casual sex.

I don't care.

I need to be fixed.

Catching his scent, pheromones launch into the air like arrows and attach themselves to me. I pull his lips to mine as he lowers me down onto the blanket.

Not that I can't see myself with Simon. I guess maybe I can— in a different life. Maybe.

While he puts the condom on, all I can think about is how much better I will feel once we're in the act. It takes all my thoughts, all my pain, away. But I know the sorrow, the guilt, the fallout from all this will follow. It always does. It will come quick and hard, and I'll wish I hadn't done it. I'll wish I'd have made a better decision. I'll leave Simon with the intentions of never meeting him again.

But come the morning, the bitter, painful monkey of despair will bite me again, and I'll feel like I don't have a choice.

And the whole sick cycle will begin again.

When I get home from my trail-of-bad-decisions escapade, the walk of shame and remorse in tow, Tracy has gone to work. In the kitchen, on the oven, is a plate of food and a note.

EAT!

LOVE, MOM

I grab the plate of food and pop it in the microwave. I lean against the counter and pull my phone from my back pocket. Cao has texted me seventeen—no, wait, eighteen times. Another just came in.

> Cao: If u don't text me back, I'm calling the police.

> Me: I'm fine.

Since we were three, Cao Smith has taken on the role of best friend and Belle's Hollow's resident ninja. Stan, her father, is the karate instructor in town, which makes it a no-brainer that Cao has every color belt, including the black.

Ed Sheeran-obsessed, closet chain-smoker, valedictorian nominee, Caltech bound, she's an overachiever with an outspoken way about her. She also has no idea about Simon. Part of me wants to tell her. I don't want to keep this black hole of a secret, like it's a nasty, dirty hush-hush that no one would believe because of how I carry myself. How well I play the character. That makes me feel more like a liar than thirty seconds ago. She'd probably laugh in my face. And then she'd cry because I had lost my virginity and didn't even tell her.

My phone chimes again.

Cao: K. See you tomorrow morning. P.S. Tomorrow will be great. Love u.

Tomorrow will be my first day back at school. I'm a senior at Belle's Hollow High. The therapist, Dr. Elizabeth, convinced Tracy it would be the healthy thing to do.

I don't much care for Dr. Elizabeth. She does this thing with her lips when she's listening to me. She shoves her lips into her mouth and slowly pulls them out. She does this three times in a row, and then she stops. A minute later, she does it again. Three times. Then, stops. And there's a brown mole she has just above the left side of her mouth. When she does the mouth thing, it makes the mole move, and I can't focus. It's distracting. I want to ask her if she's had the mole looked at by Dr. McGoldrick. I'm sure they're colleagues. I'm sure they've met before. I'm sure he's seen it on her face. We live in such a tiny town, so—scratch that idea. I'm sure the mole is fine.

The microwave dings, and I grab the plate of food and sit in our dark dining room alone. I keep it dark because it's different from how Jasper and I used to do it. He used to grab our food from the microwave, and I'd usually set the table. He'd have milk, and I'd have water. We'd FaceTime Tracy and quickly talk about our day.

The table is big, lonely, and quiet tonight. I stand up and walk to the cupboard. I grab a plate, a fork and knife, and fill a cup with milk. I carry it over and put it at the head of the table—where Jasper used to sit.

Tucking my hands between my legs, I will the feelings of sadness in my stomach to go away. I start to believe some kind of new truth about my current reality: It's going to be a long life.

"I'm glad you're back, Livia," my dead Grandma says.

2

"Didn't mean to startle you." Poppy crosses her arms and leans over Jasper's place, her pink floral housecoat shimmering in the dark.

"You can't sneak up on me like that. In the dark," I say quietly, still feeling the tiny needles prickling at my skin from the scare.

A long, heavy silence sits in the air like cigarette smoke, thick, unmoving, stifling.

"Do you like this boy?"

I roll my eyes, partly embarrassed that Poppy knows I'm sleeping with Simon. I wonder what she's seen between us, and I feel the color rush to my face. All I know is that it feels good. Not the sex part—well, sometimes—but it's more the rush of it all. The being touched in ways others don't touch me.

But I shrug an, *I guess*, just to get her off my back.

"Eat. I'm certain that's what the note says." Poppy leans in further, trying to catch my eye.

My eyes are fixated on the green leafy substance—also known as broccoli.

"Your grandfather and I lost a child." Her words are quick, diplomatic. "Before your mother was born. Tracy doesn't know about it."

I take my fork and poke the broccoli now, listening. I look up to see her take her fingers and gently pull her tight, tiny curls to the side of her forehead. Then, she takes both hands and pats her hair down. She used to do this as a nervous habit when she was alive.

Poppy pulls her eyebrows up, staring down at my food. "Your grandfather took it very hard." She smiles. "He processed his grief in some of the same ways you do. Searched for a fix, I suppose."

I set my fork down and wipe my mouth.

Our grandfather died when Jasper and I were barely ten. I remember riding shotgun. Jasper and I would share the front seat to the bowling alley where Grandpa would feed us French fries until our bellies popped and soda until we couldn't contain our laughter.

"I know you feel abandoned, Liv. By your father and now your brother. But this is out of your control. You won't feel less abandoned by seeking acceptance through another's affection." She pulls at her curls again.

Stop, I want to say.

I would just as soon eat my broccoli and not take on the woes of my sorrows that stare at me from across the table like a big blob of a monster.

"Hello?"

I hear Cao's voice.

I look to Jasper's spot before I answer Cao. Poppy is gone.

"There you are. Why are you sitting in the dark?" Cao asks, clearly not waiting for an answer because she continues, "Not that I am providing twenty-four hour surveillance or anything or that I'm your keeper or whatever, but you've got to let me know where you're at. I worry, Liv."

Cao walks to the fridge, grabs some grapes, and sits back down, opposite of Jasper's table setting. She looks at his spot and back to me, back to the table setting and back to me. Worry colors her face, but she doesn't ask any questions. She chews a few grapes and then leans back in her chair, crossing her arms.

"What?" She pushes her long black hair to the side and leans forward now.

Cao is eclectic in her choice of clothes. She'll wear just about anything. Her style makes her unique in her own right. From her jam pants to her leg warmers, she's a trendsetter. With her tiny waist and tall frame, she can squeeze into just about anything.

"You hate grapes," I say, putting my fork down.

"Why are you sitting in the dark?" She pops another in her mouth.

Maybe, sometimes, it's easier in the dark. When the world doesn't seem so loud, so chaotic.

"Why are you eating grapes?"

"Why are you sitting in the dark?"

"Quiet, I guess." I always give in first.

She spits her grape out into her hand. "Thank God you caved. My mom made some Chinese meal again for dinner. I gave most of it to Rosie." Their golden retriever. "I'm starving, and grapes were my only choice in your empty refrigerator."

Cao's mom, Beth, has been making traditional Chinese meals for the past three weeks, she tells me. She rests her head on the crook of her arm. "And"—she pauses—"they found my stash."

I want to say, *I told you so.*

"When?"

"Yesterday. They waited."

Cao chain-smokes out her upstairs bedroom window to prove cigarettes don't cause lung cancer. She claims it's a research study. But I think she got addicted somewhere along the way.

"My parents think I'm going through some sort of identity crisis. Adopted from China. White parents. Their words, not mine. 'We want you to feel like you can be yourself, baby. We feel like you might be using cigarettes to escape whatever you're feeling.'

"So, what does my mom do? She's been packing me rice in my lunch, and just this morning, I found Amy Tan's entire book collection on my desk. And the thing is, Amy Tan was born in Oakland. And, if they knew me, they'd know, I've already read all of Tan's books. You'd think, if they wanted me to embrace my culture, they'd send me to some camp in China or something. I don't know." She huffs. "That's me. Now, you." She stops. "Why are you really sitting in the dark, Liv?"

I want to tell her I'm sleeping with Simon. That I can't control it, and every time I walk away after being with him, I feel disgusted with myself, with the decisions I've made. Hence, it's easier to face myself in the dark. But I don't want to get into it. I don't have the energy.

I grab at my necklace pendant—the one with Jasper's thumbprint, the one my dad had made for Tracy and me when Jasper passed away—trying to hide behind the wall I've put up around me.

11

"You know, I don't think the AC/DC shirt will fly tomorrow at school with them canceling their show in Orange, California. Lots of kids at school are pissed."

I know what angle Cao is working. She's trying to help by not telling me that wearing my dead brother's shirt is weird, borderline creepfest. And that somehow I need to buck up and wear a different shirt to school tomorrow. I get that all from the look she is giving me right now.

"Wear that pink one," she insists. She tries to pop another grape in her mouth but quickly spits the whole piece into her hand again. "Nope. Just can't do it." Her face contorts.

Really, I didn't plan on wearing the shirt. I didn't have anything else planned because I don't care. So, I make a mental note not to wear the AC/DC shirt. Maybe I'll wear the pink one Cao suggested—and my necklace and pants, of course. Jeans. Maybe. But pants nonetheless.

"I'll pick you up for school tomorrow." I force the conversation that isn't coming easy on my end. "Wait, who drove you here?"

"My mom. She's in the car. Do you want me to stay with you tonight? I can grab my stuff."

I shake my head. "I'm good."

"You're not good, Liv. But I understand why. And I'm not going to push myself on you, but I will text you, and if you don't respond, I'm calling the police." She points her finger at me.

"I texted you back, and you still showed up."

"I know. I was bored at home." She bites her lip. "And worried."

I nod and grab her grapes, my plate, and then I head to the kitchen. Cao follows me. She leans against the counter, facing me, as I put the dishes in the dishwasher.

She looks back into the dining room—to Jasper's spot. "What about those?"

"Can you grab them?" I ask, turning on the disposal.

When I stare back at the empty spot, a sob chokes in my throat as Cao turns away from me, but I'm able to push through it before she returns.

Cao walks back in with the empty plate and the glass full of milk. Watching her carry the contents into the kitchen makes me feel like I'm losing my mind.

"Thanks," I say.

I wonder what Poppy thinks as I dump the milk down the drain. While growing up, Poppy salvaged everything. From leftover scraps of a quilt she'd made to her coffee grounds. And, when I say *leftover scraps*, I mean, a tiny piece of fabric that could be mistaken for confetti. And food. If you had two bites of a pork chop left, you'd better believe it would get eaten. Half of a piece of bread? Saved for a sandwich later. When Jasper and I spent the night at Poppy's, she would make sure we ate all our dinner. Even if it was liver and onions. Once, I tried to hide my mushy broccoli in my milk. She found it. Made me eat it. Four hours later.

"Earth to Liv. Are you there?" Cao sits on the counter.

I try to play it off, that I was paying attention the whole time.

"Are you still seeing that counselor? What's her name? Dr. Elizabeth?"

"No." I wipe the counter with a sponge. "So she can tell me that setting the table for my dead brother is not normal and that wearing his shirt for three weeks that I'm a borderline mental-institution-committal-straitjacket-live-in-a-loony-bin-forever candidate? No."

God, I could really use one of those little white pills right now.

"Maybe you should try a different counselor."

"Cao, I'm good, all right? I'm fine." My voice is louder than intended.

She lets out her ungodly cackle. The one she's known for. "That's seriously the biggest line of shit, Liv. Ever!" She stops the cackle on cue and stares me dead in the eyes. "You and I both know, you aren't 'fine.'" She uses her fingers to make air quotes. "Your freaking brother just died of something awful. Your twin, no less. It's been a month. You wear his favorite shirt."

She looks at Jasper's shirt I'm wearing with a spaghetti stain down the front. And I'm sure the smell is rancid, but I'm too scared to wash it because, when I wash it, his scent will go away forever. I quickly make a mental note to check his hamper for any other shirts that might be cleaner that I can wear.

Shit.

I'm crazy.

Cao interrupts the chaos in my head, "At what point are you going to admit that you're not fine?" She collapses her hands on the counter.

13

Cao talks a lot with her hands. She blames that on her parents being part Italian. I don't know how being Italian provides a direct correlation to talking with your hands, especially when one considers the nature versus nurture argument with her being adopted and all, but I don't question it.

"Look, it's my duty as your best friend to recognize what you can't see. Why don't we do what we used to? We'll head to Bob's Footlongs for dinner on Friday nights again. Go to the movies on Saturdays."

I want normalcy. I want to go back. Rewind to thirty-three days ago. Better yet, two days before when Jasper was at home. Safe. With me. Go back to Simon being just best friends with my brother and not a sex partner with me. Go back to when things were less messy. More average. Natural. Unforced.

"Yeah," I say as I look Cao in the eyes, now standing.

"Good, then. And no Jasper's shirt at school tomorrow."

"Yeah," I say again.

I collapse into bed. Usually, after my third night of no sleep, I can fall right to sleep. Exhausted, I pull the covers over the top of me, and the darkness settles around me. There are only the natural creaks of the house, and my senses feel more normal than they have in the past month.

Poppy used to make an appearance in my bedroom at night, but I told her it freaked me out. I don't know if it's the whole idea of ghosts, nighttime, or our old Victorian house that sways when the wind blows, but she hasn't made an appearance since then. I guess, too, I don't actually think of Poppy as a ghost or whatever. Not dead. Maybe a perception of my reality.

A hot sensation comes over me.

What if Poppy is just my crazy? Nobody else can see her. Nobody else can hear her. She only started appearing after Jasper died. What if I'm really delusional and I can't see that I'm delusional because I believe what I see? And what if what I see is really just a facade of what I think is there, and it's really not?

What if I'm going crazy?

My stomach grows queasy with this new thought information.

I roll over, facing my bedside table with the bottle of anti-anxiety medication, and I reach for them like it's natural. Like water.

I read the label, *Take one tablet every four hours, Livia Stone,* as if the bottle is speaking to me.

I almost expect the bottle to grow lips and give me another lecture in Dr. Elizabeth's tone with her holy-moly mole about self-care and sleep.

Too many kids at our school have grown addicted to medication. Some buy them on the streets. And, when I say *streets,* I mean, from the Gabriel Struvios of the world—the rich kids who live on the hill behind the gate. Rich kids are the biggest dealers. Some prescribed, some stolen from parents. Whatever they say about small towns, it's not true. In fact, alcohol and drug abuse grows more rapidly per capita in small towns. And this isn't based on data stored somewhere in a database; it's what I've seen.

I turn the bottle of pills so that the label faces my dresser, hoping that it will deter me from taking my normal two at night. I see them piled on top of each other, waiting to be swallowed.

If I take the whole bottle, would I stop breathing? Would I be able to see Jasper again?

A need deep inside me wants so badly to see him again. Just for a moment.

What if I take them? What if he comes to me just like Poppy? Who'd find me if I overdosed?

Most likely, my mother, and the thought of taking the pills quickly fades because I know Tracy couldn't handle losing both her children. One was hard enough. She doesn't think I can hear her quiet sobs, the ones she tries to hide from me in the shower in the early hours of the morning. Although Tracy and I have a strained relationship, I know she loves me. The past two weeks, I've woken up to her arm around my middle and her head buried into my back.

I glance back at the pills, reach for my phone, and set my alarm for school tomorrow.

I click off the light and pray for a few hours of sleep.

Tick-tock.

Tick-tock.

Tick-tock.

Tick…

I click on the light and take two of the white pills that Dr. Elizabeth prescribed.

Simon: C u @ school. Good luck.

A text from Simon comes in as I head to my white 2002 Honda Civic. The text isn't an I'm-sleeping-with-you text; it's clearly a boyfriend text. He's a boyfriend with a girlfriend. My stomach knots as I throw my backpack in the backseat. It's kind, and I know he means it that way. But it's too close. Too boyfriendly.

Me to Cao: Be there in five.

She makes fun of me because I can't—correction, *won't* type things like *B4, N, B, TY, LOL, ROTFL*. When I text, there needs to be full sentences and correct grammar. Call it the writer in me— the writer who hasn't written a word since Jasper passed.

Passed sounds so much better than dead. Dead seems final. Passed seems more open-ended. Like Poppy. Whether she's a figment of my imagination or not, she feels real. And, if she comes to me, why can't Jasper?

My phone chimes again as I take a left onto Main Street. The rain begins to fall. November has started, and so has the rain. Thinking it's Cao, I glance down at my phone just in case she's sick or something, which really makes my stomach double over. All the anticipation of my first day back without my brother builds up. I can't go to school without her.

What if she's sick?

Don't panic, I tell myself.

But it isn't a text from Cao.

It's from my dad.

Dad: Good luck at school today, Mimi. I love you.

His nickname for me. *Mimi.*

Jasper and I had a hard time calling each other by name when we were little. So, I was Me, and he was You. But Jasper never got the name You-You. Maybe it was too close to *yo-yo,* or maybe because it sounded funny.

The last time my dad texted me was the day of the funeral, and all it said was, *I love you, Mimi.*

I wanted to be angry that day. I didn't want him to come to the funeral—for selfish reasons, of course. He'd just lost a son after all. So, I didn't do the unthinkable. I didn't make a scene and tell him how much I hated him. I didn't call him a homewrecker. I didn't call him out on his cheating. I didn't even give him a nod when we caught each other's eye. I only stared.

The funeral was a blur to me. Gray. Spotty. Some parts, I remember, and some, I don't.

Dr. Elizabeth said that was shock. *"The body's natural response to trauma."*

I take my pendant and pull it across the chain as I turn onto Highway 36 and go down Weaverton Gulch. I weave through the redwood trees, darkness just beyond the tree line.

Jasper's service was closed casket and was held at Belle's Hollow First Christian. We aren't churchy, what with a cheating father and secrets of the Stone family swept under the rug. I was certain there was a qualifying application for having a funeral in God's house, right? The big white church in town with the steeple that can be seen from outer space. But they didn't ask for an application. They agreed we could have Jasper's service there.

Pastor Randy delivered the eulogy. The only words I can recall from Jasper's service, the ones that stuck for me anyway, were, "We were victims once. We will not be victims again."

Tracy and I planned the service, as if nothing had happened. As if we hadn't lost Jasper. It was like our endorphins had kicked in, and we were on autopilot. Tracy asked me to write the obituary, so I did. I managed to write it. *Managed* being the operative word. Operative means, functioning, having effect. I'm not really sure what I wrote, but I sent it to Goble's Mortuary—the only mortuary in town, family-owned since before Christ and down the street from Belle's Hollow High. I'm sure they did what mortuaries do to fix shitty obituaries.

Is there a class you can take on shitty obituary writing?

Shitty Obituary Writing 101 with Dr. Shitty.

Some emergency personnel from Los Angeles showed up in our sleepy little town. The responding police departments and several members of the FBI showed, too. I think the hardest part of the whole situation was making eye contact with one of the first responders as we followed Jasper's casket up to the front of the church that day. She made the face that people did when something awful happened. Her face contorted, her tears fell, and she reached for my hand. She spoke with brokenness. Though she tried to prove her conviction, she couldn't hold it together. And her look altogether made my insides turn shaky. Cold even.

Was what she saw on scene that awful?

Simon and Whitney showed. And that was really awkward. By the time of the service, we'd slept together only once. But it was hard, looking Whitney in the eye. And Simon was a mess. He hugged me and wouldn't let go. And I don't think it was out of love for me, but more for the emptiness my brother used to fill.

Before the funeral and after we got Jasper's body back from the FBI, he asked if he could see him, so I took him to the mortuary.

I'd never seen a boy cry so hard as he sat with Jasper. I stood back and let him have his time with his best friend. Watched as he shook because the tears didn't fill the need of his loss.

When his sobs became louder, I walked to him, placed my hand on his shoulder, sat, and rested my cheek on his back.

All I could muster was, "Same."

And all Simon could choke out was, "He's so cold, Liv."

I pull up to Cao's house, the crunch under my tires bringing me to the present moment.

She's bounding to the car as her mom, Beth, calls after her, "There's rice in your lunch, Cao. I packed you the chopsticks that you like, too. Love you." Beth pauses. "Hey, Liv." Her tone changes, becoming softer. She walks over to my window, reaches in, and pulls me into her.

She doesn't have to say anything that hasn't already been said. Beth has been at the house several times since Jasper's passing. She organized the biggest meal drop-off in Belle's Hollow history. Tracy and I were grateful—don't get me wrong—but I don't know how I'll ever eat chicken again.

Chicken and dumplings.

Stuffed chicken breast.

Chicken casserole.

Chicken roll-ups.

Garlic chicken.

Lemon chicken.

Baked chicken.

Chicken cordon bleu.

Chicken.

Puke.

It was as if Belle's Hollow had gotten together and said, *Let's make the Stones chicken for every meal.*

Chicken. Chicken. Chicken.

Over half of it is still in the freezer and will probably remain there for the next forty years.

Beth taps the hood of the Civic, and we drive back toward the Gulch.

"I don't know how much longer I can take this, Liv," Cao says while digging in her backpack. She pulls out her lunch, opens her rice container, rolls down her window, and dumps it out the window.

"I don't think that's good for the birds."

"It's a rumor. I Googled it." She shoves the empty container back in her lunch bag. "Birds actually love rice and eat it until migration. And"—Cao holds her phone to my face until the blue bird becomes blurry and the white is almost blinding—"Ed Sheeran liked my tweet!"

Cao has had a fascination with Ed since we were eleven. Last year, we went to one of his concerts in Sacramento, and I think she cried the entire time.

"When's the wedding?" I say, begging myself to return to the old me. But I feel like I'm inside out and upside down. Nothing feels right. And everything feels wrong.

"I'll let you know," she says, typing into her phone, her eyes blazing. "There. Now, it's on my Instagram page and retweeted, tagging him in it." Her tambourine earrings swing from side to side.

Cao leans down and reaches into her backpack again. She takes a set of chopsticks out, slides them out of the paper, and chucks them out the window.

That's littering, and there's a fine associated with that, I want to say but don't.

We're reaching the crest of the Gulch, and I notice a red jacket. And, by the height of the walker, I can tell he's male. Most girls our age aren't that tall.

"You know what my mom did? She bought the mondo pack of chopsticks at Costco, Liv. The mondo pack," she says, rolling her eyes. "She's never going to get it. I even told her that, if she stopped being so stereotypical with her attempts to have me embrace my culture, I'd never smoke another cigarette again."

I slow down.

Who walks the Gulch?

I peer through my windshield at the suicidal maniac. Not a local, but perhaps a local with a death wish?

Weaverton Gulch is a notorious life-taker—from car accidents to pedestrians being struck and killed by logging trucks. Locals all know this. So, I've narrowed it down to he's male, and he's not from our area.

Cao squeals and claps her hands to herself. "There he is! The infamous new British kid that Blog Heiress has been talking about. Slow down. Slow down." Her fingertips graze my arm. "Let's ask him if he needs a ride."

Dark red hair escapes through the back part of his beanie. His school bag rests at his side as he turns to face my car.

I slow to a crawl, so slow, I hear the rocks twist, turn, and pop underneath my tires. We follow him on the side of the road like creepers.

He stops.

I stop.

21

"Hey. You're the new kid, right? The one from the UK?" she asks.

"Kingston upon Hull actually." He's slow with his words. "It's like asking, *Are you from the United States?* But the United States is vast. Gigantic, right?" He pauses again, as if having a deep need to get the facts straight distracts him from the conversation at hand.

Cao's eyes slowly make their way from her phone and back to him. "Actually, the UK is roughly the same size as Oregon and half the size of California, so comparing the US to the UK is laughable when referring to dimensions." Cao takes a breath. "Oh, do you need a ride?"

His eyes grow wide. "I'm not even going to ask how you know that."

His light freckles, like stars making their debut at dusk, pepper the bridge of his nose. And he pronounces *ask* as if it starts with an *O* instead of an *A*, which gives my stomach a nervous feeling. It makes me feel like the time I was fourteen and watched *Sixteen Candles*, the part where Jake kisses Sam while sitting on the dining room table.

Un-fucking-believable.

"Oh, I'm Cao, and this is Livia."

"Daniel," he says, reaching in the car to shake our hands. His eyes get stuck on mine, as if I just appeared out of nowhere. "You know what? I really appreciate the offer, but I think I'm all right."

The rain has subsided, but the clouds are angry. I look up toward the sky through my front windshield.

"How do you know I'm not some psychopathic serial killer?" His eyes are still sizing me up.

I *almost* grin for two reasons. One, Jasper and I used to watch *Dateline* all the time. And, oftentimes, I'd end up on the floor of his bedroom because the creaks in our house got so loud, I was convinced someone was coming to murder us. Hence, psychopathic serial killer. Two, my face wants to smile at the way he tilts his head at me, a more concerned look on his face now, as if to say, *You shouldn't have stopped the car.*

"Psychopathic killers don't have red hair. Research suggests that their hair color usually varies between brown or black," Cao says, clearly bored with the conversation.

Daniel bites his lip. A small grin displays the dimples on either side of his mouth. "How do you know that?" He looks from me to Cao and back to Cao.

"I read an article in *Newsweek*." Cao stares down at her phone for a moment.

He finds my eyes again, and I pretend not to be staring at his cheek structure. His face is long and lean, more vertical than horizontal. I pretend not to stare at his eyes that look like two perfectly shaped blue topaz stones that God intended Daniel to have.

Daniel taps Cao's window. "See you at school."

I slowly accelerate back on the highway to head toward Belle's Hollow High.

Cao squeals. "I wonder if he knows Ed Sheeran." She grabs my arm. "I should ask him."

We take the freeway to Twelfth Street and pull into the high school.

Our phones chime at the same time.

"Update from Blog Heiress," Cao says, staring down at her screen. "She's been ruthless lately."

Blog Heiress

Well, Belle's Bitches, it's senior Livia Stone's first day back after a long hiatus from the loss of her brother and our classmate, Jasper Stone. That's all I'll say about that. Hopefully, someone can mend that broken heart. Wink, wink.

I feel my lungs constrict. Does Heiress know about Simon and me? My entire body grows clammy.

Okay, now to the juicy gossip. Mr. Lowery, tenured Chemistry

23

teacher, is going through a divorce because of his undoubted drinking problem. We shall see how this plays out. I don't know; if I was married to a fat cow, I'd probably drink, too.

P.S. The Chemistry questions for the final are accessible at www.k12.hschemistytest.questions. It seems Mr. Lowery can't be bothered with test questions for the final, as it interferes with cows and Jose Cuervo.

Next, and TOTALLY juicy! Mark Pattison, senior class slut, and—wait for it—Leah Moran—YES!—were caught having sex in the boys' locker room two nights ago after football practice. And, apparently, Mr. Pattison still had his football pads on, so says the night janitor. SAY WHAT? I know; I'm totally trippin' about that one, too.

If you need help studying for your AP English exam, have no worries because rumor has it that the hot new ginger boy from the UK has signed up to tutor you pitiful human beings who have nothing better to do with your time than take smart-kid classes. I'll bet the list of tutees will increase 100%, and they'll all be girls. Trust me, ladies, if you see him, you'll definitely want to get on that list. In fact, I'm not even taking the AP class, and I've signed up to be tutored in French, if you know what I mean. :)

That's it for now. Happy first day of November!

Later, bitches.

BeLHo

C ao and I take our seats closest to the door, front row, in Mr. Joe's AP English.

Mr. Joe, Joe Foreman, prefers that we call him Joe or Mr. Joe. Not Mr. Foreman.

"Absolutely, under no circumstances, do you call me Mr. Foreman. He was an asshole; I'm not." Mr. Joe's words, not mine.

He's new to Belle's Hollow High and new to Belle's Hollow. Fresh meat is what Cao calls him—or rather, dead meat because most of the faculty at Belle's has been teaching here since circa 1800. Baby boomers not willing to let go, I guess. Joe's maybe twenty-four. His approach is different, unique. Some of the faculty got bent out of shape when they heard us call him Joe.

My classroom, my rules, was his response when Blog Heiress interviewed him toward the beginning of the year. He uses phrases like *brah, yo, sames, killin' it, hashtag,* and *mad*—as in *very*—all in the correct context. And he uses contemporary music to convey his approach to critical thinking. He's kinda cool.

"Livia." Mr. Joe approaches me.

Smile, Liv.

I know my face probably looks awkward. Pained even. A forced smile and an eerie feeling in my stomach, I look up at Mr. Joe.

"I'm so sorry for your loss. I'd like to talk to you after class." His horn-rimmed glasses, almost metallic in color, pick up the glare of the fluorescent lights above.

I muffle a noise of acknowledgment.

Students trickle in. Kids who have gone to school with Jasper and me since we were five. Many attended the funeral. Hell, most of Belle's Hollow attended the funeral. Stores shut down to attend.

But I get it. Some don't know what to say. Some make eye contact as they come in and give a nod.

Please just ignore me, I beg silently.

Some put their heads down and walk by. Some are lost in their electronic world of fake facades.

I'm the sister of a dead twin. Who wants to acknowledge that?

They don't know me as Livia Stone. They know me as Livia and Jasper Stone, half of a set of twins. Yet I'm the new Liv, the one who sleeps with a boy who has a girlfriend and hides it from her best friend.

The vacant space between my liver and large intestine, also known as my stomach, grows the preexisting knot that's been there for a month. The lonely one.

The knot I can't shake. I can't take enough pills to make it go away.

The knot that aches when I see a picture of Jasper.

The knot that aches when I walk past his room in the morning, waiting for him to say, "Knuckles"—another charming nickname my brother gave me—"get in the shower."

I guess, when I realize he's not coming back, the knot grows, twists, and contorts, pissing off my stomach and my heart.

Benny Jacobs, Landry Pendleton, and Alicia Abbott make it down my row and touch my shoulder. Alicia murmurs something under her breath. I'm sure they're words of condolence. Words I've heard before. Standard words when someone dies.

Why do people even say these words? Because they feel the need to say something to ease their minds? Like it's their unspoken duty?

Livia Stone, brother died. Wish her well. Done. Check mark.

And then Miranda Stein enters the room. No, no, she sashays into the room, as if she's expecting "Hail to the Chief" to play over the loudspeaker. Her nose is turned slightly up though still buried in her phone. Really, I think it takes a special skill to do that. Her all-seeing tentacles take snapshots of her surroundings, the ones buried under her perfectly pink tracksuit.

28

Also, Cao and I agree that, when God created Miranda Stein, he said, *Here, do something with this.*

Resident mean girl.

Devil in a pink tracksuit.

"Miranda, phone away, or it's mine," Mr. Joe says, his light-brown corduroy pants pressing against his desk as he leans.

Miranda turns on her right heel, a look of bewilderment on her face. "Mr. Foreman—I mean, Mr. Joe, I was just finishing a text to my mother—"

Mr. Joe's expression is cool. He knows what she's doing as he comes around his desk and sits on the front part. "Graveyard." He nods toward the box by the classroom door.

The Graveyard is where our phones go when we've abused the privilege to use them between the four tiny walls known as our classroom. A place they die for fifty minutes when we can't seem to keep from sliding our fingers across the screen. A habitual rule-follower, I've never had to put my phone in the Graveyard, but since I'm changing my ways apparently—sleeping with another girl's boyfriend—I imagine my time will be coming soon.

Miranda with her perfect lips in a perfect O that match her perfectly pink top and flats in a coordinating lipstick and eye shadow turns to devilish red as her face contorts to a demonic stare. Nobody, except for Mr. Joe, has ever stepped up to the plate like this.

Everybody knows that Mr. Stein, Miranda's dad, is the biggest pot grower in Humboldt County. He's built our gymnasium and revamped our football field that includes stadium seating and a rain cover. Though Miranda will take it to the grave that he does construction in southern Humboldt. That's code for locals in the green game.

And absolutely nobody stands up to Miranda because they don't want to deal with her shit or feel her wrath. Including me.

But I will admit, she stopped by when Jasper died—not out of the goodness of her heart. Because people who do that must require a heart. Hers is gone. Left the building. Vacated the premises. She pulled up in a black stretch limo—weren't those a thing in the '90s?—and Tracy thought it might be the President. Again.

Tracy might have thought this because the President of the United States had shown up at our house, unannounced. The Feds had arranged for the President to meet those of us affected by what had happened a month ago at an undisclosed location somewhere in LA. So, Tracy and I had stayed home.

The President doesn't take, *Thanks, but no, thanks,* very well. So, lo and behold, he had shown up at our doorstep with what looked like an entire police brigade. According to Ester Williams, self-appointed news/gossip guru, Secret Service shut down half of Belle's Hollow. It really wasn't necessary—not the shutting down of the town, but the showing up part. Before the President had entered our home, Secret Service had done a sweep of the house while Tracy and I stood there, staring, hands up. Why we'd held our hands up, I'll never know. I guess it's the natural thing to do when you see men and women in black suits entering your home. Jasper would have enjoyed it. Asked the Secret Service questions about their jobs, classified information, what they thought about WikiLeaks, Area 51, America's Stonehenge.

And, if having a surprise visit from the President wasn't bad enough, Miranda showed up, unannounced, at our house in her cheesy presidential limo after Jasper passed with a freaking chicken.

A chicken revolution. Viva la chicken! Taking over homes across the world. Please, God, no more chicken.

Tracy thanked her and sent her on her way. And, like everyone else, it was considered kind, but from her, it was not nice enough to be trusted. Miranda Stein always has ulterior motives.

P.S. Miranda is the CEO of the Virgin Club—as known to us students, but better known to teachers and staff as the Healthy Choices Club. But everyone knows it's a joke. I bet, now, they'd burn my application on the spot. Or God would. Not that I want to join because I don't. Though Miranda's prim and proper ways—manners, brains, words—suggest one thing, her attire suggests another. With her skirts just shy of the fingertip rule and her tiny butt-hugging shorts that slide up her crack during track practice, her provocativeness is so passive-aggressive, and it proves to be evil. She's just one decision shy of falling from her throne leadership with the rumors we hear via Blog Heiress about her and boyfriend, Anthony, a boy who attends Eureka High School, thirty minutes north of here.

The classroom phone rings, bringing me back to reality. Mr. Joe answers as Miranda takes her seat, her demonic death stare blowing holes in Mr. Joe's face.

"Livia?" Mr. Joe's tone is louder than usual. "Did you hear what I said?"

Lost in Miranda Stein, I try to register what Mr. Joe said. I shake my head because I'm not sure what he just said.

Does grief cause hearing loss?

Poppy's voice is loud. "Your attention span is the problem, not your hearing, Livia."

Poppy is nowhere in sight, and I hate when she does this—this thing where she projects her voice, but she's nowhere to be seen.

"Mrs. Brimm wants to see you in her office. Take a hall pass. Come back to class when you're done."

Reluctantly, I pull myself from the comfort of my desk and look to Cao, who's motioning me toward her.

She whispers in my ear, "Routine protocol for counselors. Dead sibling. Chat about it. A box to check. Don't stress."

I try to gather my uniformed, prepared response for Mrs. Brimm. My stomach clenches on the pieces of last night's dinner. She'll give me the look the Have-Nots do.

The Have-Nots—those I haven't seen since Jasper's passing.

The Haves—those I have seen.

Mrs. Brimm will tell me she's extremely sorry for my loss. She'll ask me a variety of questions, probably about self-harm, grief. She'll do this to protect her job, not me. Maybe I'll tell her about the pills on my nightstand. But maybe I won't. I probably won't because, in a matter of seconds, I'm no longer heading to the office but instead to the janitor's closet.

I'll wait here until the bell rings, I tell myself.

I'll explain to Mr. Joe that time ran out with Mrs. Brimm. Then, I'll tell him I don't have time to talk because I'm too distraught over my conversation with Mrs. Brimm. Knowing him, he'll arrange a later time for us to speak because he cares about his students. Mrs. Brimm is at Belle's Hollow High to collect a paycheck.

I take a sharp left into building B. I open the door to the janitor's closet and shut it behind me. I feel around for a light. It would have been smart of me to grab my phone from my backpack before I left. But there was no way I was going to be able to get it past Hawk Eyes—Mr. Joe.

I feel around and find a bucket. Carefully I turn it upside down. Resting my back against a shelf, I take in a deep breath as the tears start to sting my eyes. My chest grows heavy, and all I want to do is cry. This sort of tear debacle comes and goes quite a bit.

Dr. Elizabeth says I need to breathe through it.

You know what I want to say to her?

Sex. That helps. A lot of sex. It helps a lot with the tears. You should try it, Dr. Elizabeth. You're stiff as a board.

I want to text Simon. Immediately, I want him to come to the closet.

Stupid phone.

But, before I can think another thought, the door opens and closes quickly.

Shit.

Please, God, don't let it be Mr. Lee.

He's the sixty-eight-year-old janitor who has been at Belle's Hollow High since Tracy and my dad were freshmen here.

And I'd like to believe that I wouldn't be responsible if I scared him to death, and he had a heart attack. But I'd probably be blamed for murder.

Headline: *Grieving Twin Murders Janitor with Scare Tactic.*

The tall, dark figure punches the door as hard as he/she can.

Nope. Not Mr. Lee. He doesn't pack that much punch.

I'm assuming the person is male because I don't think a female could hit that hard unless she was Ronda Rousey.

"Fuck!" he whisper-yells. He—confirming my suspicions of a male—pronounces *fuck* like there was an *O* in it and not a *U*. He punches the door.

It's Daniel—aka lone hiker on the Gulch.

Part of me prays he'll walk out once his tirade is over. The other part of me is unsure and curious.

"Same," I whisper from my bucket that's becoming a nuisance.

"Bloody hell!" Daniel rips around and stares in my direction. "Who's there?"

Hold your breath.

Don't say a word.

I need to say a word. I just scared him half to death, I answer myself.

But part of me doesn't care—the disconnected part of me.

"This was my closet first," I whisper.

I can now make out his outline. His shoulders lower, and his breathing becomes paced, as if me being a girl changes things.

"I'm sorry, but it isn't. I called dibs on it quite some time ago." He runs a hand through his hair. "Besides, you haven't recently been in here to stake your claim, so I took over."

I've never once set foot in the janitor's closet until this morning, but I'm trying to prove a point. "I call override dibs. Been at Belle's Hollow since freshman year. I have ancestral rights. It overrides your *quite some time ago*."

"What? You make up the rules as you see fit?"

I can see him leaning against the shelving, still trying to relax.

J. Lynn Bailey

"I don't make rules, Daniel. It's written as a law in the constitution of Belle's Hollow High." I shrug. "You can see it for yourself. It's on a scroll, hidden in the school's trophy case." I'm totally lying. And I can't explain why this is pouring from my mouth.

"You're a liar, Livia."

How does he know who I am? Can he see me somehow?

I let him sweat the silence. Because I have no idea what I'm going to say next. He's called my bluff. "Truce?"

He casually pulls the string for the light, and the tiny closet illuminates. He's even taller than I remember from this morning. His hair is a darker red with his beanie off. His chest is broad, as if he works out to keep in shape. But it could be muscles or a rare chest deformity. I've seen those on the Discovery Channel. He's still wearing the same red jacket, though it's unzipped now.

"Livia Stone," Daniel says in an accusatory tone. "Since you don't know where the light is, I call your bluff and your override dibs. And I'll raise you rights for next week. But I'll share today since today is your first day back." His next words are paced, calculated, well thought out. "I won't give you the words I'm certain you're used to hearing." Daniel's words are hushed. "But, for what it's worth, I'm sorry about what happened to your brother."

He said *brother* like *brotha*. As if Jasper were just a friend.

That removes me only momentarily from my grief, and I like the way this makes me feel. Like, just for a millisecond, I can eat minestrone soup and read a book and pretend like life hasn't been flipped upside down, as if Jasper never died or he never lived. Relief rushes through me, but the sinking feeling rubs up against my shoulder, forewarning my grief's return.

"Jasper. His name is Jasper," I say. Saying *is* rather than *was* confirms I'm still his twin. But he's still dead.

And nothing has changed. And everything has changed.

He leans back, still waiting for me to continue. Patient.

The moment of silence seems to sting and drag on.

"What was he like? Jasper, I mean."

The bell rings, but neither of us moves. Daniel clicks off the light.

Nobody has asked that before. Maybe it's because everyone knew Jasper, or maybe it's because they didn't want to ask a

34

question that would beg for an answer that perhaps they didn't want to hear.

Jasper hasn't become a memory yet. His hands. His heart. His laugh. I can still hear it, and this makes my eyes sting.

But I give Daniel the most honest answer I have, "Half of me. And only the good parts."

Because I think of the unsavory things I've done in the past month. The decisions I've made, not like the Livia and Jasper Stone I used to be. The meticulous, soon-to-be Ivy Leaguer whose passion for achievement and dream-chasing was lost between October 1 and now.

"I lost my dignity on Hawthorne Hill."

Shut up, Liv.

My mouth betrays me as I continue, "I lost my self-worth between here and LA. And I think I lost my pride on purpose." I begin to chew on my thumb.

Jasper always used to slap my hand away. He hated the fact that I bit my nails. I do, too, but I can't help it.

I reach for the light and click it on to see Daniel's face. "Why are you here in Belle's Hollow?"

The tardy bell rings, signifying to students that those late will sit in detention.

"You'll need to leave first. Just so the rumors don't start. Not about *us*, but about who owns claim over this closet." He smirks.

I see the scar under his right eye as he pushes the door open for me, shedding in more light.

"It would be dumb if this turned into a custody battle."

"You didn't answer my question." I stay seated and dagger myself to death with the *whys* of what I just told him.

"Another conversation for another time." His lips are in a thin red line.

I stand and step out into the light of the hallway. I look back at him. "I'll send an eviction notice."

"And I'll see you in detention." He lets the door slowly shut in front of him.

What was I thinking?

I kick myself on the way back to Mr. Joe's to collect my things.

"I lost my dignity on Hawthorne Hill."

Christ. I'm sure he couldn't wait to get this loon—me—out of that closet.

I peek my head in, but the classroom is empty—except for Mr. Joe.

"You're late." He doesn't look up. He continues to work at his desk on his computer.

I sigh and push myself through the door. "Sorry. Got caught up with Mrs. Brimm," I lie.

He stops typing. "No, you didn't. You didn't go, Liv."

Why can't I stop lying?

I sit down because Mr. Joe, I've learned, likes to talk. And this is going to be a long one.

He takes off his glasses and comes around the side of his desk to sit on the front part. "Livia, you're an amazing writer. You're smart." He pinches the bridge of his nose and closes his eyes. "I heard back from Dr. Livingston at Harvey College, Liv. He's really impressed with your sample we sent him. He'd like to see more."

We sent him a writing sample of mine during the summer, one I totally forgot about.

"I believe in you. But what I care more about is your well-being. The person you are versus the student with all this potential." He's not using slang, so I know he's serious. Not that he's ever not serious, but sometimes, he just tends to be more *not* serious. Now isn't one of those times.

"Look, I told him what happened with your brother. And, of course, he'd already heard." Mr. Joe pauses. "Liv, there's a lot you need to make up in this course." He drums his fingers on his desk. "I'm wondering—"

"What? You want to give up on me? Because my brother died, you think I can't hack this? The pressure of getting into college and everything else?"

Mr. Joe is taken aback.

Hell, I'm taken aback.

"No. Actually, quite the opposite. You need a tutor to pass this class, and I will set aside my personal time to work on your essays for Harvey. And maybe we can do an additional essay if Dr. Livingston would be willing to give us feedback." He crosses his arms. "It's a lot of work. But I have no doubt in my mind that you'll meet the challenges set out in front of you. But let's be clear, Liv. You give me one hundred percent, and I'll give you one hundred percent. And absolutely no lying. Or the agreement is off." He extends his hand. "Fair?"

"Yeah, fair." I shake on it.

Mr. Joe walks back around his desk. He slides his finger across the stack of papers. "You need to get one paper to me tomorrow, so I can send it off to Dr. Livingston. I'll also double count it for the class. Can you do that?"

"Yes."

"Here." He hands me a slip of paper. "Get to class." It's an excuse for being late to second period.

"Thanks," I manage to say and grab my bag.

"You're welcome. And, Livia?"

I stop and turn around.

"I know what you're going through. I know what loss feels like."

I nod. We all know about Mr. Joe's heartbreak.

He stares at me. *The tragedy of life is not death but what we let die inside of us while we live.*

"Norman Cousins," I say, tilting my head.

"Brah," he says as a smile pulls at the corners of his mouth. But it quickly disappears as he looks back down at his paperwork— a scapegoat for the sadness I see that creeps in and around his eyes. He carelessly bites his lower lip.

As if the quote were written for Mr. Joe and me. As if Mr. Joe's tone and his pitch were the absolute truth of Mr. Cousins's intent. Because, when Mr. Joe said it, I felt every single word.

"Now, go. You're already late." He shoos me away.

I don't see Daniel for the rest of the day, and I'm grateful. I know I will inevitably have to face him. He'll probably ask what I meant but maybe not. I hope not.

It's the end of fifth period, and I'm waiting in the handicap stall in building B for Cao.

I get a text from Simon.

Simon: Hawthorne Hill. After school?

My body fills with anguish and need. Every inch of me, my skin creeps, as if ants are holding it hostage just above my muscles. My grief is not only matched by Simon's, but it's also understood in ways that others cannot understand. And, in some weird, sick way, it makes the loss so much less. It makes the heart ache less.

Me: Yes.

"Nana-nana-boo-boo, I can't see you," Cao says.

"Seriously, that was, like, the second grade. I'm in the handicap stall, like you asked me to be." I roll my eyes.

Cao laughs and opens the door to the stall.

"I need to tell you something," I say. All of a sudden, I need to clear the air with her about Simon.

"Yeah, I know; it's obvious." She slips her phone back into her pocket but not before it chimes. She looks at the text. "Damn it, Mother. Enough with the Chinese shit."

I run my fingers through my hair, and the bile gathers in my throat, ready for takeoff. "I'm sleeping with Simon."

Cao slowly looks from her phone. "Wait. Hold the food cart. What?"

I chew on the inside of my lip. My eyes dance from the toilet to the stall door and back again. Cao looks like I just told her that I'm pregnant. I might as well have.

In all our years of friendship, I've never seen her speechless.

"Please, say something, Cao. Please."

She hears the desperation in my voice, the need to feel okay, the need to feel the sense of normalcy I felt just a month ago.

"Well, there goes the city."

Cao has a knack for taking cliché sayings and changing the words—whether on purpose or not, I'm not sure.

"There goes the neighborhood," I clarify, still in shock that I've finally told someone, someone who isn't red-haired and blue-eyed and from the UK—or Hull.

Poppy: "Lying by omission is still lying."

Poppy, seriously.

"Liv, you have got to put a stop to this. He's got a girlfriend. A friend of yours."

Friend *might be a strong word for Whitney and me*, I try to justify.

Poppy: "Justifying your behavior is for the goats!"

Poppy, would you please just be quiet for a minute? I can't think.

Cao reaches for my hand. "Look, I've done a lot of reading up on grief lately, and you're trying to fill a need. A void. I know Simon was extremely close with Jasper. But this isn't going to bring him back." She gently rubs the skin between my thumb and index finger.

I know.

And yet I keep lying.

I know.

And yet I continue to make the wrong decisions.

I know.

And yet I seem to push the right ideas out of the way. The good ones. The solid ones. And pull the wrong ideas, the bad decisions, back into the forefront of my mind.

"I know," I say but for my personal reassurance and justification.

But do I? Do I really know? Or is this just a vice that grieving people use to protect whatever truth they want to believe?

"Come on. Let's go to Bob's and grab some cheese fries and a large Cherry Coke on the boulders."

"Rocks," I say as she puts her hand in mine.

Bob's Footlongs is the hot dog, burger, cheesy fries capital of the world, according to anyone who steps foot inside.

Right across the street from the high school, Bob's is where I've worked for the past year and has been in existence since the 1950s. The look, orange-and-white stripes, and the logo, a wiener dog in a bun, are just a few of the rarities that makes Bob's…well, Bob's. We take orders with a pen and paper. Cash and local checks only. And the cash registers are considered antiques. It's like stepping back in time when customers come in. It has Belle's Hollow High memorabilia dating back to the 1950s with yearbook pictures, football trophies, and even an award for Humboldt County's Best Eatery in 2006. From fishing pictures to family photos of Linda's, the owner's family, both past and present, it's a fixture in Belle's Hollow. It's where you can get hush puppies and nacho dogs and frozen burritos. And they make the best shakes in the county.

The old-fashioned cowbell that hangs from the front door to signify a new customer rings as Cao and I walk in.

The Have-Nots, I tell myself. Not all of them, but some. Panic sets in my chest.

Linda turns from the fry station and gives me a toothy grin. She doesn't come over to hug me because Linda isn't the warm and fuzzy type. She and Al, her husband, attended the funeral. She hugged me then, tears leaking from her eyes. That was enough.

I look over at Jasper's spot, the one in the back corner by the window next to the big stuffed husky that's suspended from the ceiling. There's a tiny plaque there. Though I can't read the writing, the plaque is new, and I see his picture.

Fuck.

Linda gives me a wink as Whitney approaches us from behind the counter.

Fuck again.

I feel Cao's hand tighten around mine.

Don't run.

"Hey, Liv, Cao," she says the way most Haves say. It's a cross between a singsong voice and a try-to-act-chipper tone. "What can I get you?" She flips to an empty white page on her notepad.

Her long blonde ponytail rests on her shoulder while her innocent blue eyes stare back at me. I want to tell her I'm sorry and that I can't control myself.

"When did you start working here, Whit?" Cao removes her hand from mine, knowing I have nowhere to run now.

"Linda needed some help with Liv gone." She's awkward about it, as if she's taken my job or something.

"Well, that's fantastic," I blurt out loudly. Clumsily. Like I'm totally comfortable with the situation when I'm not. Like I have something to hide. And this really makes me look like an ass.

There's a really loud silence between us, and I know I should follow up with something else because my *fantastic* comment is the one that created the weirdness.

Whitney pulls her lips inward and pops them out to say, "Cheese fries?"

Cao pulls out a ten-dollar bill. "And a large Coke, please."

Whitney gives us our Coke, and we go sit while we wait for our order.

Cao stares at me. Hard.

"What?"

She shrugs and puts her lips around the straw, batting her long black eyelashes, her eyes barely visible. "Remember when we were twelve, and we found a half-smoked cigarette in front of the movie theater?"

Where's she going with this?

I pull the Coke to my lips and take a sip while Cao takes the straw's paper and wraps it around her finger.

"We bought matches at Hollow's Grocery and then went to Rohner Park, behind the skating rink, and to the trees to smoke it."

I take another long sip of Coke, so I don't have to answer her question.

"You told me not to do it. That it was a bad decision. You recited the facts on teen smoking and cancer rates and what cigarettes do to our insides. But I did it anyway. I smoked the entire thing by myself." Cao's looking down at the wrapper now. "You've always been the good decision-maker, Liv. And, now that the cards are flipped, I don't know how to help you." She pauses. "How do I help you come back from this?"

Cao has never been a crier. Dramatic, yes. But tears? Never.

Until now.

I roll my eyes. I'm frustrated with myself because I've done this to her. I've caused these tears, and I don't know how to make this right. And I don't know how she can help.

"You can stop crying. That would help."

"I'm not crying. My eyes are leaking. It's a condition I have."

I try not to laugh. "Yeah? What's that? And since when?" My voice is softer this time.

"There's a name for it. I just don't remember it." Cao takes a napkin to her nose and blows. "What if you get pregnant?" Cao's eyes make their way across the table to me.

My face turns hot, my hands sweaty.

Condoms, I think.

And then I remember the statistics on condoms. In 2010, forty-two percent of unintended pregnancies in California resulted in births, and forty-five percent in abortions. The remainder resulted in miscarriages. The teen pregnancy rate in California was fifty-four per one thousand women, aged fifteen to nineteen in 2011. The national rate was fifty-two per one thousand. This is all according to The Guttmacher Institute. I Googled it soon after Simon and I started our dirty secret.

Whitney approaches our table with our cheese fries. My gut twists into tiny pieces, littering them all over the chair where I'm sitting. If my guilt doesn't eat me alive, my conscience will. The floral scent that trails her makes me wonder if Simon likes her scent. I don't wear a scent—unless you consider Jasper's AC/DC shirt, and that's probably not a good one.

Whitney turns to leave.

She stops.

Turns back around.

Sighs.

"Liv, can I talk to you in private, please?"

I stand and follow Whitney toward the pinball machine.

My stomach is dancing in circles, and I prepare myself for the punch she might throw. I picture the final fight between Apollo Creed and Rocky—Jasper's favorite Rocky movie.

I've never asked Simon if he and Whit have ever had sex. It didn't seem like a pertinent question at the time. And, now, it seems like the only question I need answering.

Please, God, don't let me ask it.

I look back at Cao, who looks like death.

I look back to Whitney. "What is it, Whit?"

Please don't let this end badly.

"I know you're going through an unimaginable time right now." She twists her fingers together uncomfortably.

Please don't be nice to me.

She looks down at her heart-shaped ring. Probably one that Simon gave her.

Dear God.

Here.

It.

Comes.

I hold my breath.

"It's hard to think about anything else. I know that Simon is having a really rough time with it, too." She eyes me like an eagle now, taking in my every movement. Eye twitch.

I imagine her sitting across the table from me in a dark room. A bright lamp in my face, and her incessant questioning only worsens in my hypothetical situation.

Why did you sleep with my boyfriend?

Are you a whore?

Did he wear a condom?

Are you on birth control?

WTF?

"Liv?"

I look at Whitney. My heart is pounding out of my chest. "Sorry. What?"

"I said, I'd like to talk about Simon." Her words are clear. Her tone justified.

I play dumb. "About what?" I hear the gush of blood pumping, pushing through my ears.

"It's his birthday. And I was wondering…look, I know it's the last thing you're thinking about. But I was wondering if you had any pictures of Simon and Jasper together that you could loan me for the party? I promise, I will get them back to you in perfect condition."

Wait.

What?

"What?"

"A party. A surprise party for Simon."

I've borrowed your boyfriend, and you want to borrow pictures.

"Yeah, of course. I'll look." Abruptly, I turn and walk toward Cao, whose panic has subsided with my steps toward her, as I try my best not to pee my pants. Looking at Whitney was killing me, and I couldn't do it anymore.

"I think I almost peed my pants," Cao says as I sit down.

"Me, too!"

I look back toward Whitney, who is walking back toward the counter.

"She asked for pictures of Jasper and Simon."

Cao puts her fingers to her temples, her eyes searching the table. "I thought I was going to have to get all Jackie Chan or something."

"Cao—"

She continues rambling on about a dead conscience, Chan superpowers, and whatever.

46

"Cao," I say louder.

Rambling still.

"Cao!" I whisper-yell. "She asked about pictures for a surprise party for Simon."

"Party for Simon?" She stops.

We're both silent as we lean back in our booth, not in the mood for cheese fries anymore.

"Wow, this is going to be really awkward," she says.

"I know."

I drop Cao off at home with no sign of Daniel along the way.

"This thing with Simon is nothing but trouble, Liv," she says before she shuts the car door. "Teen pregnancy rates are higher than they've been. Plus, the girlfriend factor. Plus, STDs—oh my God." She shakes her head.

"Bye, Cao."

Before I pull away from her drive, my phone chirps.

It's a text from Simon.

Simon: Ran into Old Man Morris. He didn't know about Jas. I told him.

I throw my phone into the passenger seat and make my way home to change for work. I have the five to nine p.m. shift tonight. My phone chirps again.

Simon: Hawthorne, right?

Shit. I forgot I agreed to meet him after school today. Really, what I want to do is just curl up in Jasper's AC/DC shirt—my shirt now—and listen to his Low and Slow playlist.

I grab my phone.

Me: Rain check?

Simon: 2 late.

What?

I pull into our driveway. Our restored Victorian sits on Tenth Street and high enough above town that it overlooks Belle's Hollow. Everyone knows the one and only palm tree in Belle's is located just to the right of our house. I imagine my parents know who planted it when they bought the place back before Jas and I were born.

Why plant a palm tree in Northern California where it rains eighty percent of the time?

Jasper's favorite spot was just under the palm at ten p.m. sharp.

He'd ponder.

He'd think.

He'd listen to music.

I see Simon is sitting in Jasper's spot—under the palm tree—and my stomach doubles over because, for a second, I think it's Jasper. That he's alive, and this has all just been an awful, sick dream—him being dead—and not a twist in fate.

Too late, Simon said.

Makes sense now.

I quietly let my car door pull shut and throw my bag over my shoulder. As I approach him, he doesn't move. His black sunglasses shield his eyes from the permanent fog layer that seems to drift in and out from the ocean, almost never allowing the sun to make its debut.

His hands are clasped in front of him, and he's staring out over Belle's.

"Hey," I say as I walk over and sit beside him.

He doesn't say anything.

Our backs resting against the strong, solid wood of the palm, we sigh together, uniformly, as if the world expects us to.

Palm trees are a sign of victory and peace. It's said that a large oak tree trunk can support a huge weight of branches but has limited flexibility. The palm trunk has lots of small roots just under the surface of the soil, which provides stability, and has far more flexibility and can bend forty to fifty degrees without snapping.

The palm can move, flex, and take whatever is thrown at it. It survives.

Simon bites his lower lip and takes a breath, as if holding back what he wants to say—or do—right now. "I, uh—" He coughs. I can feel the tears that get caught in his throat, the push of sadness.

"I told Jasper before he left that he'd better come back because he owed me twenty dollars." His voice is brash, hoarse, and is cut off with his own feelings.

He swallows, and I can hear the groan, the familiar one, the one I feel all the time. I know it so well, I can feel it in my own throat.

"I didn't...I didn't...that was the last thing I said to him—that he owed me money." He tries to hide a sob by covering his mouth with his clenched fist.

I rest my head on the tree and don't say what's on my mind.

He takes off his glasses, and his eyes are the color of a deep red rose. Like he's been at this for a few hours.

"I go to bed, in my bed, every night. But I always wake up in his." I try to quiet my heart. "Guess I just need something to hang on to."

He pulls my head to his chest, and I smell his shirt. He and Jasper wear the same deodorant, and immediately, all I want to do is listen to the beat of his heart. So, I push my ear closer, grab on to his shirt, and try not to allow my tears to become too loud.

I feel Simon's hands tighten around me. I close my eyes and pretend it's Jasper.

When we were kids and our mom and dad fought, it would scare me. Jasper would quietly tiptoe into my room and motion me to follow him to his room, and we'd climb onto his bed. He would hold my head to his chest and cover my ears until the shouting stopped. I'd listen to Jasper's heartbeat instead. That was the place I'd go when life got too hard.

I pull my head away from Simon's chest and look at him. Tears stream down his face.

I put my lips to his because I want him to forget his sadness, like it's some act of valor, like I'm saving his life. But the truth is, I want to forget my sadness, too.

Simon's hands have always stayed where they should. I've always been the one to push him further, I hate to admit. Maybe it's my degrees of grief. Wanting so badly to escape my reality, I trudge further into my dark abyss that has no end in sight.

But it's Daniel who enters my mind.

The question he asked earlier: *What was he like? Jasper, I mean.*

My answer: *"Half of me. And only the good parts."*

I wonder if Daniel would have liked the old me. The less haunted one, less sad, the better decision-maker. I wonder what he'd think of me if he knew what I did in my spare time to meet the needs of my grief.

And poor Daniel, the boy who met me as a single, not a double. The boy who met me as Livia, not Livia and Jasper. The boy who met me after the sadness and not a minute before.

I try to push Daniel and my answer to his question from the tendrils of my hair, the same tendrils that sop up the remnants of my tears, my memories. The same memories I pray that stay with me, yet I yearn for their departure, so the pain won't be so much.

Simon pauses before he reaches my breast, as if to ask if this is all right.

I nod, lean back, and wait for the momentary relief.

I walk away from Simon. The momentary relief is gone already, and the guilt drags behind me.

The numbness is fading, and I know I have the cure hiding in a little bottle on my dresser.

Pulling my bag up closer on my shoulder, I turn and look back to the palm tree where Simon still sits, alone with his own stuff.

It happens every time. The old feeling returns too quickly, and I wonder why I did it in the first place. I wonder if Simon feels the same.

Locking the front door behind me, I run upstairs and pull Jasper's shirt on but not before grabbing two white pills from the bottle on my dresser. Quietly, I go into Jasper's room and fall into his bed with the day's dirt wearing on me like a tight sweater made with scratchy yarn. I pull his headphones on and hit play.

My mind flashes to mere minutes ago with Simon's hand on my breast, his hardness between my legs.

Whitney's face.

Cao's face.

Tracy's face.

Poppy's face.

Jasper's face.

Daniel's face even.

Disgusted with myself, I turn on my side and face the wall, waiting for the music and the pills to take me to another dimension.

It's four thirty p.m., and the two pills have done their job. I feel more relaxed and less feely. I need to get ready for work. Pushing off Jasper's bed, I look out the window and down toward the palm to see if Simon has left. He has, to my relief.

I pile into the adjoining bathroom and wash my face. I stare back into the mirror at someone I cannot recognize. Deep, dark holes where my eyes used to be, a glimmer of blue, recognizable only by an intent stare. My lips, not even a shade of pink, but a shade of sadness. The tiny stud in my nose, I barely notice. My skin's so white, I try to scrub it away because I don't want to be this person anymore.

I scrub harder and harder until my face burns, and I look back at her. The twin of the twin. I feel separated by glass, the old me just out of reach.

Over the cold running water, I hear my phone.

It's Tracy with a text.

Tracy: At the store. Just thought you might need this. :) Thought we could watch Us and eat the entire thing when you get home.

It's a picture of a half-gallon of cookies-and-cream ice cream. And *Us* is a show Tracy and I started watching together. It's one of the first bonding things we've ever done.

Jasper said he wasn't into it, but partly, I think he would have sat down and watched it but wanted to give us time together.

He wouldn't interrupt us or say, *Why do you watch shows that make you cry?*

He wouldn't flick my head just to annoy me as he stood behind me while I sat on the couch.

His body doesn't exist anymore, just remnants of ash that sit on our mantel.

Me: Yeah.

Tracy: I love you.

Me: Me, too.

I'm tying my apron when Linda comes up behind me and finishes tying it for me.

"Ain't the same without him," she whispers under her breath. "Put somethin' up to remember him by." She motions to Jasper's spot.

"Saw that," I say.

Her lip twitches as she leans up against the counter, staring at the plaque from across the room. She shakes her head. "Ain't nobody deserve to die like that, Liv. Nobody. But, your brother, he was somethin' special. Some people are just at the wrong place at the wrong time." A small tear forms at the corner of her eye, but she wipes it away before I can verify the evidence.

Some people tiptoe around my heart. Don't say the stuff that's blatantly obvious. People are unsure of where to stand, what to do and say to me, the girl who sits at the base of the palm tree, having sex with a boy to ease her pain.

But, when Linda says this, I connect. I hear her words and the hurt in her tone. She's affected, too.

What if Jasper was at the wrong place at the right time?

My heart drops to my toes.

"Glad you're back because Whitney ain't worth a shit. Think she broke every glass we own." Linda rolls her eyes, wiping her hands on her soiled apron. She places her hand on her hip and winks. "Get to work."

I was worried about coming back to work because of the Have-Nots. I don't want to hear how sorry people are over and over and over again. How heartbroken they are for us. The if-there-is-anything-we-can-do people who say that just to say it. A check-off item.

The Silvers walk in first—Annette and Rick. Dr. Silvers is the local OB/GYN. He's probably delivered half of Belle's Hollow, if not eighty-five percent of our population. Tracy works close with Dr. Silvers. He took her under his wing when she was just starting out in the field. They've been like grandparents to Jasper and me.

Annette comes around the corner of the counter. She gives me a kiss on the side of my head and a weak bear hug. "I love you." She brushes her thumb against my cheek.

I don't say anything, except for, "Thanks."

"Call me, you hear me? If you need anything, you'd better call. Or I'm coming over."

Rick reaches over Annette and also gives me a kiss on the temple.

They set up a scholarship in Jasper's name at the local university, I think—or something like that. I heard Tracy rattling on about it one night. The scholarship covers four years of tuition.

They place their order and then walk to Jasper's small plaque in his spot.

"Order up," I say, putting the order in. I walk back to the counter.

I know they came in just to see me.

The Abbotts.

Oh, God. Not the Abbotts.

James and Annabelle. Nosy. Self-centered, egotistical, and greedy. They're both real estate agents in Belle's. "The Best," according to their brand.

Annabelle purses her lips together like she's going to cry when she sees me at the counter.

Before Annabelle can preach her fake words of condolences, Linda walks up behind me.

"Annabelle, you feed Livia one line of bullshit, I'll choke you with this spatula. You got me?" She points the spatula across the counter.

"When are you going to sell this place, Linda?" Annabelle is cool, her demeanor changing instantly. "It has become more of an eyesore than anything." Annabelle looks around the restaurant. "The upkeep must be hard for your age. See if this dive stays in business." She pulls her left eyebrow up, staring at Linda, as if calculating her next words.

James is nervously jiggling change in his pocket.

The Abbotts are transplants from Sacramento. Moved here about three years ago. Their daughter, Alicia, is a junior, and she's the opposite of her mom. Shy. Tends to hang out by herself. Smart, which her mother is clearly not because she wouldn't have said that to Linda. Alicia is more on the techie side. She's probably already

STANDING
SIDEWAYS

been admitted to an Ivy League school or whatever for computer programming. Rumor is, she's some sort of computer prodigy.

"We don't serve assholes. Get out!" Linda barks and walks back to the fryer.

Annabelle laughs. "Let's go, James," she says but not before dropping her business card.

But Linda is too red-faced to care. I push the business card off the counter and to the floor.

But it's the next bell that catches my attention. It's eight ten p.m. It's the red hair, the glassy clear-blue eyes that make their way up to the counter. It's the dimple that appears just below his mouth when our eyes meet that makes my stomach flip.

"Adrian," I whisper.

Jasper would have gotten it.

Daniel cocks his head to the left. "Who's Adrian?" Confidence follows his words.

I try hard not to smile. "Nobody. What can I get you?" I put my pen to paper and push the nerves down.

"What's good here?" he asks, placing his injured hand on the counter.

"Looks like it hurts," I say, my eyes falling to his hand.

"It will heal."

In this light, his hair looks different, as if the fluorescent overhead lighting has changed his hair color from a deep red to a dark brown. I watch as Daniel's eyes scan the menu board in a way that makes me curious.

"Cheese fries." I write it down and walk it to Linda. "Order up. And a banana Oreo milkshake." I meet Daniel's eyes. "You're welcome."

A puzzled look he's giving me, not a oh-thank-you look.

"Or whatever you want. I can change your order, if you want. But you're going to want the cheese fries." I pause.

Don't, Liv. Just shut up, and allow him to go sit down.

But I can't.

"Here's the deal. Let's say you sit down. You're waiting for your food, and you see several cheese fries go by—because that's the popular thing to order here. And then you'll second-guess yourself for not ordering the cheese fries. And you'll probably have nightmares about not getting the cheese fries. Then, all you'll eat is the cheese fries, and then you'll get obese because you've eaten too many cheese fries due to your craving for them. And then your heart will stop, and you will die." I take a breath and whisper, "Death by cheese fries." I stop. "You can order something else, if you'd like."

Daniel's face is stoic. But it softens slightly, as if he, too, is trying to hide the elusive smile. "Seriously?"

No. You just make me talk too much, and then I can't stop. Why do you do that? I want to say. *It's me not having the ability to control my mouth when you're around.*

"I'll get the cheese fries. And the banana Oreo milkshake." He reaches into his front pocket for his wallet, and I can't help but want to smile. "And I prefer you call me Mickey, not Adrian. She was a bit of a whine bag, if you ask me." He pulls away from the counter and sits at a table in the corner. He pronounces *ask* like the word leads with an *O* instead of an *A*.

I turn around to make the milkshake, and Brandon, Seaton, Lira, and even Linda are staring at me.

"What?" I put the ice cream in the stainless steel cup.

All four of them turn and go back to work.

A few minutes later, I slide the tray onto the table that Daniel's sitting at. "Death and a milkshake."

He stares down at the cheese fries. "These aren't much different from cheesy chips that we have back home. Though the caliber of the potato might be different. I hear there are better potatoes in the United States than the UK."

I haven't heard that. But I don't study potatoes. Does he?

"What happens if I have a heart attack?" he asks, staring at me as he takes a cheese fry and drops it into his mouth. His Adam's apple slowly moves with the swallow. "And it'd be worth the heart attack because these are really good." He puts another in his mouth.

I'm staring, and I need to walk away. But I can't.

Think of something quickly, or he'll think you're a zombie, Liv.

"I wonder if eating cheese fries will affect your health insurance. Like smoking." I turn, kicking myself the whole way back to the milkshake machine, wondering why I have the keen ability to make an ass of myself.

Slowly time passes and I watch Daniel as he walks to the trash receptor, dumps his trash, and brings the empty tray to the counter. "It seems I'm in quite a predicament." He's cautious with his words, even shy a little. Shaded behind the mask that he wears, that I see right through. "The cheesy chips were delicious. Though my heart seems to be acting a bit funny. Peculiar, I'd say. But I'd also add, certainly worth it. So, if I die from a heart attack tonight or obesity years down the road, please know it wasn't the cheesy chips—or, as Americans call it, the cheese fries—that did it." He slowly turns toward the front door. "It was the waitress who explained the ramifications that my life was at stake. Thank you, Livia, for saving my life." He nods modestly. His dark flames of hair follow him out to his car.

"Now, he's a keeper," Poppy whispers.

Livia, Age Six

"Daddy?
What's wrong with you?
Why won't you talk?
Why are your pants off?
Daddy?
Wake up."

Present Day

Tracy's home, her car in the circular driveway, pulled forward, allowing room for mine. I'm annoyed that she's home. I shouldn't be, but I am. Lately, when I look at her, which isn't often, I'm reminded that I'm the wrong twin. The twin she adored was killed. This works against me because it only makes me miss Jasper more, because I adored Jasper, too. He was *my* favorite twin. I look at the clock—9:47 p.m.—and glance at the palm tree, looking for my brother. But, now, the palm tree has an imprint of my guilt, and it eats away the tiny layer of happiness that I had just moments before with Daniel.

"Mom?" I quietly shut the door behind me.

"In here, Mimi."

My stomach drops.

Not because Tracy calls me Mimi, but because it isn't her voice.

It's my dad's.

An electric shock shoots through my entire body and reaches my fingertips. I follow my eyes around the corner to see my mother and father in the same room—opposite sides but nonetheless in the same room.

Sitting.

Talking.

Seemingly a simple task between a mother and father but not ours. I'm hit with the realization that I now have to deal with the two of them on my own.

Tracy, her elbows resting on her knees, leans forward, and I slide down to the arm of her chair, showing my allegiance. Jasper would have sat in the middle because he was the good twin. The fair twin.

I look at my dad across our large sitting room. The same room our parents sat Jasper and me down and explained the divorce. And co-parenting. All the bullshit lines parents feed kids when they separate. All that never comes to fruition.

I wish Jasper were here. This takes me back to a memory.

We'd been camping the whole weekend. While my father drank the weekend away, my mom nagged him, making the whole weekend almost unbearable. When we got home, she'd gotten so fed up with him. We had to help her get him to the bathtub. She turned on the cold water—and not just a slow trickle. Full blast.

"Maybe you'll sober up this way," she said.

Jasper grabbed me by the arm and pulled me outside to the palm, and we watched the world below us. Cars moved. Stoplights changed. People walked. Laughed. Life went on functionally without the Stones. Yet here we were, in this big, beautiful house on a hill, surviving.

"What do we do?" I asked him.

"We weather the storm, Mimi," he said.

"Mimi?" I hear my dad's voice.

There's something in his tone? Reservation?

I don't speak. I just stare at the floor, attempting to pull together the pieces, the signs Tracy would have given that she was ready to call on my father for help. The last person on earth she could stand. The last person she'd ever call. Even if we'd received word that the end of the world was coming, she wouldn't call my dad.

I guess she's more worried than I thought.

"I'm here until your mom tells me to leave. I think you need me right now."

I laugh. "Need you? Jasper is dead because of you. I don't need you. I need you to leave. That's what I need," I spit.

My father eats my words, as if they are deserved.

"And you aren't allowed to call me Mimi anymore. You lost that luxury when you left for Los Angeles with what's her face. Remember that? Leaving your family, Dad?" I stand.

"Sis, where are you going?" Tracy gently puts her hand over mine. Her fingers linger, and it reminds me of the way we wake up in the morning, her arm around my middle. Deep down, I desperately need her, but up-front, I don't want to tell her that.

"To weather the storm," I say and walk to the front door, slamming it behind me.

I take in the cool Northern California air.

Tracy isn't in my bed this morning.

The pills stare back at me from my nightstand. Maybe I should count them, see how many I have left.

It's 5:05 a.m., and I can't sleep.

My dad is back after his three-year hiatus.

I lost my virginity to a boy I'm not sure I like in that way. I can't stop sleeping with him.

Mr. Joe has faith in me, and I don't want to let him down.

School sucks.

And Whitney is nice when she should really hate me.

And my brother is still dead.

But, through this, there's a boy, Daniel, who seems to smooth out some of the wrinkles, making life a little more bearable.

I turn the bottle of pills again. And stare at its silhouette. *What would it feel like to take three this time? Two is good, but three might be better, right?*

The dread of a new day. The anxiety that exists in my veins, turning on me. The dread pumps through my body and makes my hands sweat, my body hot. And my stomach turns to a bed of knots, making me want to throw up.

Poppy: "What about Dr. Elizabeth?"

"Mole? No," I whisper.

"Why not?"

"She doesn't get it, Poppy."

"My dear, nobody will. Ninety percent of the population have not experienced what you've experienced. But she does have the education to be able to give you some direction, some advice perhaps." Poppy is sitting on the side of my bed. Her bright-colored housecoat shimmers, just like in the movies when ghosts come out of doors, chandeliers, windows even.

"I feel like I'm going crazy. Am I crazy?" I whisper.

"Oh, my dear girl." She shakes her head, and I feel the warm rush of her hand slip right through mine, just like the Santa Ana winds. "Grief is colored in so many different ways."

Poppy used to have big brown spots on her hands. They're gone now. But she used to have the softest hands. Big hands. We used to cuddle in her chair on Friday nights and watch reruns of *The Golden Girls*—her, me, and Jasper.

I remember, one night, I thought I was going to die.

While I was lying next to Poppy, she snored like she was screaming. I swallowed a penny. I must have been about nine years old at the time. Jasper was out on the couch in the living room. Though I could breathe through the whole ordeal, I thought it might have gotten lodged in an organ. What about the coming-out part? The penny would eventually have to exit my body since it went in through my mouth. Surely, it wasn't good. Panic set in. I snuck out of bed and went to Jasper.

"Jasper?"

He didn't budge.

"Jas?" I shook him.

"What? What's wrong? Are you all right?" He stirred, his eyes sleepy, hair in disarray.

"I swallowed a penny."

*He blinked. Stared at me. A smile crept into the corners of his mouth.
"You swallowed a penny?"*

*"It's not funny. Will the copper kill me? Will it get lodged somewhere in
my lungs or something?"*

*"It's going to take a lot more to kill you than a copper penny. You're fine.
Now, go back to bed."*

A creak in our old house brings me back to the present
moment. Poppy is nowhere in sight.

I pop three white pills into my mouth and creep out of bed.
Jasper's AC/DC shirt dangles at my mid-thigh. Quietly, I open his
bedroom door, and everything is in its place. I go to his closet with
his shirts hanging, clean, waiting to be worn. And a cold, lonely
feeling enters my body. With an ache I've felt far too many times, I
sit down in his closet, on top of his nine thousand pairs of
immaculate Vans he took excellent care of. Surrounded by him, I
close my eyes and hug my knees in the secret spot that seems to
make the grief a little less heavy.

It's Tracy's sobs I hear that wake me up. I must have fallen
back asleep. The familiar early morning sobs from the shower.

Tracy.

I want to go to her. Hug her. Tell her my pain matches hers.
But I don't because my body is shaking, too weak to move.

I think fear keeps us from a lot of good.

The sobs grow silent. The water is turned off. And, slowly, I
creep out of Jasper's closet but not before I see my father, which
makes my insides instantly freeze.

My silent breath grows even quieter, and the swoosh of my
blood pumping in my ears becomes faster and louder.

Swoosh. Swoosh. Swoosh. Swoosh. Swoosh.

Swoosh.

My left eye peeks through the crack in the door, and I try to
swallow, but there's nothing to swallow.

My dad is sitting on Jasper's bed, holding his football jersey.

I've never seen my father cry. At six foot four, he was always a
giant to me.

He had a full ride out of Belle's Hollow on a basketball
scholarship. But he decided to stay back because Tracy had gotten

63

pregnant. And it wasn't with us. Before us. Instead, he went to Skagit Community College, just twenty minutes up the road. Worked during the day as a cashier at Hollow's Grocery and went to school at night. Finished his bachelor's degree and Juris Doctor online.

The baby before us didn't make it. I think that attributed to the demise of their relationship with my father going to school at night and my mother holding down her CNA job at Redwood Memorial Hospital—she'd done a nine-month LVN certificate to help offset some of the living costs. Jas and I didn't come along until after my dad finished law school. Tracy went back and got her RN degree after we went to kindergarten, as she didn't have to work anymore because Dad could provide for us and then some.

There's a stifled cry that makes me look up. Hunched over my brother's football jersey, my father is shaking like a toddler. His tears, unmasked, fall at an uncontrollable rate of speed, yet there's no sound.

And what comes to my mind is a memory that is seared so deep, it makes me fly out of the closet.

My dad was in a drunken stupor that night. Punched Jasper in the face for sticking up for Tracy. Yet Jasper made excuses.

"I should have left him alone," he told me as I held an ice pack over his right eye that night.

I'm staring at my dad, who looks like a lost little boy right now, all seventy-six inches of him.

"Why are you crying?" It's more of a rhetorical question. What I should have said was, *You don't get to cry.*

He stifles another cry as he buries his head in his hands. "I'm so sorry, Mi—Liv," he corrects himself.

For some reason, I cannot seem to articulate the words in my head and put them through my mouth. Anger and fear maybe serve as the barrier between us.

"Get out," I say and point toward the door. "You don't get to be in here."

10

"Hey." Cao throws her backpack in the backseat. I pull away from the curb but not quick enough to move out of earshot of Beth.

"*The Monkey King 2* tonight!" Beth is beaming, holding the DVD in her hand.

"My mom has gone effing crazy." Cao shakes her head as she waves out the window. "She's a loon, Liv! And she's driving me nuts!" she yells out the window, loud enough for Beth to hear.

"But! In other news"—she punches my arm and shoves her phone in my face—"Ed Sheeran tweeted me back. Heart eyes!" she squeaks. "I'm pretty sure he tweeted he wants to marry me."

I side-eye her, questioning the truth to her statement, wondering if she's reading more into the situation.

"Well, he said, @caobelle: *Married to it!*"

I smirk. "What did you tweet?"

"*Love the new album. Married to it.* So, if I read between the lines, I'm pretty sure he said, *Let's get married.* And don't worry; you're so going to be my MOH."

"Your MOH?"

"Maid of honor." Her fingers are flying across her phone screen.

"Are you replying to his offer?" I pull toward the left and start to ascend the Gulch.

But the red jacket catches my eye. *Why the hell would he walk the Gulch and drive to Bob's? Clearly, he's got a license—or maybe not. But why walk? Why would his parents let him walk? It's dangerous.*

I speed up to Daniel, who's at the top, and pull off on the side of the road.

I roll down Cao's window, and she's clearly taken aback by my brashness.

"What are you doing?" I lean toward Cao, looking out the passenger window. My words are direct, almost mom-like. No, almost Jasper-like. "You can't walk this road; it's dangerous. Get in."

He's standing. I can't see his face, so I'm essentially talking to his penis. I try to shake off the thought because I'm sure my face has turned ten shades of red.

Daniel leans down. Smirks. "Oh, I missed the lights and sirens. Are you pulling me over, officer, for walking on a public road?"

"What? No. Just…just get in, Daniel." I roll my eyes, still trying to shake off the penis thought.

He sees I'm concerned, and where my concern came from, I have no idea.

Daniel pulls back from the window and stands, lifting his arms. Taking off his backpack maybe. The bottom of his jacket rises, and I see it—his long, lean washboard abdominal muscles that scream at me to stop staring. Defined, like God knew what he was doing when he matched Daniel's deep red hair with his work ethic to hit the gym every morning or something.

Cao's face is red as she slowly moves her head to mine and mimes the words, *The V!*

She's referring to the V that guys have just above the big, ugly snakes that no one likes to look at per se. I though remain opinionless because what I'm staring at right now could work all day long.

Cao fans her face.

I realize he's pulling his bag off his shoulder. Daniel is far too modest in a confident sort of way. That he doesn't have to show you or tell you just how good he is or looks with his shirt on or off. Or—

Shut up, Liv.

Without another word, he climbs in the backseat and sits directly in the middle seat, so when I look in the rearview mirror, he's all I see.

I pull onto the highway again.

Don't use your rearview mirror; you don't need it, I tell myself.

But I do. I look in the mirror, but he's staring out the window.

Cao turns around. "So, Daniel, you're totally coming to my wedding, right? You can be Liv's plus-one."

Her words don't catch Daniel off guard. "Who's the lucky mate?"

Cao's lip curls, and then she gushes—I swear, her eyes have turned into hearts as she looks at me—"Mate?"

"Um, yeah. Lad? Dude? Man? Dude-man? Friend? Not quite sure what term you use."

"No, *mate* works just fine." Cao turns to me. "Ed Sheeran."

He slowly moves his eyes to mine. "Ah, Ed." Daniel is still staring in my rearview mirror. "When's the wedding?"

I realize I haven't told Cao about last night at Bob's when Daniel came in because she's a bit confused by Daniel and my newfound forwardness with him. Christ, and I haven't told her about Daniel in the janitor's closet.

"What happened to your hand?" Cao asks.

Daniel looks down. The bandage is gone, but the marks remain—half-scabbed, some wounds still open. "Janitor's closet. Got lost."

"Liv's mom is a nurse. I'm sure you can pop over to her house after school, and she'll take a look at it."

I feel Cao's stare in the side of my face.

I shake my head and stare out the window. I know what she's doing. Our phones chime in unison as we pull into the parking lot at school. Daniel's doesn't.

"What is that?" He leans forward and looks to the front seat.

"Blog Heiress," Cao says, opening up the notification.

BLOG HEIRESS

Belle's Bitches! Well, it's official. Daniel Pearson has eaten the cheese fries at Bob's. He's officially a Belle's Hollow resident now, served by the one and only sad girl, Livia Stone, who returned to work yesterday.

So, get comfortable with the hot new ginger with a nice set of abdominal, pectoral, everything. What I wouldn't give for two minutes alone with him. Perhaps in the janitor's closet?

Daniel leans in closer, over my shoulder, so close that I smell cinnamon from his mouth and feel the warmth of his breath on my thumb that hovers over my home screen.

"Me?" He looks at the name of the blog. "Blog Heiress is blogging about me?" He's completely taken aback. "Why does she care what I do?"

Cao cackles. Her cymbal earrings chime when she leans her head back. "Oh, you're the latest piece of meat, and BH has it bad for you."

Daniel is clearly still trying to wrap his head around the idea that a blogger is blogging about him. "Is she a bit mental?" He reads on. "*Nice set of abdominal muscles?* How the hell does she know?"

My face turns red.

We shrug because nobody knows who writes Blog Heiress. It started about two years ago, and the stuff she digs up, nobody knows about. Or it comes to fruition weeks later, proving what she said—or he said—was in fact true.

We keep reading. Daniel hasn't moved an inch, and neither have I.

From a source I cannot divulge, for those taking Chemistry, the test is up. The questions and answers are below. Make sure you copy this shit down, as I'm sure some AP kid will rat me out. (Hey, Anthony Cartwright, I see you, douche.) Then, I'll have to change the IP address to the blog again. Seriously, you didn't think I'd find out? Oh, and you'd better stop beating off in the boys' restroom at lunch in the third stall, or I'll tell everyone.

Oops ;)

Rumor has it that Principal Lundberg is on the prowl for the Ritalin pills that were taken from Gabriel Struvio's backpack. Word is, he actually needs them. So, please make sure you hide yo stashes before they bring in the county drug dogs.

Let's do a riddle, shall we?

One plus one is two, right?

What's one plus one plus one? A threesome? A threesome is defined as three people consummating together.

But what if there are two consummating relations without the third? And what if that third person doesn't know?

I'd call that a bit of a stab in the back. Maybe some things are better left alone. Or not. ;) This twosome will surprise you.

Best!

BeLHo

"Liv, you're blotchy. You have red blotches on your neck. Are you all right?" Cao asks as we get out of the car.

Daniel leans back. I feel his eyes staring at the back of my head.

I touch my neck, but the fire is burning in my chest.

Shit.

BeLHo knows.

"Just hot," I lie again. I lie to cover another lie. Soon, I'm not sure I'll be able to keep up.

I can't make eye contact with Daniel because I'm scared he'll see the whore inside me. The bad decisions I've made.

I don't think Daniel is buying my I'm-hot excuse.

Why would I feel guilty toward him anyway? We aren't a thing. I mean, we've discussed cheese fries. And my misgivings on Hawthorne Hill. And my brother.

Oh my God. What if he puts one plus one plus one together?

"I've got to run. Thank you for the ride, Livia. For saving my life again." He looks down at the ground as he walks past, brushing my shoulder.

"Liv," Cao whispers, pulling on my arm, "if BeLHo is talking about you and Simon, you need to end this. Now."

I don't answer.

We make it to first period with Mr. Joe.

As if BeLHo's latest blog post, which reminds me of Anthony Cartwright—ew by the way—isn't enough and the fact that my dad is back, I forgot the paper Mr. Joe asked me to get done by today. The one that I agreed to get done so that he could send it off to Dr. Livingston.

He eyes me as I walk in and pulls his left eyebrow up—his signal for me, saying, *Is it done?*

I break eye contact and feel as though I'm being buried alive. The metaphorical stack of bricks on my chest gains more weight.

Mr. Joe doesn't approach me. He knows.

He lectures on the colonial American poet, Anne Bradstreet, and never once looks at me. As if I've let him down. I have. I made a commitment, and I fell through.

Running is easier than seeing my mistakes come to life. I take the hall pass to use the restroom, but instead, I head to the janitor's closet.

It's dark, and all I want is to be swallowed into darkness, so I step inside and wait for the darkness to hold me down. Life was so much easier, more conquerable, and more moving in the right direction just a month ago.

Lies have created the basis for my current life. *The Livia Stone Life.* Not *The Life of Livia and Jasper Stone.* Two different lifetimes and two different concepts.

Disappointment spreads itself thickly on top of the layer of lies. The multiple lies.

Selfishness drips into the layer of disappointment, casts itself into the lies layer.

And fear. Fear wraps up the layers, ties a bow around it, and says, *Fuck you, Liv.*

"I'm glad to see you don't punch things when you get upset."

I jump off the bucket and grab my chest as a thousand needles of scared shitless attach to me all at once.

"It's a bad habit, I'd say. Don't start it anytime soon," Daniel says.

I grab for the light string, and click it, and Daniel is leaning against a large box, his feet crossed at his ankles.

He holds up his hand and shields the light from his face. "Want to talk about it?"

Slowly, I ease back down on my bucket, turning my body in his direction. And here I go. I can't seem to shut up when he asks me things. "I failed to get a paper to Mr. Joe. For a special project we're working on." I pause. "I can't seem to make good decisions that don't destroy my life."

There's a long silence that looms in the air, like a thick layer of cigarette smoke.

Daniel does this thing where he slightly opens his mouth and then closes it, only to open it once more to say something. "It's my experience that bad decisions are easier to make when forgiveness seems to work in our favor." He pauses. "Confession?"

I hear him swallow.

"Yeah."

"My mum is sick."

11

"That's why we came to the United States. She wants to die among the redwood forest. I got a map, and she pointed to this tiny little blip called Belle's Hollow," Daniel says.

I want to hear more about Daniel's mom. But I don't want to push him, just like he hasn't intruded on Jasper. Treading lightly. "Death is shitty." I bite the corner of my mouth.

"Confession?" Daniel says again. He pronounces it like *cone-fession*.

But I try not to let on that I like the way he pronounces: *seriously, laugh, United States*, and *ask*.

"This is your closet. You overrode my dibs," I say. "And, by the way, there's no constitution of Belle's Hollow High in the trophy case. I lie. A lot. It's one of the bad decisions I've managed to make since Jasper died."

Daniel moves his tongue round in his mouth, as if allowing an idea, a statement, to bounce around inside his mouth before he lets it come tumbling out—like, *liar*. I wonder what his tongue would feel like against mine. *Would it be soft or needy like Simon's? What would it feel like against my neck? My jawline? My breasts?*

Oh, God. I think my face has gone red because Daniel is cocking his head. Maybe the red splotches have come back.

"What?" I push the thought of tongues and breasts from my head.

"Don't laugh, all right?" Laugh is pronounces with an *O* instead of an *A*. He rubs his face with his hands and quiets his tongue. "I lied to the police."

I stare at his shoes.

"I wanted to keep a dog. I was about ten at the time. Found the dog roaming the street near where we lived in Hull. It didn't have a collar on it, so I asked Mum if we could keep it. She said no, as my father was allergic to dogs, and told me to hang Found Dog signs around our area." He pauses. "So, I made up this story. It's silly in hindsight. I told my mum that a man had tried to kidnap me, and the newly acquired dog had saved my life."

"Did they let you keep the dog?"

"They were adamant that I could not keep the dog. And then they got on the house phone and called the police."

"They didn't."

"Indeed, they did. And what happened next was quite a blur. But I must say, the police officer who showed up at our home was tall and quite intimidating to a ten-year-old lad. But, when he asked me to give a description of the man who'd tried to take me, I fed him a line of bollocks."

"Bollocks?"

Daniel shrugs. "Shit."

"You didn't." I feel more human. "You lied to the police?"

"I did. As eloquent and as believable as a ten-year-old chap could, I told him about the man's brown hair, his facial hair. His blue eyes."

"You made it up?"

"No, I described my uncle. So, half-lie."

I half-laugh but more smile because, for the first time, I see a piece of the honest truth through his smile.

I'm not sure if he's smiling because of the story he's telling or if he's smiling because I'm laughing now.

I cover my mouth. "You lied to the police."

"Yes. And there's probably a warrant out for my arrest right now. That's really why we came to the United States, Livia. I'm running from the police. That's why I hide out here." Daniel looks around the janitor's closet.

He laughs, a deep, throaty laugh that reminds me of his tongue. That reminds me of my breasts. I want to tell him I like his laugh, but I don't.

"That's not the worst part of the story. The extra-tall police officer came back to our flat to tell my mum and father that he'd found a man who fit my description."

"No way."

Daniel nods. "Thank God he had an alibi."

"Did you get to keep the dog after all that?" I lean forward, intrigued by his ability to tell a story aloud so easily. My stories exist in my head and in journals I keep hidden.

"I did not." He shakes his head. "I guess the moral of the story is, perhaps lying won't get us what we want. I think, too, God might have had his hand in it."

I freeze. "Do you believe in God?"

"Sometimes."

Same.

It's getting warm in here, and I'm not sure if it's my hormones because my face is extremely warm or the temperature of the small closet. I trace the word *hot* in my hand and stand to leave.

"Thanks." *For making me feel almost human again today,* I want to say but don't.

"For what?"

"For calling dibs." I don't look back at his face to see if he's smiling. I grab the knob of the door, but something beckons me to turn back to Daniel, who's staring at me. "Do you ever feel like the world is too small?"

"No." Daniel looks impatient. As if he wants to do something about my leaving, but he doesn't. His hands fidget at his sides.

"I'd like to meet your mom. And I like your smile. It's big. With lots of teeth." Without giving Daniel a second look, I allow the door to close behind me, wanting Daniel to follow me out, wanting to feel his calming presence again. Wanting him to tell me stories that make my life seem less chaotic. More right. Less wrong.

But he doesn't follow me out and save my life.

I make my way back to Mr. Joe's classroom. My phone chimes before I go in, and I look down.

It's a text.

Simon: Hey. Caaaaaannnn u com ge me? Drunkkkkkk.

Me: What? Where are you?

75

Simon: Idk.

Me: What do you mean, IDK? SIMON, WHERE ARE YOU?

Simon: n ur car.

Me: WTF?

He doesn't respond as I march over to my car.

I'm more worried about Whitney. I can deal with whatever comes my way.

You should have thought of that before you let Simon touch you in places that only a boyfriend or girlfriend should touch, I tell myself.

And there is no *us.* We're two people just trying to get by.

Me: What was your plan after you got drunk?

Simon: IDK. Stuck n seat belt. Need help.

Stupid seat belt. I should've fixed it a long time ago. It works so well that, sometimes, you can't get out of it.

I walk/run to my car, and I think about texting Cao to ask her for her help, but I second-guess that idea. I don't want to draw her into this or out of class because of the lack of my better judgment.

There he is. Stuck in the passenger seat of my car. I reach for the door handle, but it's locked. I never lock my car. Nobody ever locks the doors to their houses, cars, or anything else in Belle's Hollow. We don't need to. It's the type of town that closes up shop for town functions. The type of town that hangs signs in their window—*Be back in five. Ran uptown for some change. Leave your money on the counter.*

Simon looks at me from the driver's window.

"Open the door." I'm mad. Pissed off. Fuming. But, really, who should I be mad at? Clearly, this wouldn't be an issue if Simon and I weren't sleeping together.

He laughs a drunk laugh, and it pisses me off more.

"This isn't funny, Simon. Unlock the door."

He hits the unlock button, but when I go to pull open the door, he locks it again.

"Simon James, you asshat. Unlock the damn door."

He hits unlock and pushes the car door open.

"What the hell were you thinking?" I lean in, so my face is practically in his lap, and I'm jiggling the seat belt. It's a jiggle-jiggle-pull method.

But I feel Simon's hands in my hair.

"Stop it," I say as I feel the beads of sweat begin to form on my forehead.

He laughs.

"Livia? Is everything all right?"

Immediately, I stand and whack the back of my head on the roof of the car.

Simon is laughing uncontrollably now.

It's Daniel.

What do I say?

You lie, Liv. Because that's what you've grown accustomed to.

No, you tell the truth. You haven't done anything wrong.

But everything about this situation is all wrong.

"Hey, Daniel." I'm extra peppy with my *hey* and my *Daniel.*

My Daniel. Again, sounds weird.

"Uh, Simon, this is Daniel. Daniel, this is Simon. And he seems to be stuck in the front seat of my car."

"Yes, so I see."

Simon reaches his hand out. "Nice-to-meeee-you," he slurs to Daniel, coming out all in one word. He laughs and hiccups again.

"Oh, a bit wankered, are we?" Daniel examines the seat belt.

Simon laughs so hard, he falls forward. "Wankered!" He tries to give Daniel a pound but completely misses his knuckles.

Daniel steps in without getting too close to Simon and jiggles the seat belt, and it comes loose. Just like that.

Simon falls out of the car.

"I need to get him home," I say, placing my hand on my forehead in frustration.

Daniel's eyes don't meet mine this time.

Daniel helps me get Simon to his feet and into the backseat. Simon groans as he falls into the seat.

He slurs again, "I love you, Livia."

I shut the car door in a panic.

The right decision right now would be to tell Daniel what's going on. The right decision right now would be to stop lying.

Daniel casually leans on the side of my car, but his eyes say something different. Concern maybe. And then he asks the question I saw coming minutes ago, "Is he your boyfriend?"

"No. No. No. He's Jasper's best friend. Was. He's got a girlfriend." I wave it off like it's crazy Daniel even asked. "But, wait"—I always feel the need to clarify with Daniel—"the only reason I said he had a girlfriend wasn't to say that, if he didn't, I would date him because I wouldn't. I said he had a girlfriend because—oh, God, never mind."

A tiny smile spreads across Daniel's face, as if knowing I'm flustered gives him pleasure.

His face grows more relaxed, and then he does the methodical-thinking thing—where he pauses, mulls the words around his mouth—*Liv, don't think about his tongue again*—and then pauses again, only to say, "Do you have a boyfriend?"

He's concerned I have a boyfriend.

"No, no boyfriend. Boyfriend clear." *I'm so awkward*, I hiss at myself. "Girlfriend? For you?"

He shakes his head. "Do you want me to help you get him home?"

No, I don't want to invite you into my complicated, totally messed up life, Daniel.

"I'll manage." I open the driver's door.

Daniel taps the roof of my car with the side of his fist. "See you."

Simon is snoring as I take a left on Twelfth Street from the high school and another left on Randolph Street.

"What did you do, Simon?" I whisper under my breath.

He murmurs something. And then he starts to whimper.

I park in front of his house and open the backseat door. "Simon. Wake up."

He doesn't budge.

I pull on his arm. "Come on. Wake up." I lightly tap him on the face a few times. "Simon James, your Vans are on fire!"

He opens his eyes. "Wha?" He looks around. "Ouch! Head…" He holds his head in his hands.

"Come on, let's get you inside."

I help him to his feet but not without a lot of effort on my part. A piece of me thinks he's enjoying this. With his arm around my neck and my arm wrapped around his waist, we make it up the steps of the porch and get inside his house and to his room, the only neat place in the house.

His house is a pigsty from the overflow of dirty dishes on the counters and in the sink to the coffee can full of cigarette butts—half of them in and half of them missed shots on behalf of the smoker.

Still groggy, he says, "Come-on, Liv. Lay-wi-me." He eases back toward his pillow on his bed, his eyes closed.

I stare at him as he peacefully sleeps. I wish he could sleep like this all the time. I wish the hurt didn't eat him up. The regret I know he has for not going with Jasper to LA.

"Liv," he says through squinty eyes, "I love you."

My insides turn out. "No, you don't, Simon. We're just two people healing our hearts."

"What's going on in here?"

I turn to see Whitney standing at the door.

How long has she been standing there?
What did she hear?

"Nothing," I lie. "Whitney, we've been friends since we were kids. Of course he loves me; we're like family," I manipulate. *Because she heard that part, right?*

Whitney tilts her head to the left, trying to get a better read on me, knowing there might be more to what's being said than meets the eye. "What happened to Simon? He smells like alcohol. He doesn't drink." Whitney looks to me again, more questioning than anything. "Why are you with my drunk boyfriend in his room? Let me smell your breath," she says.

"What?" I gawk.

She turns to me. "Let me smell your breath."

"This is asinine. Smell my breath? You can't be serious?"

Whitney gets in my face. "Blow."

I roll my eyes. Whitney this close to me makes me feel uncomfortable.

I pause.

I sigh.

"Blow," she says louder.

I blow.

She smells.

"How did Simon get like this?"

I shrug. "No idea. I found him like this." I don't, however, tell her he texted me.

"Where?"

"In the gym."

Liar.

Whitney looks back to Simon and then to me again. "I'll take it from here."

I turn to leave.

"Livia, did you forget?"

What? My cheating ways?

"The pictures."

"Right. I'll get those to you."

"We work together tonight, so you'll bring them," Whitney states in a diplomatic tone, almost forceful, as she eases onto the bed next to a passed-out Simon.

I nod and do everything but run outside to my car, and I head back to school as fast as I can.

At school, I reach in the backseat for my backpack. *Shit.* It's in Mr. Joe's classroom. I realize I have to put my tail between my legs, march back in there, and grab it.

Second period, his prep period. No students. No distraction. I make my way to the classroom.

He'll want to talk about the paper and my lack of attention, that my commitment to our agreement might not be one hundred percent. That maybe Harvey College doesn't deserve such a distracted student. A flake. A cheater. A liar.

Outside his open classroom door, which is unusual, which is weird, which is totally unlike Mr. Joe, I take a big gulp of air as I prepare my defense.

It's dark.

"Mr. Joe?" My eyes slowly adjust to the dark, windowless classroom. "Hello?"

"He left. Won't be back until tomorrow, Livia," Mrs. Brimm calls from behind me. "Missed you the other day," she says casually, like a high school counselor would.

The ones that don't probe just sit and stare. No accusatory tone. No blame.

I know what she's doing. *I'm not stupid. I know what you're doing, Mrs. Brimm.* But I hold my tongue.

"Help me, would you? Before you go to math?"

I give her a what-do-you-want-from-me stare.

STANDING
SIDEWAYS

"I'll write you a note." She walks to the wall behind Mr. Joe's classroom door.

Am I wrong about Mrs. Brimm? Is she really not here just to collect a paycheck?

I grab my backpack and follow her.

Behind Mr. Joe's classroom door starts the I AM wall, something Mr. Joe started when he first got to Belle's Hollow High. In his class, my sophomore year, Mr. Joe asked us to write down on strips of paper ways that we were judged, stereotypes, the things we were not. Then, after that, he neatly piled all the strips of paper together and asked us to move our desks into a large circle. He threw them up into the air, and pieces of paper danced around the classroom like confetti. We didn't know who wrote what.

I am NOT:

Athletic
Racist
Sure of myself
Often included
Loving
Helpless
Muslim
Who you think I am
Christian
Just a band nerd
Skinny
An American
Confident

Then, Mr. Joe asked us to pick up five of these white strips of papers that we identified with most. He asked us to write down why we were connected to them. Asked us to write how we could shatter these stereotypes.

I feel Mrs. Brimm's eyes on me as I stare at the colorful wall that is the outcome of our project that we started two years ago.

After the first activity, Mr. Joe asked us to focus on what we were and to write those down, each on a colorful notecard—the I AM statements. Our class took to Twitter and Snapchat, using the hashtag #iam. Soon, it exploded everywhere. National news organizations came in to film us. Coffee shops, bookstores, other high schools, and colleges started their own I AM wall.

Without noticing, I trace my hand against the coolness of each card, a space to see who we are and what we represent.

I look for Jasper's first. I look for his writing because the I AM wall is constantly evolving with notecards and black permanent markers, growing every day, students adding to our massive wall that wraps around the building. His statement once caused me confusion, my eyes unable to grasp the fact scribbled across the card in his chicken scratch.

I find it. His.

I AM not straight.

My heart begins to ache, knowing how long he kept the secret. Not feeling like he could tell his own twin sister. His parents though, rightfully so, since that was when Dad left. At a time when Jasper needed him most, which makes me angrier with our dad. He wasn't there for Jasper. But I wasn't either.

I AM self-involved.

Jasper came out on a wall, for the world to see, though hidden behind a black Sharpie and a neon-pink notecard. The thing is, I never brought it up. I pretended not to notice.

I find mine.

I AM an awful sister.

I need to look away because the stupid tears come to my eyes. I was his twin. I should have noticed, right? Felt something the day he put the black ink to paper.

Immediately, I turn and walk to math and leave Mrs. Brimm to the I AM wall.

"Where are you going?" she asks.

"Math."

Stupid fucking wall.

"Livia? Your note." Mrs. Brimm extends her hand. "For being late."

I reach back and take it.

"And, Livia?"

I roll my eyes, my back to her. "Yeah?"

"Stop by later?"

"Yeah." *Not a chance.*

My cell phone chimes. It's Cao.

Cao: Where are you???

I hastily shove my phone in my back pocket, angry with myself. And my dad.

I try to sneak into Ms. Sund's statistics class—not because I'm late, but because I don't want the attention. The pitiful looks.

"Livia, glad you're here," Ms. Sund says as she clasps her long, slender fingers together.

Everyone tiptoes and is sympathetic to my loss; nobody cares if I'm running a half-hour late to class. There's no, *Where's your excuse for being late? You get a tardy for the class*. Nothing. Just a, *Glad you're here*. As if people are making excuses for behavior because of what happened to my brother.

I take my spot next to Cao, and she gives me the death stare, the you-have-some-explaining-to-do look.

Ms. Sund is tall, thin, and wears her gray hair in a bob. And she smells like baby lotion. She speaks softly, and her explanations are always far more in-depth than most students require; I'm sure of it. Her eye glasses, thick. Things are passed, unnoticed, in her classroom without her so much as batting an eye. Her class is known as The Exchange because you can exchange pretty much anything without being detected. Except for drugs. We have drug-sniffing dogs on campus that periodically pop into classrooms, especially Ms. Sund's.

According to BeLHo, she's been known to cut loose at Breck's Tavern—on a tabletop with red heels. It happened only once. But, still, I have the mental image to hold for collateral, just in case.

> **Cao: Where'd you go? Joe seemed pissed after you left.**

> **Me: I had to get some air.**

Part of this is true.

"Cao, is that a phone I see on your desk?" Ms. Sund looks through her glass lenses, then through her bifocals, and then back to her regular lenses again.

"This? Ms. Sund, it's my calculator," Cao lies.

"Oh, my mistake. Apologies."

Cao and I sit at Jasper's table.

Linda brings out cheese fries and a large Coke.

The cheese fries make me smile because Daniel comes to mind. I could text a picture to him.

Thinking of you. Love, Liv.

Death by Cheese Fries. Liv.

Cheesy chips anyone? ;)

But I realize I don't have his number. Maybe I should ask him for it. The look he gave me as I pulled out of the parking lot, a drunk Simon in the back, was uneasy. Unsure. I need a second opinion on all this.

"You going to tell me what happened during first period when you went all MIA on me?" Cao drops another cheese fry in her mouth, and a piece of cheese falls on her *Psychedelic Research Department* T-shirt. She pulls off one of her red suspenders, so she can clean the spot. "For Jimmy's sake." She rolls her eyes, takes a napkin, and wipes it.

It's *Christ's* sake. But I don't remind her.

I fill my cheeks with air and tell her what happened with Simon and Whitney and with Daniel in the closet. Two days in a row.

"Simon is her boyfriend, Liv, after all."

"I know. But all I was doing was helping him. Besides, he'd texted me."

Cao's eyes narrow. She drops her cheese fry back in the gooey mess of cheese fries. You never drop a cheese fry back into the pile. It's against the law. Cao knows this. She's proving a point.

"Do you think he would have texted you if you guys weren't doing the flamenco on the side?" She picks up another cheese fry.

It's *deed*. But, again, I don't correct her.

"Liv, he was drunk in your car. He told you he loved you."

"Ugh." I lay my head in the crook of my arm and bury my eyes into darkness.

I hear Cao say, "No-girlfriend British boys are way hotter and far more available than American boys with girlfriends." Cao reaches across the table and picks my head up by my forehead. "Besides, have you seen Daniel's body that he keeps hidden under that jacket? Shoot me dead." She catches herself. Slowly, she covers her mouth. "Oh my God, Liv. I didn't mean that. I just—it's a—"

I nod. Everything is different now.

There's a long silence between us.

"Do you want my egg rolls?" She tries to recover as she reaches into her backpack and pulls out her lunch. Cao rolls her eyes. "It's pathetic, Liv. I'd rather stick my eye with needles than eat another bowl of rice. Or watch another Chinese film. Or read another book by Tan. Now that she's all Tan, I'm, like, not all Tan. Why do we do this—rebel? It makes no sense."

"Tell her. Tell her you don't want any of it and that you're happy being *Chi-American* and raised by white parents."

Cao bursts out with her cackle. *Chi-American* is a term we made up in eighth grade. She did actually.

"Don't look now, but Hotty McBritish is walking this way."

D aniel doesn't walk. He doesn't swagger. He steps. He steps as if the world isn't watching him and in the humblest way possible. His strides are long and flowing and even. As if his family owns the walk, like he's been doing it for years.

With his hands in his front pocket, he approaches the table.

Our table.

But, this time, it's as if he hasn't thought about what he is going to say. As if this whole approach-the-table thing is out of his comfort zone, something he's not used to.

His eyes are on me.

I try not to twitch or move or breathe. I try not to make him feel like his coming over here is a bad decision because it isn't. It is certainly the most right decision. I bet Daniel always makes unerring decisions.

Well, except for when he lied to the police. But he did it with the best of intentions.

And, right now, all I can think about is sex with him. Maybe it's the way his hands in his pockets make his pants bulge. Maybe it's his broad chest in his maroon sweatshirt. Or maybe it's his black-rimmed glasses that I don't see him wear often. Except the night he came into Bob's.

My face grows hot. Extremely hot. Temperatures that surely a teen could die from.

Death by hot. And cheese fries. Maybe it's the cheese fries. Maybe this is my death by cheese fries. Not Daniel's.

Oh, God.

"Hey." I try not to sound too breathless, too desperate.

Hot.

Hot.

Hot.

The sound of a submarine in Mayday mode pulsates in my ears.

"Hey," he says. I can hear his British accent, even with one word. "Cao, how are the wedding plans moving along?" he asks.

She smiles, as if her wit isn't matched. Like she's the wit queen. "Ed wants red napkins. I want maroon. Whatever will be, be it, be it."

Daniel stops. Smirks. "Isn't it, *Whatever will be, will be?*" Daniel sits down.

Next.

To.

Me.

Our.

Legs.

Are.

Touching.

Cao pulls her shoulders up. "Whatever. I'll give him the earth."

"When do we get to meet him?" he asks.

I watch his face as his eyes fall to me only quickly, and maybe he's unsure if this is all right with me. Yet an even bigger part of him doesn't care. When he sits, he brings his freshly showered scent, like Irish Spring or something. And there's something about this scent, or him, that makes my stomach twist.

Poppy: "The British are bold, aren't they? And handsome."

I stare at his side profile. His freshly shaven skin makes me wonder what it feels like to the touch. As if the world has given us consent—two living, breathing humans, one with a penis and one with a vagina—to sit next to each other.

Penis.

Vagina.

Penis.

Vagina.

Oh, God. Shut up, Liv. Just shut up.

But he does the unthinkable. Something I'm not ready for.

He turns to me and says, "I'd like to come over after school, so your mum can take a look at my hand. Would that be all right with you?" He looks down at the cheese fries and back to me.

"Yeah," comes out without a play-by-play future trip of what might happen if he came over. I've never brought a boy home. No, wait, once. I take that back. Once. Maybe twice.

Benton Greggs.

Michael Martinez.

Oh, and Lance Renner. Two were for projects when I was the studious Livia, the good decision-maker Liv. And the other was a date. Sophomore year. Semiformal. I hated wearing dresses, but Jasper wanted to go with Lance's sister, Brittany, so he paid me one hundred dollars to go. It wasn't that Lance wasn't cute; he was, but he was kind of short and awkward.

Oh my God. My dad's at the house. Shit. I can't back out now.

Yes, I can.

No, I can't.

Yes. Yes, I can.

Penis.

Vagina.

Face hot.

Poppy: "No, you can't."

Daniel boldly takes a cheese fry, not breaking eye contact with me. "Meet you after school in the library?"

Now, sex is the only thing I can think about. And Daniel.

All I can manage is a, "Yes."

Wait. Why in the library?

But I don't question it because I'm afraid of what will come out of my mouth.

"It's decided then." Daniel stands.

Please don't go. I've grown accustomed to your body next to mine, I want to say. An appendage of sorts.

I'm sure my face registers relief though. And I think I'm somewhat relieved because the bad thoughts I was having mere seconds ago have disappeared. Thoughts like, sliding across his lap right here in the middle of Bob's at lunchtime and putting my lips to his clean-shaven face.

"Livia, I'll see you later," he says and turns and walks out of Bob's just the way he stepped in, quietly and confidently.

"He's hot. Taller." Cao grabs another cheese fry and drops it into her mouth.

"My dad came home," spills across the table.

Cao is mid-chew. "What? I mean, I heard you, but what? Why?" She takes a sip of Coke.

"I think my mom called him," I sigh and sit back on the bench, glancing down at the spot where Daniel sat.

If I slide over a few inches, our butts will have touched.

That's a weird thought, Livia, even for you, I think to myself.

But I slide over anyway, so his invisible butt is touching mine but not touching because his is gone.

I'm so weird.

It's a hard transition from butts and thoughts on intercourse to my dad. Yuck. But I make the transition because I've started the conversation.

"Is he sober?" Cao's lips are pulled tight. She does this when she's thinking.

"Seems to be. This morning, I was in Jasper's closet, and I watched him cry on the side of Jasper's bed with his football jersey in his hands."

Cao's shoulders drop. Her concern for my welfare comes through in her eyes. "Liv," she whispers, "you were in Jasper's closet?"

For the first time, I'm smacked with the realization that sitting among my brother's stuff, in his closet, is odd. I toy with my fingers just below the table, staring at them, praying she'll give me some words to meet relief I have stored somewhere in my body.

"Are you still sleeping in Jas's shirt?"

Now, I'm hesitant. I don't want Cao to worry, but now, I know that sitting in his closet is weird because she's worried.

"No, I washed it," I lie.

She reaches across the table for my hand.

"I told my dad he needed to leave," I say.

Cao's methodical with her words. "He's grieving, too. He lost a child"—she pauses—"in a way that most people will never be able to grapple with. Did you stop to think that maybe he's got demons, too? And that maybe, for the first time in a long time, he's trying to do what's right by his daughter? His family?"

I stare ahead and let her words resonate in my head. "You're taking his side?"

Cao shakes her head. "I'm not on sides, Liv." She stalls. "Maybe the focus needs not be on the relationship between you, Tracy, and Ned, but more on healing together. You guys need each other, Liv. Let him be there. And stop calling Tracy, *Tracy* in your head because I know you do that. Let her be your mom. Get over what was done in the past."

Fifth period. Chemistry.

Mr. Lowery doesn't know we have the Chemistry exam up online, so nobody is really paying any attention to his lecture on converting moles to liters because everyone knows Lucinda Brandt will fill in all the test answers for paying customers.

But I can't even focus on that right now because there's an incessant ringing in my ears. For the life of me, I can't drag my eyes to the open seat two rows over, fifth seat from the front. Jasper and I had Chemistry together. I'd convinced Jasper he needed to do the minimum requirements for the state university system, just in case he wanted to go to a four-year out of high school. Now, I wish I had never told him that because staring at his empty seat is only further confirmation that he isn't coming back. The hole in my chest expands, stretches, and rears its ugly head. It laughs at my feeble heart.

Mandy DeClan sits in the front row. Jasper went to prom with her our junior year. Did he feel he had to go with a girl? Jasper had a way about him that made every person comfortable in a room. Did he feel if he took a boy that it would make others uncomfortable? Maybe he wasn't comfortable with who he was?

We had a conversation just weeks before he died. We talked about college. As weird as it sounds, I couldn't imagine leaving Jasper behind and going to college somewhere else without him. Our plan was that we'd go together.

Truth be told, I think he just told me he'd go to shine me on. So that I'd make the right decisions for me and commit, and then he'd bail.

A few weeks before he died, he said, "Do you ever feel like your future feels fuzzy and hard to see?" He looked at me dead in the eyes. "I can't imagine myself growing up, going to college."

I told him it was because he didn't have a plan, and that was why it looked fuzzy.

Sadness eats away at my stomach. And the hole only grows bigger. Maybe he knew he was going to die.

I come to the present moment. My foot is shaking up and down, and the inside of my cheek is chewed raw. My stomach is in knots. I just want to leave my body.

I need my pills.

Finally, Mr. Lowery closes down his lecture—thank God—and I'm the first one to pack up my things and head for the door.

Belle's Hollow Library is at the center of our high school. It's circular and surrounded by classrooms on the outside. Each classroom is accessible via the library. From Dickens to Plath, the classics and then some are all here. The smell of old books and musk surrounds me.

My phone vibrates. And I look down to an unknown number.

Unknown number: I'm up here.

Daniel is sitting on the second level at a small table with a green lamp, looking down through the center of the library.

Me: How'd you get my number?

Daniel: The soon-to-be Mrs. Sheeran.

I smile because he takes Cao in stride, just like I do. And I save his number in my Contacts.

Making my way up the wide staircase to the second floor, I take a breath.

Don't think of sex or invisible butts touching, Liv. It's just plain wrong.

"Hey." I slide into the chair across the tiny table. *What if our knees bump? I ask myself. Do I pull back? Do I apologize? Do I purposely bump his knee to get a reaction?*

"Hi."

"How's the hand?" I ask, trying to focus on the conversation and not awkward topics that keep randomly popping into my head.

I cross my arms and lean forward but not too forward, like I'm trying to kiss him or something. This table is small enough for us to exchange oxygen; the air around us is either taken by him or me. The kissing space.

"I need to tell you something," he says.

I lean back in the hard wooden chair and throw my shoulders back for good measure, my best attempt at reflecting confidence. I bet if they gave us more comfortable chairs in the library, students would stay longer. Kick up their feet. Take a break.

But it's what Daniel says to me that forces me back to October 1 all over again.

When my dad called with his six words—"I need to tell you something"—they weren't paced or well spoken. They were rushed. Broken with fear. All one word it seemed. Those words were followed with, "I can't reach Jasper, and there's been an incident." His lawyer jargon for emergency.

Dad, are you there? Tell me what happened to Jasper, I wanted to say.

That was when we turned on the news.

Daniel says, "Why we're here."

And I can't remember what he said before this. Or why he's saying this now. Oh, yes, I do.

"I need to tell you something."

Daniel scratches his head and pushes his glasses further up on his nose. I think his glasses are a distraction and also misleading. I think they're a cover-up for the rebel he might really be. The body that he has underneath the clothes that he wears. Clearly, he's not a nerd. I wonder if he has the same color hair on his chest that he does on his head.

Topic at hand, Liv. Not Daniel's chest hair.

Penis.

"I must tell you something." He leans forward in the kissing space.

Penis.

Vagina.

Just coping.

Maybe it's the pills that do this to my brain—push my thoughts out to random planets.

But, now, unfortunately, all I can focus on is his chest, and the thought of touching it swims in my head like a school of fish. Sardines specifically. Maybe. Or guppies. Forage fish.

It's as if each is a sardine, glistening and shiny with pretty colors. One fish makes me look at another and another.

STOP.

I inhale.

Reconstruct your focus. Inhale. Exhale. Repeat.

"What is it?" My voice attempts its best to stay calm.

I don't dare lean forward in the kissing space out of fear that my lips will fly off my face—my tongue, too—and kiss him right on the mouth.

"I don't like Chinese food," he sighs, leaning back from the kissing space.

Thank God.

He intertwines his fingers and places them behind his head. "Writing songs is my outlet. I've come to love scented dryer sheets." His voice is low and deep, and it creeps through my chest like cracked glass. "I walk to school because I won't give my father the satisfaction of driving the car he bought me."

Daniel says *bought* like *boat.*

Vagina.

Vagina.

Vagina.

Help me, God, please.

I put my hand to my mouth, pretending to clear my throat that doesn't need clearing, only to give my hormones a rest.

Quiet, please, I tell them.

"Well, first of all, if you haven't had the Chinese chicken salad at Hunan Village in Belle's, you don't know Chinese food."

I used to like to write, too, before Jasper died. Underneath the table, I trace an *X* on the palm of my hand for *walked away from.*

"Second, I read that scented dryer sheets cause cancer. But everything causes cancer these days." *Please, Liv, don't go off on another tangent.* "Like cell phones, genetically modified foods, the sun, genes—with a G, not with a *J*—smoking. Mexican food."

"No." He mocks.

"Yes."

"Shit," Daniel says, skeptical but funny. "How does Mexican food cause cancer?"

"The amount of aflatoxins in corn tortillas, rice, processed sauces. There's been links to liver cancer and breast cancer."

Daniel leans forward in the kissing space.

But, this time, I loosen up just a little bit. Maybe it's because he's looking everywhere but my eyes, and it makes me feel like I might have the upper hand. More confidence. "I'd like to read something you've written," comes out too quickly. I'd rather discuss cancer and Mexican food, things lighter on the heart.

"All right." He pauses and extends his good hand across the kissing space.

Damn you, kissing space.

"I'll give you something I've written if you give me something you've written." Daniel pronounces *written* like *wree-tun.*

I immediately make up a rule because I don't want him to feel the sweat bags I have for hands right now. "I don't shake on anything."

Daniel jerks his head back. "Why not?"

Be honest. For once since Jasper's death, be honest, and let someone in.

I chew on this statement for a few seconds.

"You make my hands sweat." *Nice.*

Now, I feel like some underweight sweaty boxer looking for a time-out. A truce.

My best idea is to divulge the truth and embarrass whatever dignity I held just seconds before? Wonderful.

His face turns a soft shade of pink, even the tips of his ears. "I make your hands sweat?"

He pronounces *your* like *yor,*

"Yes," I whisper, my eyes staring down at the table.

We just met. This is weird. He's probably freaked out, and he'll get up and leave any moment. I would, but I can't remember how to walk, and if I did, I'm sure my vagina would go splat against the hardwood floor beneath us.

I roll my eyes. "You're gloating."

"Not gloating."

Our eyes connect.

I wipe my hands on my jeans. I muster courage from deep within me and reach across the kissing space. "Deal."

With long, lean fingers, his hand slides in mine.

Why do your hands have to be so manly?

Daniel doesn't let go. Doesn't move.

My phone vibrates, and it breaks up the moment.

Daniel doesn't let go. "Are you going to get that?"

Absolutely not. "No."

"You should. It might be your mum." He releases my hand with reluctance.

It isn't my mom, but instead, it's Cao, telling me that she doesn't need a ride home. That Beth is coming to get her for a doctor's appointment.

The bell rings.

"We should probably get to my house, so my mom can take a look at your hand."

"Right."

"Mom?" I push the door open, Daniel behind me, close.

Shit.

Dad.

I look through the kitchen.

Daniel comes from behind me as my dad approaches. "Daniel Pearson, Mr. Stone. I'm a friend of Livia's."

My dad is caught off guard in a good way. Maybe it's Daniel's forwardness.

"Please, call me Ned."

Their handshake reminds me of two grown men meeting for business.

My dad doesn't say, *Livia didn't tell me she was bringing home a boy.* Because he doesn't have any right to these words. He doesn't know what I've been doing for the past three years.

There's awkwardness between my dad and me; Daniel must sense it.

"Mom?" I call out, walking back toward the staircase.

She's coming down, putting on an earring.

"Hey. Can you take a look at my friend's hand?"

"Cao?"

"No, actually."

She stops at the last step. "Who?"

A boy, I mime the words, my fingers growing fidgety.

"A what?"

I feel the redness in my face.

Tracy comes around the corner. "Daniel? What are you doing here?"

Clearly embarrassed, Daniel pushes his shoulders back. "Tracy, I was...I was wondering if you could take a look at my hand."

"Wait, you guys know each other?"

Confusion streaming from my face, I look between the two of them.

Daniel speaks first, "Um, our parents work together, I guess. I mean, I didn't know Tracy was your mother. I mean, I guess I should have known, being a small town." He pronounces *small* like *smoll*.

British accents are stupid on seventeen-year-old boys. They make hormones sway to music that isn't there. Light unlit candles. And play slow, romantic songs that make American girls rip off their shirts.

Penis.

Vagina.

My face is completely red now.

"He's the new surgeon from Hull. I told you about him." Tracy looks at me, reaching for Daniel's hand. "Ned, can you flip on the light, please?" she calls to my dad, who's leaning against the doorway of the kitchen, watching this play out.

"Wait. Your dad's a surgeon?" I look to Daniel, crossing my arms. "Why wouldn't you have your dad look at your hand?"

I know Daniel is definitely not a liar when this statement pours from his mouth with both of my parents in the room. I see him mull over the words before he says them, "I just wanted to spend time with you."

A slight smile tugs on both sides of Tracy's mouth, though she's still wearing her professional nursing face. It's probably the same one she wears when blood spills from a head wound. When a baby is born. When she has to deliver good news. And bad.

But I haven't seen her smile since Jasper died. And this makes my guilt double. That I forgot about Jasper. Just for a moment. I forgot him. And, somehow, I convince my mind that forgetting him means he's one step closer to being forgotten, and my heart can't handle this thought right now, so I push it out of my head and remember not to smile.

"Looks all right to me, Daniel. I'd say, just some ointment for infection. What'd you do anyway?"

"Doors can be finicky," is all he says.

Tracy's eyes drag from Daniel to me. "Liv, can you show Daniel where the ointment is?"

"This way, Mr. Pearson." I push my hand through the doorway that I'm standing in.

The right of the staircase leads up to my bedroom—also another kissing space, also another space where two people can sit in close proximity, on a bed. But, here, in the safe space—the non-kissing, non-sexual space—is a downstairs bathroom where we keep the ointment. It's a half-bath, so it's small with a toilet, a sink, and ointment. Lots of ointment and creams. From anti-itch cream to burn cream to healing cream. It's a one-stop shop for all your minor medical emergencies.

"What are you thinking about?" Daniel towers over me in the cramped space, ready to take his cream punishment. A slight smile pulls at his mouth.

"Running the Boston Marathon," I lie quickly before the truth falls out of my mouth. Two truths in one day to a boy I barely know is just stupid.

I take his hand in mine, and I'll be damned to hell if my heart doesn't stop as his hand drapes over mine. The colorful winged monarchs explode in my stomach.

"Has anyone told you that you make a horrid liar?" He pronounces *liar* like *lie-uh*.

I carefully let go of his hand and turn to wash mine before I apply the ointment. "Truth?" I don't look in the mirror because I feel his eyes on the back of my head.

He doesn't answer, so I assume there is only one answer.

"I was thinking how much I don't want to be in this small space with you."

Daniel laughs. "Yeah?"

I turn back to him and pull his hand to mine, taking the ointment in my hand. "Can I use my fingers?" I look up at him.

His lips slightly part. Still. Quiet. Taken aback by my words, I think. "Yes," he whispers.

I put the ointment on my other finger. His fingertips barely graze my midsection, and I feel an explosion of stars in my head.

Butterflies have hatched.

Stars align.

A new universe is born.

I'm screwed.

It's Saturday. And, somehow, I've managed to steer clear of Simon since Daniel came to my house.

Several texts from Simon, but I haven't responded. But he's more concerned about what he doesn't remember from last Tuesday in my car. How I got him home. And what he knows is just what Whitney's told him, I'm sure.

Daniel hasn't texted me since our lovefest in the half-bath without kissing but with hands and explosions of worlds.

The rest of the week, I haven't gone back to Hawthorne Hill for any quick fixes. I also haven't gone back to Mr. Joe's class. I dropped it after talking to Ms. Brimm. I used excuses like grief, too much right now. Tears I manipulated.

And, thankfully, I haven't had to face Mr. Joe either. Since I dropped the class, I hope he assumes that our agreement, our handshake on his help, has disappeared, too. But a little voice inside me—not Poppy—tells me I am a problem-runner extraordinaire.

Cao went down to San Francisco to the Chinese Historical Society of America with Beth, and I have the day off of work.

Jasper's room is getting smaller and smaller, the longer I lie here, on his bed, waiting for him to deliver an answer to what I should do about Daniel.

My phone chimes.
It's Daniel.

> My heart throws itself into a rhythm that makes me dizzy. A beat. A band. A band full of drums. Bongo. Bass. Cabasa. Loudly orchestrating the solo that will finish as soon as I read Daniel's text. I need to see you.

Bang.
Bang.
Bang.
He didn't say *want*, or, *I'd like*, or, *It would be nice*. He said *need*. A verb.

And defined as: *require (something) because it is essential or very important.*

Maybe what he needs is to see me to tell me something, and the need to see me justifies the reason. So, maybe it isn't what I think.

I overthink. Perhaps he should have typed, *I need to talk to you. So, maybe he does need to see me? Maybe he wants to see me?*

The British seem to have a funny way of conveying information, I think. Or maybe it's the American way of overthinking everything. Complicating something simple. Maybe a play on words. A lost-in-translation sort of thing. I try to downplay my hopes. Maybe it's not an American versus British thing at all.

I start to text back. But he starts typing again, as I see the bubble with dots.

I stop typing.
And so does he.
Maybe it's like an, *I need to see you about a matter.*

Me: What's your address?

Because I should tell him why I can't see him. I'll explain the grief. The issue I have with taking the pills that help the grief. A drug addict, I'll tell him. That will get his feet going in the opposite direction. The gall has been discovered under my need to give him reasons—or excuses—as to why the world exploding and stars being reborn can never happen again.

There's a long pause on his end. And mine.

Still nothing.

It's been thirty seconds. Ten more. Five more. A minute passes.

He starts to type again. The bubble appears. Then, it disappears.

He said need, Livia.

Daniel starts to type again. The bubble moves. I swear, it moves quicker and quicker.

Light-years have passed.

Daniel: 4723 Rockwell Lane

I map the address on my phone. Daniel's road is just off the Gulch, which I had a feeling it would be.

Quickly, I stand, ripping off Jasper's black T-shirt to put on another T-shirt that I grabbed this morning from Jasper's closet. A clean one. Suddenly, there's an overwhelming scent of something distinct. It's the woods and fresh laundry. Jasper was an impeccable dresser. It wasn't what he wore; it was how he wore it. I feel as though I'm not alone because the scent, his scent, keeps getting stronger.

I step away from his bed, being beckoned toward his closet. The closet I've buried myself in time after time, sitting on his pristine collection of Vans shoes in the dark, begging for him to just let me know he's there.

I take a few more steps toward his closet. The door is closed, and I wonder if my father has been in here again. This thought agitates me. But something tells me to breathe, to calm down. Jasper's scent grows, as if he were here with me right now, something I've never felt since he left.

Taking two last steps to the closet door, I reach for the doorknob. I don't pull the door open just yet because, now, I'm afraid of the letdown, my big expectations imploding right in my face.

What if it's nothing?

What if I've created this scene all in my head, and what if it's nothing?

A sense of urgency comes over me, and I pull open the door.

105

It's dark in the closet, so I flip on the light.

What I find, my mind cannot quite put the pieces together the way it wants to because what I see...

There's a rhyme and reason if Jasper is here, but it's unexplainable if he isn't.

I reach down and hold a sob in my throat, too scared to let myself exhale. Too scared to move because, if I do, maybe it will chase away what I'm witnessing.

The light begins to sputter, as if the lightbulb is going bad, and Jasper's scent increases, almost overpowering. All this is happening so fast.

At the bottom of the closet, lying neatly on top of his shoes, is Jasper's phone, vibrating, with his name across the screen.

As if he's calling his own cell phone.

15

S*hock: 1.) a disturbance in the equilibrium or permanence of something. 2.) a sudden or violent mental or emotional disturbance.*

Immediately, I am transported back in time to when Jasper was alive.

"I believe in what I see," is what Jasper said to Poppy and me one day when we had a long, drawn-out conversation about God.

Does he still hold true to that on the other side? Should I?

My body sways between what's real and what I'm actually witnessing with my own two eyes.

Breathing picks up pace.

Real: Apples. Books. Coffee cups. Cats. Clam chowder. The flu.

Real.

My whole body lunges for the phone, my heart reaching, too, I answer it. "Jasper!" I gasp. "JASPER!"

This feeling inside me is real, and I believe every inch of it.

First lie I tell myself, *What if he's not dead?*

Second lie I tell myself, *What if the FBI missed something?*

"Jasper? Please, I'm here." Tears stream down my face. "Please, I'm here." Desperation is in my tone.

But all that's on the other line is static. Loud static.

I wait. Believing there's more to this. I wait, holding the phone to my ear, as tears consume my face, and my insides go numb.

I fall among his Vans and immerse myself in him.

His shirts.

His Vans.

Everything.

Just his.

With an ache so deep—a void that can only be filled by him, the other half of me—my entire body begins to shake.

Grief makes us do funny things. Our minds, once ours, are now blind by eternal light. Where we wait for our loved ones, in limbo, somewhere between heartbeats.

Pleading to see Jasper one last time, I tell him what I didn't get to tell him before he died.

"I'd do it all different, Jasper," I whisper, not recognizing my own voice.

I try to pad my mind with the burden of proof. Physical evidence that what I did see did indeed actually happen.

When the static finally stops, I wait. I don't pull the phone from my ear, for fear I'll miss whatever Jasper is trying to tell me.

After several minutes, I pull the phone from my ear. The screen is now black with a thick layer of breath fogging the screen.

I go to his Missed Calls log.

And there, under last caller, isn't Jasper calling Jasper. It's Tracy, and it has the number forty-seven next to it. I know Tracy has called Jasper's phone forty-seven times—not to reach him, but to listen to his voice on his voice mail.

"This is Jasper. You know the routine."

Beep.

Bile sneaks into the lower part of my throat, burning on the way up. I make my way back to my room and grab my keys and the bottle of pills before shoving them in my bra. I need to get some air.

My parents are in the living room.

Mom: reading—*pretend* reading because she doesn't want to worry others with her grief.

Dad: scanning the Sports section of the *Times-Standard* newspaper.

"Not so fast, young lady. We need to talk." Tracy's mom tone can be captured usually once a month. "Mrs. Brimm called and said you'd dropped your AP English course."

I don't care anymore. All this caring is ridiculous. It's overrated and a lot of energy. The not-caring part or the bile, maybe both, slowly moves from my throat to my chest and down to my stomach. Where it belongs.

"What's the worst that can happen?" I smirk. The not-caring makes its way to my mouth.

"Liv, Harvey's been your dream. Don't you think they'd like to see your AP scores once you pass the test?" Tracy asks.

I know she cares. But, for some reason, I can't stop spewing hateful things from my mouth. "And, all of a sudden, you care?"

Tracy looks exhausted. Like the songs of love and peace, heaven and earth are over. I watch her turn inside herself. Her mistakes are met with a, *Fuck you. My* fuck you.

A piece of me feels bad. But the grieving part of me just wants to make her hurt more than I do, and I hate it that I do this.

"Livia, don't speak to your mother like that," my dad says.

"Oh! Dad of the Year has returned because it's convenient. Nice try, Ned. Hey, how long are you staying this time? And where's the whore you left town with? You know, since you traded your fucking family in for an upgraded model? Is she pregnant yet, Ned?"

"Livia Stone. What has gotten into you?" Tracy's eyes are wide as she tries to piece together her family with one huge missing part. "Never—" Her voice quivers, and she stops to gather her thoughts.

My heart breaks.

She continues, "Never have you ever talked to me like this. Acted like this..." Her voice follows her once-red heart, now black with tainted trauma.

"Don't like it? Not my problem." And I slam the front door behind me.

I hear Tracy call after me and hear the deep embers of my dad's voice trail behind hers, slow and calm for once.

I text Simon and tell him to meet me on top of Hawthorne Hill because I just need a quick fix, something to forgive me or to relieve me of the guilt that is creeping its way back into my stomach again.

Shaking, I put the keys into the ignition.

I feel like I'm spinning out of control.

Poppy: "Baby, this is no way to lead your life. You're going to make one wrong decision, and then you won't be able to go back."

But, instead of taking a right onto Main and up the hill to Hawthorne, I turn left toward the Gulch.

"Go away, Poppy. Go away. Nobody has a dead grandma following them around. You're not real. And I'm going crazy. Leave me alone." I pause, pushing the tears down deep inside me. "Wait. Was it Jasper?" I say it out loud to see what it sounds like.

I shake my head and feel the emotion begin to build again, this time harder.

I beg Poppy, "Was it him?" Frustration pulls at me. "I don't need one of your philosophical answers right now, Poppy. I need the truth."

Poppy is in the passenger seat. She rolls down the window.

Why? Does the wind feel different when you're a ghost? A spirit? A figment of my imagination.

"Just drive," she says. "Spirits have a way of manipulating the world around us."

My phone directions clang, "Take a right onto Highway 36. In one-point-six miles, take a right onto Rockwell Lane."

I forgot I'd programmed the address into my phone earlier.

I turn to Poppy, but she's gone.

I follow the directions that my phone spits out.

"Take a slight right onto Rockwell."

I do, and it takes me down an unpaved road where the tall redwoods provide guidance, as if to say, *Don't veer off the road, or you'll hit me and die.*

At the end of the lane, I pull into a clearing. "Jesus."

A gigantic meadow and up against the trees, a castle awaits made of brick.

Taking the pills out from my bra, I hide them under my seat but not before I take three. Just three. I need them, right? My brother died. They're prescribed to me. I justify the importance the pills play on my reality to only myself.

I text Daniel to let him know I'm here.

I think I've got the wrong house because this isn't a house. It's a palace.

"You have arrived at your destination: 4723 Rockwell Lane," my phone chirps.

Where do I park?

I assume closer to the house, maybe by the water fountain or by the half-naked porcelain sculptures sitting just outside the castle walls.

My car—my much older car, the one I now feel totally incompetent in, embarrassed by—creeps slowly toward the colossal house, the rocks crunching under my less than capable tires. My entire life now seems less. Just less. But the pills, they sneak into my mind, twisting around and inside my brain. The incompetence fades slightly, and I feel cool. Like I'm supposed to be here.

Daniel opens one of the massive front doors—there are two—with a T-shirt and jeans that hang loosely on his hips. With no shoes, his hands in his pockets, he comes out to greet me.

I completely swallow my incompetence and tell it to stay away until I leave.

"I'm glad you're here," he says as I get out of my car, shutting the door behind me.

"Nice place. How's the hand?" is all I manage.

"Fine." Daniel looks down at his hand and back toward the house, as if it's an item of insubstantial consequence. Just a thing. "Did you have trouble finding the place?" He stares down at the ground as we make our way to the front doors.

The grand entryway. The entrance to the palace.

"No, actually." My voice seems small and so far away from my heart.

"Good."

I can't think of anything to say. Good is good, right? I go with, "All right."

The comfort of the pills makes my shoulders ease away from my ears. Confidence fills my insides, and I pretend to be someone I'm not. My problems fold themselves into a perfect origami and hitch a ride to the moon.

Relief fills every dark corner of my heart. My body.

"It's new, this place, off the beaten path. My father had it built before we moved here." He shrugs.

I stare at the entryway, which opens to the living room, the kitchen, dining room, and formal dining room. A wall of windows overlooks a meadow.

"Should I take off my shoes?" I ask, already in motion.

He laughs. "We have stone floors, Livia, so I doubt you'll ruin the floor. But do what makes you comfortable."

I stare up at the vaulted ceilings made of redwood. Up above the living room and kitchen is a huge loft, which looks like another living room, or game room.

"Would you like to go upstairs?" he asks.

Yes, yes, I would. Is it a good decision? No. Probably not, but my inhibitions are no longer here.

Daniel smiles. "But"—he runs his hand through his hair—"I'm afraid you'll have to take my hand. We'll pass by the dragon quarters, and sometimes, people get a bit spooked."

"I've wrestled dragons before, Daniel; don't worry about me. It's an Olympic sport in America."

The stoic face I'm managing to hold is not only surprising to me, but to Daniel, too.

He shakes his finger in the air as my hand slips into his. My fingers slide between his.

Simon's hands don't feel like this, and my heart doesn't do the strange things it's doing right now when I'm with Simon, not any boy for that matter.

I have a flashback.

Dr. Elizabeth made me visualize my grief as a dragon. She said, as her mole pulled to the left, "What do you need to tell the dragon?" She said, "Use this time to be honest with the dragon. Come on, let it all out." But my personal favorite was, "Do you feel the dragon roar? Do you feel his fire?"

When I left her office that day, I was more confused than when I had gone in.

That was the last time I went to Dr. Elizabeth. I haven't told Tracy yet. She still thinks I'm sitting with the dragon on a weekly basis, and it's been two weeks. When Tracy asks, I lie about it because it seems I'm good at that now.

"Livia?" Daniel asks. "Are you all right?"

I nod as he leads me upstairs to a whole new level of big. Vast. Large. Expansive. Oil paintings hang, representing the Elizabethan era well. Men and women in formal wear, their collars like cones you see on dogs and cats treated at the vet. They don't look comfortable either. Smiling seemed to be against the law back then, or nobody was happy because each painting we pass is something drab, less enthusiastic, and sad than the painting before.

"Who are these people?" I ask as I feel Daniel's thumb slightly rub against my hand while the butterflies begin to flutter, making my hands sweat.

"Family." He stops in front of one particular painting of a man who is sitting. He looks miserable.

"Who is he?" I whisper as I trace the word *envious* against my leg.

"My great-great-great-great-grandfather. This was done after his wife's funeral." He pronounces *grandfather* as if there is an O in place of the A in father.

I stare into the eyes of the man. "Looks jealous."

Daniel stares into the eyes of the painting and then back at me. "How so?"

"Well, he looks to me as if he wanted to go first. As if it were prearranged—that he would die first and his wife would die second."

"One stare?" He pauses and turns to me, my hand still in his and my body still facing the painting, tilting my head to one side.

"Absolutely."

It's as if the pills allow me to reach a deeper level of thinking, creatively touching places I've never touched before. Perhaps a deeper psyche. A psyche newer to me, built on the lies I tell myself when I use.

"Huh."

We walk past several doors down the large hallway, and we stop at the end of the hall, facing a door.

"I'd like you to meet my mother. Would that be all right?"

I question why his mother is behind a door in a room and not in the kitchen. The feeling this gives me is not a good one. *Why isn't she in a living room, reading Pride and Prejudice, or in the backyard in some sort of organic garden she's created from scratch?* Because I bet that's what Mrs. Pearson does.

"What's your mother's name?" My hands noticeably grow sweatier, so I not so casually pull away from Daniel's.

Caught off guard, he responds, "She's my mother, not the Queen of England, Livia."

I rub my hands on my jeans, attempting to be nonchalant, trying to wipe away any evidence of nerves. "No, I know. I just…" I swallow my gum on accident.

He reaches down and takes my hand anyway, pulling me closer to where my ear meets his mouth. "Rose. My mum's name," he whispers.

I count the seconds his breath is against my ear, so it will distract my impure thoughts of heavy breathing. Sex even.

"You shouldn't swallow your gum, Livia. It's bad for you, so says my father. Blocks your intestines." The way he pronounces *swallow* is as if the *A* is actually an *O*, and he says it as if his lips are pulled tight, which they aren't, but it sounds like they are.

I panic because his breath on my neck makes me sweat even more, like I'm a sweaty cesspool, dripping away, melting.

Get it together, Liv, I tell myself.

"I didn't know your father was the leading authority on gum-swallowing."

"Indeed."

He pulls open the door to a massive bedroom, full of windows that show a path through the giant redwoods, beautiful curtains, antiques, antebellum curtains, wallpaper of pink flowers to be exact, and remnants of time travel. As if we'd traveled back in time.

The room or ballroom—I'm not sure which because it's so big—smells antiseptically clean.

A voice calls out—a feeble one, cracked, full of breaths that break up the words—"Daniel, is that you?"

Daniel, wide-eyed, looks back at me, and a slow grin appears across his face. "Yes, Mum."

Smack dab in the middle of the room full of natural light but protected by the redwoods that sit just outside the windows is a hospital bed. Her back is to us, slanted up.

My stomach drops. I try to pull my hand from Daniel's, but he doesn't let me, and this makes my heart pick up pace as he leads us to her bedside.

Withering in the bed before us is a frail woman, though her thinness must be a direct result of her condition, making her look years older than she is. Her eyes are gray with a slight twinkle when she catches mine.

The beanie covers her head. It looks like the one Daniel wore on the day Cao and I passed him when he was walking up the Gulch. I think about telling her the ramifications of her son walking on Highway 36 and the deadliness that the curvy road provides, but I don't because she speaks first.

"Ah," she breathes, "you must be Livia." She carefully reaches for my hand.

He's made no mention of his mother, except for the fact that she is sick. And I wasn't sure if it was cold sick or flu sick, but not *this* sick.

"Rose, it is nice to meet you." I'm thankful the pills are still taking the edge off.

Her hands are cold, her fingers thin, weak, her skin almost transparent with blue veins leading to hidden places.

"I've heard a lot about you." She speaks just like Daniel. The way she moves her mouth. "Did my son offer you tea, Livia?"

"I did not, Mum." He turns and walks to a cart located in the back of the room.

"Your home is beautiful, Rose. And your view…" I glance out the wall of windows to the redwood forest.

"It is." She takes in a deep breath. "God's country. Isn't this what they call Humboldt County?" Her head rests at an angle against the hospital bed.

I try not to stare, but through the corner of my eye, I see pill bottles blanketing the top of a makeshift nightstand.

"I'm very sorry," she whispers, either from lack of oxygen or fatigue, "about your brother."

My insides twist and move in an uncomfortable display of inner turmoil, only visualized by God. If only someone could see inside my brain, they wouldn't apologize. If she knew the things I did to cope, she'd tell her son to run in the opposite direction.

"Thank you," is all I manage, trying not to trip over my words with my tongue.

Rose closes her eyes and takes in a deep breath. She's peaceful in this moment, and I wonder if this is our sign to leave.

I glance back at Daniel again. He doesn't move, so I don't either.

A minute passes and then another. Rose's eyes remain closed.

Is she dying? She doesn't look well, but would she just up and die the moment I got here?

Her hands are warm. Dead people have cold hands.

Poppy chimes in, "She's not dead. Just listen."

To what? I answer Poppy in my head. *Rose's eyes are closed. Her lips aren't moving, Poppy.*

Daniel waits.

I cock my head to Daniel, as if to say, *What gives?*

Rose stirs. And her eyes flutter open, as if she were napping. "You know, Livia, I had to let go of a lot in my short life." She pauses to catch her breath. "Just accept situations for what they are. We come into this life with nothing." She pauses again. "And we leave this life with nothing but our character." She weakly adjusts her head. "I don't think God will be waiting for me in heaven, a clipboard in hand," she breathes, "asking what my annual income was, what make of car I drove, my career"—Rose pauses to cough—"if I had everything I wanted in life. I think he'll ask if I was kind to everyone I met. Patient. Tolerant. Loving." She pauses one last time. "When I faced tragedy, adversity, did I change as a human being, or did I carry my character all the way through? One of love, patience, and kindness." Rose coughs into her tissue, this time pulling away a little bit of blood. She wraps up the tissue to conceal her hurt. She looks at me dead in the eyes. "When life gives you the ultimate test, how will you handle it?"

I can't breathe.

I want to run away.

It's easier, softer than facing life on life's terms.

Rose's hand is still in mine, her fingers tightening around mine. She winks.

Rose nods, breathing.

Breathing is good, Rose. Breathing is good.

"He says, 'Stop sitting on my shoes.'" Rose laughs hoarsely, almost a crazed laugh as it continues.

My heart stops beating because she and I are the only ones who know what this means. And I'm not sure whether I'll laugh or cry or both. I want Rose to stop and continue, all at the same time. I want to get lost in her words. Roll in them. And push them away and leave them in the dark by themselves to find their own way out.

Breathe, I tell myself.

My throat constricts.

Now, I want, more than ever, for the pills to just take me away from my body. I want to hear Rose's words, I do, but I don't want to feel what I'm feeling right now.

And my tears fall one by one, staining my cheeks, creating dark spots of wet on my T-shirt.

I nod.

She pulls her hand from mine and tells me to lean forward. "I'll be with Jasper, watching over him. Keeping him safe." Rose reaches for the pendant that my dad had made after Jasper passed. After Rose is done examining the necklace, she slowly drops her hand back to her side with a pat on my hand. Her body looks exhausted. Rose closes her eyes again for a long time this time.

Daniel takes my hand and leads me toward the door. "She gets a bit crazy in the head when the pain medication kicks in. Says things that are off."

He takes me to the kitchen, lets go of my hand, and leans against the massive island in the middle of the kitchen. He folds his arms against his chest.

I don't say anything. I don't think I can.

Daniel bites his lip. And does the go-to-speak, hold-back, and-then-speak look. "Grief is grief, Livia. We all carry it. Varies with different people. Some mask it. Some live in it. Some run from it."

I try to remember all the reasons I came here. To explain my grief, as if making excuses? Condone my own behavior? To who?

Why? Give every excuse why I need to act upon my physical need for affection from someone? But all of these excuses—because that's what they are—don't seem much like reasons anymore, not after meeting Rose. I chew on each excuse—trying to rationalize why behavior is functional, reasonable, the only option—but I can't.

So, instead, I ask Daniel about his mother, "Is your mother dying?" I probably should have worded this question differently. A million different ways would have been better, but I didn't.

"Diagnosed with stage four breast cancer. My father won't allow hospice, so he and I split the duties. A lot more me than him."

I pause before I ask the next question. "What's your relationship like with your dad?"

"It's complicated."

"Complicated is my life. When was she diagnosed?" I'm standing two feet away from him.

"When I was thirteen. On my birthday actually." He smiles, most likely at a memory that has come up in his mind.

I do that, too, with a good memory. Not a bad one.

"When is your birthday?" I want to keep the smile on his face for as long as he'll have it there.

"October 8."

I choke out a cough.

"Livia?"

"Ours," is all I manage to say as I try to collect the pieces of fate that are seemingly falling from wherever fate comes from. "That's our birthday." Mine now. Just mine. Jasper stopped having birthdays on October 1.

"Your birthday is October 8?" Daniel tries to soothe the mistake I've just made with my words, and all I want is to take his mom's cancer away.

I begin chewing on my thumbnail to refrain from taking my hand and touching his lips in my best attempt to hold his smile there.

Carefully, he leans over and pulls my thumb from my mouth, and his fingers linger in mine. "We're doomed." His smile grows beneath his sadness.

Jasper and Livia, Sharing a Room, Age 8 ½

"Jasper? Are you awake?"
"Yeah?"
"Do you have both arms out of your covers?"
"Just one."
"Which arm?"
"Left." Jasper lets out a sigh. "Go to sleep, Mimi."
Silence.
"What about your legs?"
"Both of them are under the covers."
"Okay."
I adjust myself by reluctantly moving my left arm from the safety of my covers, keeping my right arm and legs nestled beneath the protection of the dark.

D aniel reaches for the butter behind me, his arm brushing my hip, his face inches from mine. "Are you hungry?" he asks.

I'm not sure, I want to say because the explosion of butterflies in my stomach is hiding any hunger pangs that I might have.

I nod to be polite.

"It looks as though your thumb doesn't deserve the abuse you're giving it." Daniel finally moves away from me, away from the kissing space he's created. He releases my thumb, my hand, before he turns and walks to the one-thousand-burner stove. Whatever it is, it's huge. Maybe not one thousand burners. Ten maybe. But it's big.

I attempt to put my thumbnail in my mouth again, but I think twice and shove my hands behind my back. "What did Rose's doctor say?"

"Wait for her to die." He laughs.

I don't laugh.

Daniel turns his head, resting his chin on his shoulder. "I'm sorry. That wasn't funny."

But I understand where he's coming from. The humor in death, there isn't any. But the human response to death can be morbid. I wonder how long Daniel has been grieving.

Slowly, I walk to the gigantic stove and lean against the counter, so I'm facing him as he cooks. "How long have you had to do this?"

"Cook? Or watch my mother die?" He doesn't make eye contact and adjusts the flame, as if trying to put off the answer.

When I don't respond, he knows what I'm getting at.

"Well, she was diagnosed when I turned thirteen. Went into remission when I was fifteen. And then it came back when I was sixteen—with no hope and no cure." Daniel shrugs, as if he's shrugging off the world. As if it might be easier to cope in his own way for now. "My father read through her diagnosis, labs, etcetera, etcetera. There was no need for a second opinion. That's when we moved here. So, my long-winded answer to your initial question is: since as far back as I can remember." And he says *remember* like it ends with an *A* and not an *R*. "I'm making a bacon sarnie. You'll have one. It tastes much better than a thumb." Daniel walks to the refrigerator and grabs bacon.

I can tell he wants to change the conversation.

"Has Rose always had the gift to communicate with…well, you know?"

Daniel walks back to me with the bacon and bread. "She's always known she's different. When she told her parents, they admitted her to a nuthouse." He pulls the bacon apart and puts it into the frying pan. "I guess they were trying to scare the spirits out of her. My mum knew she wasn't crazy, so in order to get out, she played along."

There's a long pause as the bacon sizzle fills the void.

Daniel turns so that he's facing me. "She moved out when she was eighteen and never spoke to her parents again."

"You've never met your grandparents?"

"Would you like tommy sauce or brown sauce?" Daniel puts the bread in the toaster, trying to keep himself busy.

I slowly tilt my head to the left in curiosity, not knowing what either of my options are.

Daniel clarifies, "My apologies. Tommy sauce, uh, catsup, I think you call it. And brown sauce is like catsup but tangier."

"Tommy sauce," I say because it's what I know. Many years I've spent looking at Jasper for the answers to questions about life. I need to try something different this time. "No. Wait. I'll try the brown sauce actually, please."

He covers the toast with brown sauce, layers several pieces of bacon on the bread, and closes it up with the top piece of bread, also covered in brown sauce.

"This, Livia, is a bacon sarnie." He pushes both of our plates over to the other side of the kitchen counter. "Can I get you something to drink?"

Jasper bought me a shirt back when he went to New York City sophomore year. The shirt said, *Everything Is Better with Bacon.* He brought it back with a face that suggested he knew it was meant for me and no one else.

"I'll have water, please," I say, pushing the memory away "Where did you learn to make these?"

I wait for him to sit. He slides into the seat next to mine, so close that our knees touch.

"British thing."

Daniel watches me as I take a bite. The bacon, lopped up in the sweet, tangy brown sauce, crunches with each bite. I try not to moan as I chew. It's so good.

"My brother..." I pause to contemplate my next words—not because of what I'll say, but knowing that he'll appreciate me changing the subject from his mother. "He brought me back a shirt when he traveled to New York City a few years ago. It says, *Everything Is Better with Bacon.*"

An empathetic smile spreads across his face—not a plastic one put together to demonstrate sincerity, but one created deep within the heart, one that can only be generated through a felt sense of shared grief.

Daniel takes his napkin and wipes his mouth as I finish my sandwich. "Your brother was great?"

I, too, wipe my mouth. His knee pushes into mine in the softest way possible.

I nod, justifying what will come out next but feeling the desperation inside to share it with someone else. "When we got the call, one of the surgeons donated his pilot and his jet to us to take down to LA." Feelings pile into my chest like mounds of bricks. "My dad and an FBI agent were there to pick us up at the airport and drove us to the staging center."

Daniel doesn't look at me, but his knee presses harder into mine. He gently cups his hands around his water glass.

Crowded, the butterflies push on my insides, and my chest grows with an ache, making more room for the butterflies and the bricks.

"It was at the fairgrounds in one of the halls where they held the exhibits. The art exhibits. The craft shows. There were cots. And families. And sadness." I nod, as if trying to convince myself that it doesn't hurt that bad. That the sadness and despair don't come flooding back. But they do.

Reality: the world or the state of things as they actually exist, as opposed to an idealistic or notional idea of them.

The place I'm in right now, at this very moment, is hard to exist in and even harder to breathe in.

"Some people were inconsolably crying. A mother sat on the floor uncontrollably sobbing." I stop. "We sat and waited on a cot—my mom, dad, and me."

Daniel's leg pushes harder into mine.

"A woman who I assume was an FBI agent was dressed in business casual—and I remember this because it was a humid day in LA, and the hall was hot. She was in a sports coat, and I noticed the sweat rings under her arms. She got on a loud speaker. She said that the first bus of survivors was coming in. We hadn't heard from Jasper since it all went down, so we didn't know much at this point." I spread my fingers out and place them on the cool granite. "We watched a sea of people move like a body of water. Or a flock of birds, swarming across the sky, following the leader. They quickly moved together. My mom, dad, and I followed suit." I swallow my grief when I hear it come out in my tone.

But Daniel doesn't ask any questions. He lets me continue.

Have you ever felt like you can't catch your breath? Or hope the breath you breathe will be your last? I want to ask Daniel.

I didn't feel this way after my dad left.

I didn't feel this way after Poppy died.

And I especially didn't feel this way when I lost my virginity to Simon James.

But I feel this way now. Like some massive feeling is blocking my airway, and I can't breathe past it.

I look at Daniel.

He's staring at his water glass, and his leg is pushed up against mine, urging me on, saying, *Continue*, without words.

"We followed the sadness out the front doors of the hall where the bus was pulling up. It was a bright orange school bus. But, this time, it wasn't full of kids after a long day of school; it was full of post-traumatic stress disorder, probably years of therapy, and awful sadness that only those who have survived know what it feels like. The doors opened like an accordion." I laugh to myself. "My therapist has asked for this story over and over. I'm not sure why it's so easy to talk to you, but I never told her or anyone anything."

Daniel still stares at his water glass. He's biting his lower lip. He doesn't look up, as if he's afraid—not for himself, but for me.

"Survivors began to pour out. Reunited with family. Lots of tears. Kissing. And hugging. I've never wished for something in my life so fucking much, Daniel. I've never prayed so hard in my life." I shake my head, ashamed of what I say next. "Why couldn't just one of those families have been us?"

I take in a deep breath because I know the last part of this story is heartbreaking. "The sea of sadness gravitated back inside the hall—some with their loved ones, many without. Many, many, without. And, in a weird way, I was grateful. I know that's selfish to say, but I was grateful other families were hurting just as bad as we were." I stop and push back the tears, only for a few seconds.

"My mom, dad, and I sat on a cot closest to the front door this time." I pause. "In that moment, at the staging center, my mom should have been yelling at my dad. They couldn't stand to be in the same room together. In that moment, I should have been worrying about my application to Harvey College. Jasper should have been sitting next to me. But he wasn't. And the world keeps turning, and I can't understand why." My last words fall apart into a whisper.

His knee moves even closer, as if there's room to move, pushing into my leg with intensity.

"We sat there in silence; the hall was eerily quiet. Families waited. Nerves high. The FBI agent called over the loud speaker that the next survivor bus would be coming in one minute. So, the wave of people moved outside again, just like cattle. And, just like the time before, as the bus pulled up, the accordion door opened again—this time a different bus. And survivors poured out again. Some of the families we'd walked back into the hall with last time now had their loved ones—their brother, their sister, their cousin, father, or mother. They're a family again."

My chest begins to ache, and I feel short of breath. I need a pill right now.

Daniel turns to me with purpose, and his eyes burrow deep inside mine. "You don't have to continue if you don't want to, Liv." He takes a strand of my hair and pushes it behind my ear.

"I don't want to." I pause. "I need to." Now, my legs are between his, as if this were how it should have always been. "I felt like I was losing my mind. Like reality was slipping away, just out of my grasp, and I couldn't stop it. And I couldn't believe it either. Like my brain was making excuses for Jasper. Why he wasn't on the last two buses." I pause as I allow my fingers to fidget.

"We went and sat back down, but not thirty seconds later, the agent came over the loud speaker for the last and final time. Uneasily we went outside, slowly, terrified of who wasn't on the bus. I counted the families as we huddled together in the suffocating night sky. About twenty families left. The odds were good, right?" My voice quivers with hope and sadness. Like maybe, if I retell it, it will end differently. "Sometimes, I still think it's all a bad dream and that Jasper will stagger out of his room before school, complain about the time, rub his right eye, and say, *What are you staring at?*"

I cover my mouth because the heartbreak of truth is almost too much to bear: he's not coming back.

"The last bus pulled up." I try to take a deep breath, but it gets caught somewhere in my chest, only allowing me to take a half-breath. But I take what I can get. "Three buses full of survivors. Three buses."

His thighs squeeze tighter around mine.

"Six survivors. Only six survivors came off the last bus. And Jasper wasn't one of them. You start to try to deny the fact, right? He's at a hospital somewhere. They've overlooked him. He's safe; we just need to find him."

I don't tell Daniel this part because it makes me feel crazy. I begged the bus driver to give me my brother. And she cried as I begged. I screamed at her. Told her she didn't bring my brother home like she was supposed to. I used words I'd never used with anyone. But she took it. She cried, and she took it. I told her to turn on the lights. I checked each individual seat, each seat, for my brother as Tracy collapsed outside on the ground, my dad by her side. I got to the last seat, and Jasper wasn't there.

I tell Daniel the ending I want him to hear, "I checked seat after seat, Daniel. Twice. He wasn't there. I yelled from the back of the bus to the driver, 'You forgot my brother. He's at the college. Can you go get him, please?'"

"Daniel?" The British tone is short, deep. He says *Daniel* like it's one syllable instead of two.

"Shit." Daniel rolls his eyes. "What time is it?"

"I don't know. I forgot my phone in the car."

Tracy has probably made my phone disintegrate with text messages with the way I left the house this afternoon.

"It's six o'clock." He shoves his phone back in his pocket, but his legs stay around mine. He doesn't turn, and his eyes stay fixed on mine.

I'm sorry, he mimes with his mouth when a tall, older redheaded Daniel glides into the gigantic kitchen, as if the room expected him. Like he's late for a talk he's giving on some sort of innovative surgery.

Setting his briefcase on the counter, he looks down at his phone and then acknowledges us. "Oh. Hello. My son didn't inform me that we had a guest." Again, voice short.

"You didn't get the telegram I sent to the hospital, Dad?"

Ignoring Daniel's sarcasm, the Daniel look-alike but older says, "I'm Radcliff Pearson. And you are?" His glasses sit at the end of his nose, newspaper in the other hand, his blue scrubs neat, clean, presentable, as if he wears them for looks and not for blood.

I stand, tripping over my own two feet and Daniel's, like I should have stood a long time ago, but my thoughts just couldn't meet the future.

"Livia Stone. Nice to meet you, Dr. Pearson," I say in the old-me voice. Like it's all premeditated.

"Please. Mr. Pearson is fine." He tosses his hand in a give-no-mind-to-it way as he looks through the mail on the counter, shoving the newspaper under his arm.

Daniel rolls his eyes.

"It was nice to meet you, Miss Stone." Mr. Pearson pauses, looking up from the mail to me. "Daniel, you can see your friend out." He turns on his heel and strides out of the kitchen and down the hallway, just the way he came in. His running shoes—probably super-expensive surgeon sneakers—barely squeak down the stone hallway.

"I have to go," I whisper to Daniel, my mind imagining what my mother has done to my phone, text message after text message. Call after call. I'm surprised Belle's Hollow PD hasn't tracked my phone down to the Pearsons' yet.

"Wait. Sit."

I do—and not because I have to, but because leaving Daniel is something I don't think I'm capable of doing right now. He takes my hands in his while he does the mouth thing, not making eye contact, but he doesn't say what I think he's going to say.

"Do you ever feel like you're supposed to be in your life at the exact moment you realize you're supposed to be? Like your life has never, ever made sense before." He searches the floor and my eyes, licking his lips—not in some weird sexual way, but in a way of conviction, intention. He continues, "But then you have this moment, and you realize your entire past makes sense? And that maybe God put you, me, in this instance, on this planet for this exact experience right here."

He reaches up to touch my cheek with his thumb and slowly runs the length of my jaw. "I don't know why my mother chose Belle's Hollow, Liv. I don't know why I moved half a world away from a place I felt perfectly content in with a dick of a father and a sick mother and a cat—a dumb cat, no less—named Sebastian. I don't know why you stopped your car for me on Monday. But two things I believe in most: things I can see and science." He pauses. "I've never witnessed a heart break with my eyes, but I have now. I want to put the pieces of you back together. Build a mold around your heart. Made of titanium and all matter indestructible, so it never gets broken again."

This time—*this time*—I don't even notice his accent. I want to take him by the hand and lead him where heartbreak doesn't exist and sick mothers don't die. Where life can be measured, not death. Where death isn't real. And all that surrounds us is the best of what life has to offer: the color pink, unicorns, and puppies. Just good.

But then these words fall from my mouth, "That's not real life, Daniel."

Being with Daniel makes me forget, only momentarily, about what my life is like outside this house. Outside of Simon. Outside of Belle's Hollow. Outside of my life. Like I'm a stranger who's just knocked on the my-life-with-Daniel door because it's fiercely stormy outside, and I ask to come in out of the chaos.

With these feelings he gives me, I know the sadness will return. I know the heartache will eat me alive tonight as I crawl in bed. And I'd rather not feel it. Not feel any of it.

I stand, and it catches me off guard because it's not something I want to do. Maybe it's my heart trying to protect itself.

But Daniel, who's still sitting, grabs for my hand. "I'll walk you out." His fingers fraternize with mine. He doesn't tell me I should stay for dinner.

It's dark outside.

"My mom's going to freak out."

"Why?"

"I left upset this afternoon."

The rocks crunch under our feet, our pace a snail's.

"I dropped an AP course, and when my parents wanted to talk about it, I bailed."

"Why'd you drop the course?" And *course* sounds like *couse* without the R.

I think about this for a moment. I shrug because I'm not really sure. "I guess I don't know. I missed a lot of school after Jasper died. It's just that...Mr. Joe has a connection with Harvey College, and I'd written an essay that was noticed by one of the English professors there. Mr. Joe said that he'd help me get in."

"Wow. Harvey? Even the Brits are well aware of Harvey."

I kick a rock.

"So, you jumped ship? Have you talked to Mr. Joe?"

"No."

"So, you dropped the course and haven't talked to him about it?" *Couse* again. Not *course*.

"Yes." I feel the shame take shape in my face.

There's a long silence as we approach my car. I wish I hadn't parked so close. For the sake of the universe and just a few more minutes with Daniel, I wish I had parked on the moon.

"God, what a beautiful place," I say, not ready to hear what he has to say about Mr. Joe.

"It's just a house, Livia."

"Castle," I correct.

Daniel stops and takes my elbows in his hands. He looks me square in the eyes for a long moment. "What if my father wasn't a surgeon and my mother didn't have cancer and we lived in a modest three-bedroom home in town? And what if I told you, behind locked doors at night, when the moon was quiet and the dark was relenting, that things weren't what they seemed? That, on the outside, it was a perfect situation, right? But people change in the dark, Livia. People change in darkness. Would it change the way you looked at all this?"

I try to pretend it wouldn't, but wouldn't it? I think of home. My home. My dad, my mother, surviving under one roof.

"You'd be more human," I whisper.

"Is any one person more human than the other?" He pronounces *other* without the R.

"Do you always answer all statements with philosophical questions?"

He smiles.

We reach my car, and I extend my arm for my door handle, but Daniel gently takes my hand in his again and uses his other hand to open my car door. "Please," he says, "allow me."

He steps back so that I can get around the door and sit in my driver's seat.

Daniel leans in, his arms resting on the roof. "Thank you, Livia, for seeing me today." He looks at my phone, which is now vibrating across the seat.

Simon's name is on the screen, but Daniel doesn't say anything.

My heart stops, and now, it's flopping around on a bank like a suffocating fish. And, if fish could talk, it would say, *Help me.*

He bites his lip. "I'd really like to kiss you right now, Livia."

I'm dead.

My lips feel swollen and big, wanting his kiss more than any other kiss in the history of best on-screen kisses ever.

"But I'd rather wait until your heart begins to mend."

And this kills the heat that, only thirty seconds ago, began to radiate through my body.

Daniel leans in the car and softly pushes his lips to the space between my collarbone and my neck. My entire body goes limp, numb.

"Text me when you get home, so I know you made it safe." He pulls back from the car window, shoving his hands in his pockets.

I don't roll up my window as I start the car because God knows I'll need fresh air, cold fresh air, to shake off the remnants of Daniel.

Tracy and my dad are in the living room when I walk through the front door. They don't say a word. Silence covers every square inch of our living room, even the walls, and it seeps down like molasses.

I quietly shut the door behind me, my tail between my legs.

They blew up my phone with text messages. Phone calls.

This was always a Jasper move, not a Livia move. He was the one who came in late, the one who had to explain to Tracy why he was past curfew or hadn't answered his phone. Not me. I was the good girl. Followed the rules with only minor mishaps with alcohol—unbeknownst to my parents. A rule-follower, and I prided myself on it. Homework done on Fridays, always ahead of time. Now, I can't remember what homework assignments were given. It was Jasper's job to break Tracy's heart and mend it back together. He was good at that.

Livia Stone, Parental Heartbreaker.

"Hey," I say as my steps sound like loud, giant footsteps against the hardwood floor.

Tracy is on the couch, sitting next to the end table. My dad is on the easy chair, stretched out, legs crossed, shoes on the coffee table, like he has been here for the last three years. Like Tracy didn't fall to pieces every morning after Dad disappeared while Jasper and I were left with the wake of his destruction.

"Your shoes aren't supposed to be on the furniture," I tell him.

"I'll pass out the rules, Livia"—Tracy's tone is curt—"which, by the way, you've broken several." She's trying to stay sane. Trying not to explode. "I…" She pauses and toys with her nail, distracting herself or trying to find the right words.

But I know how this line goes. *I expect this from your brother but not from you.*

What did Dr. Elizabeth say about this?

Breathe. Don't react. Think. Wait. Sleep on it.

But then again, I've always been mild about my reactions. Not a hothead. Jasper and I were very different in that way. Similar in a lot of ways, ones that Mom liked better in Jasper than she did me.

"Your favorite twin died, Mom. I'm not him. But I'm holding up to his roles in the family. Staying out late. Forgetting my cell phone."

"Apologize to your mother, Livia." My father's voice has always been enduring but not now. Now, it's diplomatic, and he never calls me Livia. "Do you have any idea how much worry you caused us, Liv?"

He leans forward from his chair. Our chair. Not his. The soft light makes him look younger. Like the years of alcoholism haven't eaten away his youthfulness.

"Oh, now, you're here to play 'Dad'?" I use air quotes with my fingers, the ones Jasper used to hate.

"Listen"—he points at me—"I'll take every last ounce of what I deserve. I know what I did, Livia. And I'm not proud of it. And I can't promise that, two weeks from now, it won't be different. All you and I have is the present moment. Today. Now, you can hate me all you want, which I expect, but that doesn't give you any right to disrespect your mother or her rules. Keep your damn phone on you. Answer her when she texts you." He pauses. His eyeballs seem to grow in the orange light, but I know it's the tears building up. My dad coughs once, leaving his fist in front of his mouth. "We don't want to lose another child, Liv." His voice quivers.

Jasper was so much better at making off-the-cuff, convincing arguments. Not me. I have to think about it. I sit on the idea for days before I can articulate my thoughts and put them into a statement that makes sense. Where the validity isn't questionable.

But I have to get one last dig in. Who knows why I need to. And the regret begins before I say it, but I can't *not* say it. "You lost me a long time ago," I whisper and drag my feet upstairs to my room.

I take three pills and use the water on my nightstand. My heart is pumping so fast, and my ears are swimming. I find no solace in the last dig I threw at my dad. I feel lost. Alone. Afraid. The hollowness I have inside me is the dead tree bark, blackened grief shriveling away into nothingness.

Poppy: "Those pills aren't going to help you, Liv."

I wince, trying to make Poppy's words disappear from my head. "Leave me alone, Poppy." I just need something. I just need relief. "I'm tired."

Staring at the bottle of pills labeled Valium, I hold the bottle in my hand.

Take one every three hours as needed.

My heart is whooshing.

My head is pulsating.

And my feelings are eating me alive.

I open the bottle and take another pill for good measure.

Turning off the light in my room, the darkness greeting my needs, I pull my knees up to my chest and let the tears silently meet my pillow. And I wait for the medicine to take effect while I think of Daniel and forget the heartbreak.

Fuck you, Jasper, for leaving.

I saw the word
Written on his back window in dirt.
Fag.
I rushed to erase it,
But he was behind me.
He saw it.
Later, when the night settled in,
I reached his room, pushed the door open.
"Want to talk?"
"No."
"Can I sit?"
"Free country."
I walk in.
We sit,
In silence,
And let the world rage around us.

A bright orb from last night enters my mind, making my eyelids turn a bright red from the inside.

The melancholy of what I did the night before—four pills, no longer one, two, three…now, four—extends out of my brain and washes over my already predicted shitty day.

Why did I do that? I shouldn't have done that.

I grab the pill bottle and check the damage I have left.

Four.

Right now, I want to dump them down the toilet, so I won't make the same mistake again. Then, the guilt quiets down very quickly, but somewhere in the same brain, in the front part, my conscious mind thinks better of it.

Keep them, it says. *You'll need them, and you know it.*

I look at my phone—11:02 a.m.

"Crap!" I jump out of bed. I haven't slept this late or for this long for a month. "I'm late."

I spring into the shower that connects Jasper's bedroom and mine, and it's so automatic.

I wait for his music to start.

It doesn't.

But this thought doesn't completely fill me with loneliness, as it did just yesterday. It's a little softer this time. A tiny bit softer, and I'm not sure if it's the pills or the world.

As I let the hot water run on my face, there's a knock on the bathroom door. My head though is still a bit fuzzy from last night.

"Yeah?"

"It's me," Tracy says. "Can we talk when you get out?"

"Yeah. But I have to get to school."

There's a long silence.

"Well, unless Belle's Hollow High has started school on Sundays, I'd say you have another day off."

I take a huge breath. Relief. Instant reprieve that I don't have school and that I don't have to face anyone today if I don't want to.

Not Mr. Joe.

Not Simon.

Not Whitney.

I don't have to face life.

Tracy is sitting on my bed when I walk out of the bathroom, towel wrapped around me, my wet hair in fat chunks down my back.

"Hey," I say. "I'm sorry," comes out of my mouth.

Maybe it's the full night of sleep, plus some, or the pills I took last night. Either way, I feel good.

I sit down next to her.

"Me, too."

There's an awkward silence between us. Two strangers, related by blood, have spent the last seventeen years with useless words to fill silence. Now though, words have run out. The encounters from here on out have to count. They have to count, or we won't make it.

"Liv, we need to talk." Her words are shaky, her serious nurse face.

"I know." I reach up and attempt to run my fingers through my wet hair, a fruitless effort, yet I'm trying to divert my attention or hers. I'm not sure.

Tracy's eyes are on her hands. "What do you think about cleaning out Jasper's room?" After each word, a break and a breath.

"No," comes out too fast. I'm unprepared, and I want to take it back, or add further explanation. "I'm not ready." I pause. "Are you?"

"I don't know."

My throat feels dry, and the hair on my back causes a cold chill to run up my spine.

"Let's have lunch today, just me and you. Las Cazuela's?"

This makes me think about the bacon sarnie that Daniel made me last night. I nod at another futile attempt at quality time with Tracy.

Quiet nods.

Awkward words.

Check, please.

Tracy gently places her hand on mine. "Jasper wasn't my favorite twin, Liv. Just so you know. I have a harder time communicating with you than I did with him, I guess."

I don't say anything.

"Your AP class. I just wish you had talked to me about it before you did it."

Silence on my end.

When could I have talked to you about it? When you're working at night? When you're crying in the shower? When you're grieving my dead brother?

"Are you and Dad getting back together?" My stomach twists in a knot at the thought, between the anger and the hurt.

Tracy's hand tightens around mine. "No."

"So, he's really here to help with me? And that's it?"

Tracy searches my room, maybe looking for her own unprepared answers. "Remember when you guys were twelve, and you and your dad would go down to the library and come home with a stack of books? You'd spend the time reading each book and analyzing what worked and what didn't work about the story. And there was joy on your face when you and your dad connected on a point." She smiles through the tears that have formed in the corners of her eyes.

Before Dad's drinking became a problem.

Before Dad hit Jasper.

Before Dad left.

The Before Dad.

"As much as you don't want to hear it, Liv, he's here for you and only you. He's here to help with your broken heart. Just like when he read *Old Yeller* to you. Remember? Oh, you were so sad when the dog died."

I wish, this time, it were that easy. That my dad could say a few dad words, rub my forehead, and give me a glass of chocolate milk, so everything would seem to find its place again in my complicated universe.

"I know your world isn't the same as when you were twelve. I know this hurt is far different than anything we've ever experienced."

"I want him back, Mom." My bottom lip begins to quiver. "Some days—" I choke up. "Some days don't feel real. Like I'm just waiting for him to come through the door, and he doesn't."

Tracy pulls me to her chest. "I know, baby. I know. Me, too."

Tracy finds my ear with her lips. Through her touch, I know she'd rather heal my heart than her own. We've had this inexplicable communicational divide for most of my life, but I know, in this moment, she wants my world to be right. And the truth of the matter is, she can't fix it. Nobody can.

There's a long pause where the outside world freezes, and then finally she speaks, "How are your meetings going with Dr. Elizabeth?"

"Fine," I whisper a lie. As if there's peace of mind, comfort in lying. An unethical deed I keep allowing to happen, and I can't explain why.

Like facing the truth, the consequences, is too much to deal with. Before Jasper's death, I wasn't a liar. I also wasn't a whore.

Now, I'm both.

"Good," Tracy says.

Tracy leaves a few minutes later with my word on lunch. We'll eat. Make small talk and awkward body movements to distract us from the gaping hole that separates us.

Tracy and Jasper are more alike, in my opinion. Easygoing. A free spirit to an extent. A natural leader because of their wit and charm. Both Jasper and Tracy had a way of speaking off-the-cuff, using philosophical points that drew others together. They were the gray. They could do the gray.

I'm different. Black and white. I need time to think on things before I speak. Preparation. Type A personality.

Jasper and Tracy just had an unspoken bond that I couldn't fit into. But my dad—the dysfunctional one, the alcoholic, a lawyer—I can relate to him. His job is to prepare arguments overnight, strategize, be methodical, analytical. We are the same, the exact same.

I take the towel from my body and stand in front of the mirror. The imperfect body, the one without any bumps. But I see someone looking back at me, someone whose lack of sleep is reflected just beneath her eyes. Her deep blue eyes have changed to gray. And the gauntness in her cheeks reflects the sadness in her heart.

Though I see her reflection—remnants of me in her eyes, her hands, her thighs—it's only emptiness that fills her bones, her body. Where there was once a passion for life, for success, it is now clouded with the reflection of someone she doesn't know.

Who is this girl?

This sad girl staring back.

Has too much time passed for her to see her twin brother through her eyes? That was where people said we looked most alike. The eyes and the smile.

A void fills my insides as my memory replaces the girl's face with Jasper's. I know this is my imagination, my desperate, vain attempt to see where the world went wrong. Took the wrong person. Surely, there was a miscalculation. Somewhere in the universe, God got it wrong.

My phone chimes, bringing my attention away from the reflection of the girl who's somehow supposed to be me, from my nightstand where it puts off a tune next to the bottle of pills that alleviated my broken heart last night. Made me unfeel any sadness and allowed me to drift off to sleep. The guilt begins to retreat.

It's a text from Cao.

> Cao: My mother is the devil in comfortable shoes. I think she thinks I feel more Chinese now than before we left. I don't. Don't tell her. I figure this is my only way out alive.

> Me: LOL. When are you coming home?

> Cao: Driving now. See you tomorrow morning for school? U OK?

She's always asking if I'm okay. I'm not, but I text her a thumbs-up.

> Cao: You're lying. But whatever. You never use emojis. Just FYI. Not sure if you've noticed that or not. Call you when I get home.

I've used emojis before.

> Me: I do too use emojis. Remember that one time I sent you the middle finger?

> Cao: OK. The fact that you had to say "remember the time..." ;) See? You don't use them.

> Me: Drive safe.

I go back to my text messages and notice several text messages from Simon, and my stomach doubles over and not in a good way. How can a boy I hold good childhood memories with give off a merciless feeling of uneasiness, of loss?

Just past my phone, the pill bottle beckons me with its metaphorical claws that wrap around my shoulders and whispers, *Just two. Two will make you feel better. Your brother just died. You need this, Livia. You need some relief.*

What did the prescription say? Just one every four hours? Four every hour? Does it matter?

I reach for the bottle of pills and fight through the resistance my body gives off.

The guilt has retreated all the way back to my mind.

A conversation with myself and the bottle of pills.

Me: Remember what alcohol did to my dad?

The bottle: That's different. I'm not alcohol. Besides, you were prescribed me. Come on, your brother died.

Me: I'm bound to make worse decisions when I ingest you.

The bottle: It will help you not feel.

Me: I need not to feel.

The bottle: Come on, you deserve me. It will help at lunch with your mom. Remember? Awkward conversation. Body jerks. That whole bit. You're welcome.

And that's all it takes because I remove the last four pills from the bottle and quickly swallow them without water.

I sit on the side of the bed and wait for them to take effect.

And, when they do, it's glorious. It doesn't take long.

I remember Dr. Elizabeth telling Tracy, "They're rapid release. New on the market. These will help."

I feel better. I feel stronger. I feel as though I don't care what people think of me; in fact, they're pretty lucky to be in my presence.

Yeah.

This.

Is.

It.

I have arrived.

I'm relaxed, and there's this squishy—not sure that's a word I'd use normally—feeling that surrounds me like a bubble. A protective pink bubble that reminds me of how important I am.

"Poppy?" I whisper. "Are you there?"

Still, nothing.

Is this what Poppy feels like?

I look back to my phone and click on the text messages that Simon sent me.

I watch as my fingers glide across the screen, as if they don't belong to me. As if they're someone else's fingers. Thin, long, and lean and just like Jasper's. And the mention of his name doesn't hurt as bad this time.

See? the bottle of pills whispers from my nightstand. *You feel alive.*

> Message 1 from Simon yesterday at 4:42 p.m.: Liv. Where are u? @ Hawthorne Hill. Waiting 4 u.

Crap. But it doesn't take long for me to forget about it. *I'm just a person trying to heal my wounds*, I tell myself.

> Message 2 from Simon: Livia. Call me. Whitney is freaking out.

> Message 3 from Simon: Livia. Seriously. She's freaking out.

Missed call from Simon at 1:42 a.m.

> Message 4 from Simon: Liv. Shit. IDK where she's at, but she's gone nuts.

> Message 5 from Simon: She scrolled thru my text messages 2 you.

Lunch with Tracy Earlier Today

"Livia, are you all right?"
"Just tired, Mom."
"Did you not sleep well last night?"
"No."
Awkward conversation.
Awkward conversation.
Awkward conversation.
Lunch over.

Monday morning calls too quickly and piles on my shoulders like a bad dream when I come to the quick—and sad—realization that I have no more pills to take. No buffer. No protection against my feelings. It feels as though there's a snow cloud in the middle of my brain that sits and waits for me to try to think again.

I turn the alarm off on my phone and drag myself into the shower. It's six forty-five a.m.

I wait for Jasper. His music. His, *What are you staring at, Liv?*

But I'm met with darkness on the other side of the door.

The snow cloud separates, and my mind slowly becomes clearer.

I called Simon back yesterday, but he didn't answer. *What did Whitney see anyway?*

I rinse the shampoo from my hair.

It's not like we'd sexted or anything. We'd kept our messages subliminal. Quiet. That's it. Right?

I try to think, but this stupid cloud keeps me from doing so, and I don't like it.

What could she have seen that made her flip a lid?

Simon never got back to me.

My dad is sitting at the dining room table when I make my way downstairs. He's drinking coffee and reading the newspaper. The way he used to do.

The Before Dad.

Years ago.

Before his drinking dictated when he woke up in the morning, if he went to work, how he treated his family. Before he abandoned us.

Our eyes connect, like the time they did when I received an academic award in eighth grade. With a sea of people, Dad's eyes linked with mine, and I knew he was proud.

But this morning, his eyes are softer, more compassionate. Like he's giving me room to breathe without saying a word.

"Hey," he says. "I made pancakes."

I shake my head, and I'm not sure if it's to shake off his nice gesture or because I don't like pancakes anymore, and he would have known that if he'd hung around a bit longer.

"I'm good. Just taking an apple," I say.

I reach for the door handle.

"Liv?" he asks.

I look up, and he's turned toward me in his chair.

"Are you okay?"

No, actually, Dad, I'm not. I'm taking pills now to cope with losing Jasper. I'm taking pills to cope with you leaving us. I'm taking pills, Dad, because, somehow, taking pills is far easier than dealing with life on life's terms. And I'm a whore who's probably going to get called out on it today.

"Yeah."

Quietly, I shut the door behind me, drop down the stairs, and see Simon, who's at my car.

"I tried to call you back," he says as I approach him.

"What did she see?" I ask, trying to push away the dread building in my stomach right now.

"Nothing really. I just brushed it off like it was no big deal and that we'd meet at Hawthorne Hill to talk about J. I told her that we had a bond that no one could understand."

He tries to grab for my hand. I avoid him and walk to the driver's side.

"So, why all the panicked text messages, Simon?" I drop my hands to my waist, my backpack on my shoulder.

"That was before she and I talked."

When he texted me on Sunday, I started to feel like the cat was out of the bag, and in some weird way, I felt relief because maybe then this would be the beginning of truth. That hiding this big, fat secret was only causing more heartache than it was worth—and not the heartache of longing, but the heartache of measuring my morals against Mother Teresa or something. Like my morals didn't exist. And I thought, somehow, maybe this was our gateway to the truth.

So, when Simon goes to touch my hand again, I pull away. Making it obvious that we need to stop all this nonsense.

"Simon, we can't do this anymore."

"What?"

"This. Us. Together. Touching. Having sex," I finally say the truth.

Finally, one right decision.

Livia: 1

World: 633

Simon chews on his cheek. "Liv…" He stalls. "When…when I'm with you, I feel like the world stops. And I feel like your body understands mine. Like the grief we both feel can only rid itself when we're together." His eyes search the ground but then make their way back to mine.

"Well, you can't feel that way."

"Why not?"

"Because you aren't supposed to, Simon. We are two people grieving the same person, but it isn't healthy because I feel like a whore. *You* have a girlfriend," I sigh. "A good one."

"I can break up with her if that's what you want."

"No! I don't want that." I open the driver's door.

I chew on these words before I spit them out because I'm sure it will hurt him, but maybe by hurting him, he'll walk away and get on with his life. "Simon, I don't like you in that way. What we had were moments that held us together because our hearts were broken. We sought refuge in that. We hid from the world. We hid our dirty secret."

"Dirty? Is-is that what you think?"

I roll my eyes. "You know what I mean." I get into the car, and he leans his hands on my window seal.

He's hurt; I can tell. Just like the time he and Jasper got into a fight, a physical fight, when we were eight. I pulled them apart while they swung, and I took a hit to the jaw, but it didn't stop me. Simon's giving me the same look.

"I don't know what we shared, Liv, but it was everything but dirty. Have a nice life." And he removes his hands from my car. He climbs into his truck and leaves.

I rest my head on my headrest and text Cao.

On my way. Running late.

I wonder if I'll see Daniel today. I didn't hear from him yesterday. It makes my stomach grow with hidden anticipation.

But I tell myself, *Why would you bring him into my chaos? His mother is dying. You're taking pills to cope instead of seeing Dr. Elizabeth. You sleep with a boy to smooth out the wrinkles in your heart. A mess.*

I don't see Daniel on the way to Cao's, and we don't see him on the way toward school. And he didn't text me at all on Sunday. I begin to feel less significant.

Handing Cao my phone, I tell her to read the last text messages from Simon.

"What the fuck?" She covers her mouth. "Does Whitney know?"

I nervously bite my thumbnail. "I don't think so." My stomach feels like it's full of knives and brass knuckles. I pretend like I don't care, like it's not a big deal, when, clearly, it is. "We didn't say much through text. Simon was at the house this morning."

Cao turns to me, her mouth agape.

"He said he told her that we were just friends and that we were just tight because of Jasper."

"Oh my God, Liv. Seriously." Cao's hands are now on her head. "If I could speak Chinese right now, I'd totally be praying to the gods that Karma didn't come in and kick your ass."

"I know, I know. I told him we couldn't do this anymore." My voice grows quiet because I start to acknowledge the fear that I just brushed off moments ago. "The sex thing," I whisper.

"Well, you've got that right. Besides, what about British boy? Hot ginger. Daniel."

"I went to his house." I think about what happened in Rose's room, and I want to tell Cao, but I feel as though I can't do the story justice, or it's just too unbelievable for people who aren't familiar with that sort of thing, so I skip it. "How was your trip?"

"What? No. You went to Daniel's house, and you just want to stop the story there? Don't think so. Continue."

"Nothing to tell. I met his mom. He made me a sandwich. His dad came home. That's it." Not sure how private he wants to remain about his mother's sickness or the fact that his dad is colder than the center of an ice cube.

"Your face says otherwise, Liv." Cao smiles. "You like him."

"How was the trip with your mom?" I try to change the subject.

"Torture," Cao sighs. "She took me to an authentic Chinese restaurant." Cao thinks. "Mr. Kwan's. My mom ordered me sea cucumbers." Cao pushes on her hot-pink velveteen pants to smooth out the wrinkles. "But, Liv, the sea cucumbers thought they were a vegetable. They weren't bad. But I think I'd prefer something more like sweet and sour chicken.

"But Mr. Kwan insisted, 'Sea cucumber. You order. You love. Healthy. Delicacy.'" She imitates Mr. Kwan.

"And then he looked at me like I was supposed to know. I ate half of my dish, mostly the rice. Then, we went back to our hotel room after we went to China Town, and because I was curious"— Cao rolls her eyes—"I Googled sea cucumbers." She makes *the face*. The face that looks like she's about to puke or explode. And the probability of her exploding is highly unlikely.

"Are you going to puke?"

Cao shakes her head and slowly drags it in my direction. "Do you know what sea cucumbers are?"

I shake my head.

"They look like uncircumcised penises floating through the ocean, Liv. Uncircumcised penises! And do you know what they do to protect themselves when they're in danger?"

I'm trying not to laugh. I'm trying to be a supportive best friend because Cao still looks like she's about to explode. Or puke.

"Big, fat penises," she whispers under her breath, still attempting to push through the wrinkles on her pants. "They propel themselves to safety by expelling their guts, Liv." She huffs. "Explain that one. I don't even know if I'm a virgin anymore after eating one. Or maybe I am, but maybe I gave my first blow job and didn't even know it!" Cao shakes her head again. Her face is turning greener and greener.

Don't you dare laugh, Liv. Hold it together. Explain that she's still a virgin. And that she didn't give her first blow job.

But I decide to go deeper—without laughing. "Why don't you just tell Beth that you didn't smoke cigarettes in an identity rebellion and that you are all right with who you are?"

"You know my parents, Liv. They've overcompensated my whole life. And, when they found out about the cigarettes, they flipped the hell out and became extreme. Like…like bad." Her eyes grow big. "Anyway, the trip was a disaster. Mom tried to pretend she was Chinese, too. It was really weird. She's taking a Chinese culture class through the community education in Eureka two nights a week. Liv, she wants me to go. I told her no, that I already have a lot going on with school and that I can't handle another class. Plus, who's going to manage the Humboldt-based Ed Sheeran Fan Club besides moi?"

Why do you take to French so easily and not Chinese? I want to ask her.

"Since when?" I turn left onto Main, toward the high school.

"Since I started a page last week. While locked in the bathroom at home. Smoking a cigarette."

I pull into the parking lot, shaking my head, and look around for Daniel, knowing full well he drives.

"I don't see your ginger anywhere."

"Not looking for him. I'm looking for a parking spot," I lie and pull into a spot halfway between the school and the end of the parking lot.

"Right." She rolls her eyes, grabbing her backpack from the backseat.

Out of the corner of my eye, I see Whitney stalking toward me like I slept with her boyfriend.

And Daniel moves toward me with a certain swagger. A swagger only made for me.

Two worlds collide into one.

An explosion.

Earth crashes into Jupiter. Everyone dies.

Daniel slows as he sees Whitney charging toward me. Cao stands at my side, puffed up like a best friend should be.

Whitney's finger is pointed at me before she's close enough, before I can hear the words spewing from her mouth.

"And, for the record, I had him first. You might have known him longer, but I had him first." She heaves. "You ever come near Simon again, and I'll rip out your throat." Whitney's words are clear. Her fire continues, "I know what's going on. I'm not dumb. And here you are, playing the I-lost-my-twin-brother victim role. News flash, Liv: The world doesn't revolve around you."

The heat from her fire quickly disappears when I don't argue back. I deserve every single word she's spewing at me.

Daniel walks up behind me. "Everything all right?" he whispers, his hand slides into mine.

Please don't touch me. I don't deserve his hand. *She's right. About everything.*

Whitney stares at Daniel and then at me. "Got me? He's mine. Hands off."

"Okay," is all I say.

Whitney storms off just the way she stormed over.

"What was that all about?" Daniel's hand tightens around mine.

But it's over with Simon, and Daniel doesn't need to know. Simon and I are over. I can move on.

But this little feeling prickles at my heart. *A life built on lies is no life at all.*

For whatever reason, I can't seem to make the right decisions, the practical ones. As if I'm trying to take the easier, softer way, but it's only making life harder.

All three of our phones chime at the same time.

Cao is the quickest, as always. "BeLHo's Blog." I hear the tension in her voice because we know what this means.

We know that BeLHo is going to ignite and blow out of proportion what she—or her spies—has just witnessed. Because, let's be honest, who didn't witness it?

Daniel is staring down at his phone, too.

"Couldn't resist?" Cao says to Daniel as we begin to walk toward first period.

"I like to be well informed," he counters as we read and walk, still stealing sideways glances at me, perhaps hoping for an explanation that I don't want to give. Yet.

Blog Heiress

Well, Belle's Bitches, it's official.

Leah Moran was spotted at Belle's Hollow Women's Clinic. Why? Who knows? But sources tell me that she's looking for more than just the pill. We will see in nine months if there's a little Pattison on the way. Or a little Watson. Or perhaps an Adams baby. Keep your legs closed, Leah!

Chemistry answers have been removed from the link. LAME! So, hopefully, you wrote them down like I told you to do.

Student Council has just announced the two options for this year's prom: Haunted House or Masquerade Ball. Both stupid in my opinion, but if you feel you need to voice your opinion—I will do a write-in—cast your vote here: www.belleshollowprom2017.vote

Also, the school carnival will be held November 15. Remember last year when Levi Watts drank too much punch? Don't do that. It makes for an icky mess when throw-up gets stuck in the carpet.

LivJam...can anyone tell me what that means? It means, three's a crowd. And someone is being really sneaky.

Hawthorne Hill anyone?

Until later,

BeLHo

Jasper and Livia, Age Ten

After the Police Are Called for a Domestic Disturbance

"Jasper, do you think Mom and Dad are getting a divorce?"
"Go to sleep, Liv."
Quietness.
"Jasper?"
"What?"
"You'll never leave me, right?"
"Never."
"If they get divorced, who will you pick to live with, Jas? Please say me and Mom. Dad will kill us."
"Go to sleep, Liv."

Cao elbows me as I read.

"Liv, may I speak to you for a moment—alone?" Daniel asks.

Cao gets the hint. "I'm out." She holds the peace sign with her fingers, kisses it, and heads to her English class with Mr. Joe.

Not my class anymore. My dropped class.

"What was that all about with the blonde girl with the shrill voice?"

Lie, Liv.
Liv the Liar.
Livia Stone, Liar of the Universe.

At some point in my life, I'd like to start telling the truth again. But fear gets ahold of my mouth first because lying has now become second nature to me.

Give him the truth, Liv.
He deserves it.
You like him. Stop lying.

I give him the partial truth and partial lie. "Simon and Jasper were best friends. Since Jasper passed, he's been there for me. And I, him." *It's a convenience thing, Daniel. Really, I'm a liar. I have been having sex with Simon, and even though it doesn't feel good, it's a way I can just forget about everything.* "We text, and Whitney found some of our texts back and forth." I try to justify my actions. "It's innocent. But I think she's reading into it more than need be."

Daniel shoves his hands in his pockets. I think about going to grab for one of his big hands. But I don't.

He asks me an easy question, "Do you like him?"

"No. Not like that." I'm clear. I think. I add, "Not at all, Daniel," for good measure.

He nods and cocks his head to the right, as if trying to read my internal dialogue.

"What?" I say.

"I'm just going to be frank with you, Livia. I like you. I like spending time with you." He pauses, almost hesitant, and takes a step closer with quiet confidence. "I like the way your lip curls when someone mentions your current president."

I take notice when he says *your* president, not *our* president.

"I like the way you talk about cheese fries and death. Maybe it isn't the two things put together but rather that facts are important to you. I like that. I like the way most conversations you have take place in your head and not aloud. And I love the fact that you can't keep your mind quiet when you're around me." He pauses. "But, right now, I'm not sure you need all the added pressure of someone like me." He pronounces *all* like *oll.*

"I like the way you pronounce words," I say in a fluster because I can't think of anything better to say. "*All*, the word, I like the way you say it." *Think, Livia. You like him. Tell him so. It's no wonder you've never had a serious boyfriend.* Either way, I'm totally

STANDING
SIDEWAYS

unpolished in the boy department, unslick with no game. No game at all. *And I'm calling the No Game Police to come arrest me for lack of coolness.*

Daniel smiles and bites the corner of his cheek.

The bell rings.

In an almost panic, he slides his hand around the back of my neck, and I feel his lips brush against my ear.

I don't have feet anymore; they've left. Betrayers.

"I'd really like to be your friend. For now. And I promise I won't pull you by the neck and whisper in your ear because, trust me, it's harder for me right now to let go of you. I promise I won't touch you. Or grab your hand. Until we can decide what to do next."

In an instant, Daniel is gone, and I try to find my betrayers. I need to splash cold water on my face, so I make my way to the girls' restroom before class.

Alicia Abbott is in front of one of the stalls with Bridget Peterson. Alicia hurries by, pushing her hair behind her ears, hiding her face.

I'm pretty sure she squeaks, "Hey, Liv," but I'm not positive.

I shut the stall door behind me, the water from her handwashing still running.

And running.

And running.

How clean do her hands need to get?

I glance at the clock, knowing I'll be late to class. Again.

The water stops.

And there's a long pause.

Footsteps come toward the door, and then she murmurs, "Gabriel Struvio…" And then, "High as fuck."

Now, Alicia Abbott, the quiet type, doesn't usually use a phrase like that. But then again, I was a virgin three weeks ago, so things happen.

I remove the airplane bottle of vodka from my backpack that I took from the shed, one of my dad's old hiding spots. I imagine he probably forgot where he hid most of his stash. When I ran out of pills, I needed a quick fix, so I took it. I crack it open and hold my breath.

I take a sip, my lips tight. I swallow, and I want to throw up. But I don't. Because I know, the moment I throw it up, it won't do its job.

And I need it to do its job.

I take another sip, this time bigger.

I gag.

I swallow.

I take another sip, this time even bigger than the last.

I gag.

I take the rest of it and push the bottle back into my backpack. I take three pieces of gum from my backpack and shove them in my mouth, trying not to throw up.

I wash my hands.

I leave the restroom.

I make my way to Mrs. Etter's English class. But not without walking past Mr. Joe's classroom. His door is open, and he's giving a lecture on Raymond Carver's short story, *Neighbors*—one of my favorite pieces.

Mr. Joe and I have discussed the story before when he asked about my favorite writers.

"Why?" he asked.

Simply, I liked Bill. As strange as he was, I could relate to him.

"I think," I told Mr. Joe, "he did what most people want to do when they're in a strange apartment, but the fear of getting caught far outweighs the will to do so. And, when the Millers got caught, I rooted for them, that, somehow, they wouldn't get caught."

Mr. Joe probably won't ask his class if they liked *Neighbors* because chances are, they didn't. But he'll push them to question Carver's writing style, to think critically about the piece. And then have them write an essay on it, which I'd love to do, only if I could stop making bad decisions.

And, before I know it, I'm standing in the doorway of Mrs. Etter's class, the entire class staring back.

The alcohol has made it to my stomach and explodes.

"Sorry I'm late." It's just a gesture, a saying. I don't think I'm all that sorry. Because, right now, I'm not really sure I care.

I take a seat between Mark Pattison and Luciana Martinez, who is currently in the running for valedictorian, which I'm sure is against me. But I'm almost positive I lost my spot in the running when I dropped AP English, worth four credits and a lot of grade points.

Right now, as my head begins to fill with warmth and fuzziness, I'm not sure where I stand on abortion rights, gay marriage or straight marriage, our current president, social media and the dummying down of our society as a whole, the cost of college, or the environment. I want to yell.

My head cloudy, I try to focus and pull out my notebook as Mrs. Etter turns to the smart board and continues her lecture on…whatever. I'm trying to pay attention, but all I can focus on is a little piece of Mrs. Etter's hair that's sticking straight up.

I lean over to Luciana. "Do you see that? A piece of her hair is sticking straight up." It's not funny. It's quite serious, and I want to fix it for her.

I don't think Luciana and I have ever had a conversation. I bet Luciana makes great decisions. I bet she hasn't lost any of her siblings, and I know she has three. I bet her parents are strict, and I bet she doesn't take anti-anxiety medication at school. Or drinks. I bet she's going to a big school. A smart one. For smart kids.

Smart kids. That sounds funny.

This leads me to think of Daniel.

I wonder how Daniel would say, *Smart kids.*

I feel good.

I feel comfortable in my own skin. Finally.

I'm not sure that Luciana heard me because I haven't heard her answer my question. But maybe I wasn't listening. Maybe I didn't really care in the first place. Maybe I didn't expect her to answer. *Was it a rhetorical question?* I should know. I was the asker.

God, I feel so much better.

Luciana, I say to myself.

That's like two names in one. A two-for-one special. Lucy. Ana. Maybe her parents couldn't agree on a name. Her mother wanted Lucy, and her father wanted Ana. I bet that's it. I should ask her.

I feel the blood gush in my ears as I watch Mrs. Etter use the smart board. In many ways, Mrs. Etter has always reminded me of Angela Lansbury from *Murder, She Wrote,* a show that started in the 1980s.

When Jas and I were little, we would pile into Poppy's old recliner every Friday night and watch back-to-back episodes. Jasper used to make toast with a layer of butter, then sugar, and then sprinkles.

Every time, he'd say, "Liv, just try it. It melts in your mouth."

But I'd always want to gag, like I just did with the vodka.

One particular Friday night, I was feeling extra brave, so I tried it. I didn't puke, but it wasn't good either. "Tastes like sugar," I said, chasing it down with a glass of milk.

Jasper wasn't really into eating the right stuff. He didn't have to for two reasons:

1. He had a high metabolism.
2. Eating healthy didn't save his life

I come to the conclusion that it's Mrs. Etter's bumpy hair and her age that make her a dead giveaway of Angela Lansbury.

Everyone stands.

Lucy-Ana looks down at me. I think she sees the confusion on my face.

"The bell rang," she says and throws her eighty-pound backpack on her shoulder.

"Oh." I put my notebook back in my bag and make my way out the door.

"Livia?" Mrs. Etter—aka Ms. Lansbury—calls behind me.

I could pretend not to hear her. She's a Have-Not, and I really don't want to hear the I'm-so-sorry-for-your-loss dried-up, old statement that everyone uses. It's uncomfortable because all I can think to say is, *Thank you*. And then the awkward silence comes, and I'm not sure if I should walk away or stand and make small talk, which is a total waste of time. And stupid.

I turn back. The good Livia, the one who makes good decisions, is somewhere in this messed up body, and she turns back around and into the classroom.

Mrs. Etter, standing at her desk, slides the envelope across it. "I thought you'd like to read this. It's Jasper's Hope letter he wrote just...beforehand," she says. "I'm pretty sure this is you." She points to the name on the envelope.

I nod and deflect every single emotion that tries to pry its way through my throat and to my head.

We had an assignment the beginning of our senior year to write a letter to our best friend about where we saw our lives going in the next five years. A letter that was supposed to bring hope for our future. I thought Jasper would have written it to Simon.

But it's addressed to me.

My eyes fill with tears, and I'm not sure if it's because I see his handwriting or the fact that he addressed it to me or that he's not here anymore to see my reaction as I read it.

"Thank you," is what I manage and turn to leave.

I stare at the letter as I make my way to second period, my head still fuzzy from the alcohol. Feelings begin to seep through the wall of protection I've created. The ball of pressure that sits at the base of my throat expands, making my body feel insignificant.

Am I ready to read it?

I stare at his handwriting, his chicken scratch, that is scribbled across the page. I run my fingers over it, knowing that he wrote this a mere few months ago. Knowing his hands touched the envelope where my hands touch now.

But it doesn't say Livia Stone.

Sophomore Year of High School

"Mimi, come on."
He drags me from the party.
We're sophomores.
"But I don't want to leave, Jas." Voice slurs.
I try to push his hand away.
It's fruitless.
"You're drunk. Time to go."
He pulls.
I push.
"Just go away!" I yell.
But he doesn't let go.
"You don't need to save me, Jasper!"

The letter says, *Mimi Stone.*
  I head to my car and debate on whether I'll read it or not.
I need to read it.
I need to wait.
I shouldn't read it at school.
Who cares?
I need to read it.
It's going to hurt, Livia.

Don't read it.
Read it. Now.

"Miss Stone," Mr. Marty, our Disciplinarian, says, "where are you headed so early in the day?" He approaches me.

His khakis are hiked way too high above his hips. I bet he was more of an Anthony Cartwright in high school. Picked on because of his brain and his style of clothing. I bet that's why he takes his job so seriously. I bet, if he got rid of the fanny pack he wears, he probably wouldn't be the eyesore that he is.

"Nowhere," I lie. *Comes so easy.* I casually shove the letter in my back pocket, praying to God he doesn't smell the booze.

"Do you have permission to leave campus?" He uses a toothpick to pick the leftover egg in his teeth. His *Hawaii Five-0* glasses are upon his face but with no sun in sight.

"Not leaving." My brain somewhat returns to normal function again.

The less words spoken, the less he has evidence to analyze. And then I think about the empty bottle in my backpack. *What if I get caught with it?* My face begins to grow warmer and warmer, my head becoming a bit clearer.

"Just exchanging a few books at my car," I lie again, making sure to keep my distance.

"Don't you have a locker for that?" He puts his hands in his pockets, but they're at his stomach because of the level of his pants, too high, way too high, and extremely uncomfortable—for both of us.

"I forgot a book in the car." Lies. Lies. Lies.

And, one day, you'll get caught, Livia, I tell myself.

"Come on, I'll walk you to your car to get the book."

I follow, my head still trying to clear away the clouds. *Christ, don't panic, Liv.*

My breathing quickens.

I swallow, but all I feel is sandpaper as I peer into my car.

Thank. God.

There is a book—a fiction book nonetheless, but my favorite book—sitting between the driver's side and the passenger seat.

I turn proudly to Mr. Marty. "See?"

Mr. Marty looks in, still skeptical. His eyes dance around my car like he's looking for a murder weapon.

I open the car door and grab the book.

I slide open my front zipper to shove my book inside, and there, on top of everything else, is the empty bottle of alcohol.

Oh, God.

"What is that?" Mr. Marty asks.

My insides disintegrate, and I plan the next twenty years of my life behind bars in the next ten seconds.

I look up, anticipating his beady eyes, as my mind tries to drum up excuses. And lies.

But he isn't looking in my backpack. He's looking in the backseat.

And in the backseat is a pill bottle.

A pill bottle that says, *Gabriel Struvio.*

I feel as though I'm on an episode of *COPS.*

When the drug dog finds the drugs, the perpetrator always says, *They aren't mine. They belong to my neighbor. I gave him a ride. He must have left them.*

Likely story.

"I didn't take them," I say.

"Why are they in your backseat?" Mr. Marty asks, still picking his teeth, the pill bottle now in a baggie in his possession.

"I don't know how they got there," I say.

By this time, I'm in Principal Lundberg's office. Her long red fingernails are drumming on her desk as she peeks over the top of her sophisticated round red glasses. Tracy and my father are here. And Mr. Marty, wannabe FBI agent, is leaning against the side of the principal's desk, still picking his teeth.

What's left to pick? I want to scream.

His sunglasses are now folded over the middle of his shirt.

I twist awkwardly in my chair. I'm almost certain my parents are at a loss. My behavior lately has been totally out of character. But they don't share this with my interrogators.

The pills in question, the evidence, is on Principal Lundberg's desk.

"Look, Livia," Ms. Lundberg says.

163

Her lip gloss forms a gob when her lips come together. I find myself trying not to dab my lips together. Her impeccable fashion has always made her stick out. She grew up in Belle's. Graduated with my parents. Moved away to go to college and came back as some sort of fashionista.

"What else are we supposed to think? How did the pills get in the back of your car?" She folds her hands in front of her and leans back.

I see the empathy in her eyes. What we've been through.

I look at Tracy and my dad. Tired. Weary eyes.

Daniel has been the only one in the back of my car.

"I don't know." My voice is impatient.

Tracy stares at her feet.

My dad looks at Ms. Lundberg. "Anna, look"—his lawyer voice is in full throttle—"the car was unlocked. Liv is saying she didn't take the pills. Matt"—must be Mr. Marty's first name—"even said Liv didn't have to unlock her car. That it, indeed, was already unlocked. She has answered your questions. So, unless you have evidence of my daughter stealing the pills, we're done here."

It must be hard for my father to walk such a fine line. Not enabling his child. Having to trust me, even at my worst. My track record is unbelievably horrid right now, my own hidden issues in my backpack.

Tracy and I follow suit. My dad allows Tracy and me out first but turns back to Ms. Lundberg and Mr. Marty.

"Here's my card. Call me when you get some real evidence."

The silence between the three of us right now as we walk back out to my car puts us thousands of miles apart. By this time, it's three p.m.

Tracy turns to us. "I'll see you guys at home. We'll talk there."

"I'll walk Liv to her car," my dad says.

Silence follows us.

"I didn't take the pills."

My dad kicks a rock on the ground, casually yet methodically. His mind is probably twisting and turning in every direction. Weighing every what-if scenario.

"I trust you, Liv."

I want to sigh. I want to sigh away the lies I've told. Come clean. Because, if he knew the person I was becoming, he wouldn't trust me. Even though I didn't steal the pills, he shouldn't trust me.

"Thank you."

The rock still somersaults across the broken asphalt of the parking lot.

Again, he's staring at the ground. "No matter how mad you get at me, Liv, I'm still your father. You are part of me. I made a lot of mistakes, but all I have is today. Clean and sober. So, I'd like to try to make the best of it, if that's okay with you?" My dad peers through the corner of his eye. He stops.

I pull open the car door and check the backseat first. My dad goes to the passenger door. His face, the lines of a forty-five-year-old's face, reflects untold stories. His nose and cheeks are a soft pink due to his years of drinking. I've Googled it.

I'm honest in a dishonest way. "Can you drive?"

He tilts his head to the left. "Of course."

But I don't let him get too close, for fear of him smelling what I did this morning. Truth be told, I wasn't quite particularly in the mood for a DUI today.

I feel like I'm drowning in a pot of lies.

This thought reminds me of when we were nine.

We were at the Willits KOA, just two hours south of Belle's Hollow, on a family vacation. We took one every summer. The swimming pool was packed with kids and floatation devices. No lifeguard on duty. While Tracy read a magazine and my father was sleeping, probably passed out, next to her— whichever you prefer—a humongous hippopotamus was launched through the air and landed on my head while a kid jumped on top of it, not knowing I was under the water, struggling to reach the surface. I don't remember how long I was under, but I blacked out.

I came to, coughing and gagging on the taste of chlorine, lying on the hot cement of the sweltering Willits summer heat, while Jasper loomed over me, on his knees, dripping wet, terror written all over his mouth, eyes, and cheeks. His hands on his thighs, he heaved air into me. Tracy was panicked, and my father was swaying to an unheard tune, his eyes glazed over me.

Jasper said to me, "You need to be safer, Mimi. God, you scared the shit out of me."

What I wanted to say was, You have a twenty-pound hippopotamus land on your head, and you try to swim your way out.

But he'd just saved my life, so I figured I owed him some silence and not a smart-ass rebuttal. Plus, I knew what he meant to say.

You can't die. Me and you, not one without the other. That's always been our agreement.

He was older by a minute and thirty-three seconds after all.

His words: "The older sibling is always supposed to die first."

"What are you thinking about?" my dad asks as we make our way inside the house.

"The day Jas saved me from the gigantic hippo."

I can see my dad's face change, the guilt prickling at his lips and then moving to his eyes. He doesn't remember firsthand.

And then I think, *If Jas hadn't been there, what would have happened to me?*

What does the rest of my life look like without him?

When we make it inside, Tracy is getting ready for work, which I need to do, too. I have the five-to-closing shift at Bob's.

I thought we'd sit down and talk about what happened even though I've already explained it a million and one times.

I hear Tracy whispering to my dad in the kitchen as I make my way to my room.

"That's it, Tracy. She said she didn't take them. If she knows who did, it will come out. We need to give her the benefit of the doubt."

The Old Dad.

The Not-Drunk Dad.

The dad who also left for three years and didn't bother calling at Christmas or our birthdays. For three years.

Pushing those thoughts away, I set my backpack down next to my dresser. I sit down on my bed and pull off my pants. I see the crumpled white envelope still in my back pocket. And seeing Jasper's writing again creates a distinct punch to my stomach. It's a quick jab that knocks the wind from me.

I'm not ready to read it.

After work, I tell myself.

I put it inside the top drawer of my dresser, almost too scared to close the drawer, for fear I'll lose it or someone might take it. I take it out from the drawer and put it back in again, realizing I'm overthinking it.

I peel off my shirt and wrap myself in a towel. I go to our bathroom—my bathroom now. Jasper's door is ajar, and I almost catch myself, waiting to hear Jasper's voice say, *Turn off the light!*

I wait to hear his bed creak when he turns to the wall.

But there's nothing but awful silence. I don't look in his room because there's nothing to see. Nothing's changed because he isn't in there and hasn't been in there to make anything change.

I think about going to sit in his closet just to see if there's a sign he's watching me. I think of Rose and Daniel.

Could Daniel really have taken Gabriel's pills and left them in the back of my car? Could he have left them on purpose?

I splash cold water on my face and feel the coldness quickly make its way to the pool at the bottom of the sink. I do it over and over and over again until I feel satisfied.

I put on my purple Bob's work shirt with its logo and a new set of jeans. Linda's only requirement of dress code is, no holy jeans. She doesn't understand why we—our parents—would pay good money for holes. Tying my hair up into a ponytail, I pull out some mascara and throw on some lip balm. I always end up leaving the place smelling like a greasy onion, so I don't worry about spraying perfume.

I push back down the bad feelings that seem to creep up like bad memories.

I need another airplane bottle.

But I deny myself because I need to prove to myself that I'm not like my dad.

Once more, I check the top drawer of my dresser and see Jasper's letter. *Good.*

My phone chimes, and I see Daniel's name come up.

I t's Daniel.

　　Daniel: I need to talk to you.

Then, Cao.

　　Cao: What the hell happened?

How do they know anything? I haven't talked to anyone—
Immediately, I scroll through my notifications and see BeLHo's update. I open it.

BLOG HEIRESS

QUICK ANNOUNCEMENT:

Belle's Bitches! Boy, oh boy, do I have some juicy gossip for you today. Hot off the presses, too. Remember that little bind Gabriel Struvio got into a week or so ago? Someone stole his Ritalin medication. Poor guy. Sad face.

Well, it turns out that the pills were recovered in the backseat of none other than poor little grieving girl Livia Stone. She might need a pick-me-up after all that crying.

I feel my face grow warm, and I want to scream at the dimwit who writes this blog, *Check your facts! I didn't cry!*

But I can't. Because nobody knows who the elusive writer, who seems to be all-knowing, is.

This is libel. Slander! I call war.

I think I'll make a sandwich board and wear it to school. One that says, *I didn't take G.S.'s pills.*

Then, I'll have Cao start a Blog Heiress take-down campaign titled, *Free Livia Stone!*

Then, I'll have the FBI track down the IP address. I think I still have a few connections.

Chill, Liv, I hear myself.

This, again, is where Poppy would step in and say some magical words of clarity. Wisdom.

"Poppy, where are you?" I whisper.

Nothing.

Is it possible for a spirit, or whatever she is, to be mad at me?

I grab my keys from my backpack and shove my phone in my pocket. I think about looking for another little bottle of magic, but refrain because that might make me an alcoholic. I have the gene. My dad—attorney by day, raging alcoholic by night. Besides, it takes years to become an alcoholic, right? Isn't there a list of accomplishments one must do to qualify to become one? At any rate, I'm too young, right?

Here are my qualifying requirements I've set forth in my head to judge whether I am becoming an alcoholic or not.

Livia's I Can Only Be an Alcoholic If

Drop out of high school or college or become disqualified from the institution for lack of a GPA.

Live on at least four couches before you go home to live with Mom or Dad at the age of 23.

See? Too young.

Hospitalization due to overdose or an alcoholic seizure.

Google is a tool to be reckoned with.

Lose a job to addiction.

Still have mine, thank you very much.

Drink in the morning.

See? I've never done that.

Live under a bridge with a bottle wrapped in a brown paper bag or a bag of powder in my hand, blaming the world for my unfortunate set of circumstances.

I'm still enrolled in high school.
I still have a bed.
I've never been hospitalized.
I work.
And I'll never live under a bridge.
I take a deep breath after seeing all the facts in black and white. Clearly, I have passed the test. I think I could be if I didn't know the warning signs, but thankfully, I am aware of them.
I'll respond to Daniel and Cao on my break at work.

Clocking in, I throw on my apron. Linda's at the big fryer. I'm tired. Alcohol does that—so I'm learning—so I grabbed a tea loaded with caffeine on my way to work.

"Liv, we need to talk. In the back."

In her tiny, disheveled office, Linda is many things, but organized isn't one of them. Cooking books, pieces of paper, a blanket, her roll-top desk that's far too big for the office. She grunts as she shuts the door.

She. Shuts. The. Door.

I put a piece of gum in my mouth.

The last time Linda shut the door was when I came by to pick up my paycheck before we went down to Los Angeles to get Jasper. To find Jasper.

"Sit."

I look around. "Where?"

"Oh." She walks around her desk again and uncovers a stool.

"Lieutenant Rogers came by, looking for you, today." Linda sits back down in her chair as I take a seat. Her eyes size me up and not in an accusatory way.

My stomach grows uneasy. *Can she smell the alcohol?*

You passed Livia's I Can Only Be an Alcoholic If test, my conscience says loudly. I'm entitled.

But the alcohol isn't why I'm in here. I allow her words to settle into my brain. It's the pills.

"Linda, I didn't take the pills." My hands begin to sweat.

"I know you didn't, kid. Look, I know you're goin' through a lot. I also have known you since you were six with no front teeth." She takes her finger and points to her front teeth.

"Wh-what'd you tell him?"

"I told him that, if he's not careful, I'll tell his wife that he comes in every Saturday night before we close to get a double bacon cheeseburger. Wife's got him on some strict diet or whatever." She waves her hand because it's not the point of our conversation. "I also told him that he knows you didn't do it. So, why come up here, all official in a uniform, and scare the wits outta Liv, me, and my customers?" She pauses. "Said, if he had questions for you, he'd go to your house, not work." She stops and cradles her forehead with the palm of her hand, pushing her permed bangs out of her face. "I just wanted you to know, so you'd be prepared for when he comes to your house. And he'd better not come back to my place of business in that damn uniform unless it's Saturday night, and he's buying his double bacon cheeseburger." She tries to make me smile.

How did this life get so messy, so illegal?

Bile grows in my stomach and moves up into my throat, creating a burning sensation.

"Get to work, Stone." Linda winks.

I nod and stand. Almost out the door, I turn back to Linda. "Thanks," comes out twisted, almost sad. Desperate maybe. I didn't mean it to, but it did.

I grab a pen and pad of white paper to take orders. I push my stomach against the 1970s gold-glitter Formica countertop.

Cao walks in. Her eyes sinister.

"I'm sorry, Cao. I was going to text you back on my break."

She walks to the counter. Cao doesn't drive. Her mom's scared she'll die in a car accident. So, Beth told Cao she had to wait until she was eighteen to get her license.

The difference between sixteen and eighteen?

"Hormones and life experience," so Beth says.

Cao calls it "the apache helicopter technique." Her mother hovers.

Cao clasps her hands together and leans on the counter. "So, I have this best friend who got some pretty shitty news today. And I've blown up her phone"—she motions an explosion with her hands—"but for whatever reason, she hasn't found the time to send me a snap, text, or a call to say, *Hey, best friend, I'm all right. I'll reach you later.*"

"I'm sorry. Add me to the Shitty Best Friend list I know you have shoved between your mattress and your bed frame," I say, not allowing my culpability to cross the counter and wrap her up. I don't want to drag her into this mess.

She writes my name down with her finger on the counter. She smiles. "You okay?"

I nod, trying to pull together in my head the facts and non-facts that have come together in a matter of a day. And the added lieutenant visit still makes my stomach turn.

"I know you didn't do it."

"I know I didn't." I pause and look both ways to be sure that everyone is out of earshot, though everyone looks away quickly—the other workers, customers—as if Cao and I, together, were a two-headed tiger. "But you know when you're so sure of something and then self-doubt lingers somewhere in your brain, so you spend time trying to convince yourself that you didn't do it?"

Cao bites her lip. "Like convincing my parents that I'm okay with who I am when they're convinced I'm suffering from an identity crisis?" Her left eyebrow perks up. "So with you, sister."

"Wait. How'd you get here anyway?" I look past her to see who drove her here.

Cao sighs. "Don't freak. But I got pissed when I read the blog and immediately thought of Daniel because he's the one who has been in the back of your car recently. So, basically, not gonna lie, I called him out on private message before I knew what the situation was, and, well, that prompted a phone call on my end."

I catch Daniel's eye in the driver's seat of what looks to be a brand-new BMW, though I'm not really good with cars, makes, and models. I classify vehicles in three ways—truck, car, sport utility vehicle. The only reason I know it's a BMW is because it says *BMW* in big letters on the hood of the car, toward the grill. I can see why Daniel didn't want to give Mr. Pearson the satisfaction of driving the beautiful car. It screams arrogance.

Daniel waves.

I wave, my fingers dropping casually.

"I told him that I needed to go in first and do the talking. He argued. Liv, did he argue. He called you several times. Wanted to explain himself. He even called Principal Lundberg."

My eyes grow big. "What?" I say in my not so quiet voice.

The few customers look over.

I roll my eyes. "Come back at seven, and I'll take my break," I tell Cao, flustered. Not sure what to think.

Daniel and Cao park right up front again and walk in.

Why does he have to wear such revealing things? Like white T-shirts that hug his chest. And glasses, the black-rimmed ones that make him look far too smart for his own good. *Can he just keep his hands shoved in his pockets, so I don't have to see those either?*

They sit near the far window, out of earshot from everyone. I grab the large basket of cheese fries and two Cokes and sit down with them. Cao and Daniel are on opposite sides of the table, and I side with Cao.

He's clearly all right with my choice as he leans in. His eyes burrow into me.

"Do you want to start or me?" Cao says to Daniel with urgency.

"I'll start." He pronounces *start* like *stot*. "I took the pills from the Struvio chap." He doesn't whisper. He doesn't make it a secret. He tells me. And the world.

I'm quiet. I let Daniel speak.

"I must have gotten out of your car too quickly, and they must have fallen from my pocket." He pauses, chewing on the inside of his cheek.

"But why?" comes out of my mouth in an accusatory tone. Like I'm a saint.

Daniel leans back against the bench seat and runs his hand through his hair. "I have a difficult time when people steal things. I have a difficult time when people lie. And I have a difficult time when I see a freshman buying manufactured drugs from a senior who probably shouldn't have them in the first place." Daniel sighs and continues, "In the restroom two weeks ago, Struvio was conducting an illegal activity, which involved narcotics, out in the open for everyone to see. I walked past the two of them, and they were completely oblivious to the world around them. He told the buyer that the pills weren't his Ritalin medication and that they were oxycodone. Still, he's not very smart. I assume he disguises the bottle—for obvious reasons." He stops.

"What if he was lying to the kid? What if they were his Ritalin, and he was just looking to make a few dollars?" I say.

"Thirty dollars a pill is not a few dollars, Livia." Daniel's voice is terse, and I'm caught off guard. The first time he's ever changed his tone with me. "Besides, it doesn't matter anyway. Selling drugs is selling drugs. His pills. Someone else's pills. Oxycodone or Ritalin. It really doesn't matter. Does it?" His hands are splayed out across our small table in the corner. Daniel pushes his glasses up further on his nose with his index finger.

He's right. It's as if I'm trying to defend myself.

"So, while in sports, I rifled through his backpack and took the pills," Daniel says like it's more of a confession than an act of possibly saving a life.

Cao clarifies, "Sports is PE. The British." She rolls her eyes to be funny, trying to make light of an epidemic that's been spreading through Belle's Hollow for years now.

"But why would he report the pills missing?"

Daniel smiles. "This is the lying part I hate. His mother reported it to the school. Blamed the school and the students for stealing her son's pills."

"How do you know?"

"Right? I asked that, too!" Cao shakes her head.

"This is like telling the same story twice with the same person." Daniel shakes his head. "I was in the office when his mother came in. A bit off her head, she started yelling at the school receptionist about her son's Ritalin being stolen."

Cao says, "When her son is the one selling oxycodone. And probably the Ritalin, too. Psh."

Daniel stops.

Cao stops.

They stare at me.

"Well, you won't take the fall for this, Daniel."

My dad is right. Since my car was unlocked, anyone could have put the pills in my backseat, trying to frame me. *Do I tell Daniel and Cao this? Or do I keep it from them, so they won't have to take the fall for me in case I go down? In case I'm booked into prison at seventeen, possibly eighteen, for harboring drugs on a school campus. Shit. What if they test the drugs and find out it's not Ritalin and it's oxycodone? Doesn't that change from a misdemeanor to a felony?*

Lieutenant Rogers will be back to talk to me, my family.

I make a split decision because I'm running out of break time, and I feel like it's the right thing to do for at least Daniel and Cao. "Can you tell this same story to my dad?"

Daniel stares at me. "Yes. I've already put a call in to Principal Lundberg. Left a message," he says.

I wince. "Did you tell her why you were calling?"

"No."

"When she calls back, tell her you have a question about your school visa."

He shrugs. "Okay, but why?"

"My dad's a lawyer." A washed-up, alcoholic attorney. "There's more to the story, and I've got to get back to work. I'll explain later. Go to my house, and tell my dad everything. He'll know you're coming."

There's the old Livia. Hi. It's nice to see you again.

The old Liv waves vivaciously at the new Liv across the same street, like a mirrored image.

My heart sinks as the old Livia fades into particles, calling to the new Livia, *When did you get so ugly?*

When Cao and Daniel leave, I text my dad to tell him that they're coming over to explain the pills to him. And I also tell him about Lieutenant Rogers.

Immediately, he texts back.

Dad: OK.

He doesn't ask about Lieutenant Rogers.

When I get home, exhausted, smelling like a grease pit, I shimmy off my shirt and jeans and leave the trail of Liv behind me. Makes me think of Jasper. He coined the term *trail of Liv*. He used to say that he always knew exactly where I was when I got home because there was a trail of clothing behind me.

I jump in the shower and take a quick one. Putting on last night's pajamas, I peek into Jasper's room.

Please just let me see him there, on his bed, listening to his music, his Vans tapping to the beat that plays in his ears.

It's dark. And everything is just as I left it the other day. His headphones. A shirt he threw on his bed the day before he left for Los Angeles.

What I wouldn't give to trade spots with him right now.

Jasper, he should have taken me, not you. He should have known that you'd have dealt with my death better than I've been dealing with yours. That

179

you wouldn't drink or take pills or tell lies or create a trail of mess in your wake.

I creep into his closet and sit on as many pairs of Vans as I can feel with my hands. And I prefer the darkness, so the tears will vanish, and no one can see them. His closet smells like the woods and soap. His smell.

I rest my head at the back of his closet, and the longing for him builds in my chest.

Tracy tells the story best, but she says, as twins, Jas and I spent the first six months of our lives touching. It seemed, she explained, that every time she turned around, Jasper would have his arm around me or his foot in my face; it didn't matter. I'd say we spent the better part of our lives together than apart.

On that day, October 1, something was off. I texted Jasper once, then twice, and then three times as unease grew in my stomach. My stomach began to hurt so badly, I threw up. Even though I thought it might be the flu, I couldn't etch away the terrible feeling I had that something didn't add up. Something was wrong. And something bad was about to happen.

Then, I received a text from Jasper.

Jasper: Mimi. What? You're blowing up my phone. U OK?

I remember feeling relief. A huge relief because Jasper was all right. I could breathe again.

But my stomachache didn't go away. My hands were shaking, and they couldn't quite type the words out very well.

I texted back.

Me: I lover you.

Me: *Love.

Then, I typed with my newfound relief.

Me: Because lovering your twin would be weird.

But he never responded.

That was when mass hysteria broke out across the country—at 10:48 a.m. on October 1, 2015.

I wish I could have had just one more minute with my brother in the car when I dropped him off at the airport on September 30.

One more foot in my face while trying to explain that athlete's foot is a real condition, and it can be contagious.

One more snide remark about my yoga pants being a little too tight or my shorts too short.

One last hug.

I hear a creak in the house as my silent tears fall, completely unnoticed until now.

"Mimi?" I hear my dad's voice.

"In here," I whisper like the little girl he left behind, very quietly because I've lost my way to speak, perhaps hidden behind the sobs, unable to catch my breath. And maybe I don't want him to hear me, but maybe I do.

My dad opens the closet door and sees me in a puddle at the bottom of Jasper's closet. He drops his shoulders. He climbs into the closet with me, and I can't help but think what a mix of emotions Jasper would feel if he could see us right now. Mad because my dad and I are sitting on every pair of Vans he ever owned and sad because our dad has me in his arms while I shake. My dad—my big, strong dad—has his cheek against my hair, and I feel him shake, too, his intermittent breaths telling me the story of his regret, his own loss.

Death is awful.

Death brings about the worst feelings. Ones you'd rather die from than face.

A loneliness that I've never known before.

And one I'm not sure I'll be able to escape.

181

I wake up, unable to breathe. Sweat is the only remnant of haunted dreams that I can't remember just yet, my mind too foggy. My eyes swollen from tears, I turn on my bedside lamp, the darkness creeping in on me like sneaker waves.

I breathe. Finally.

How did I get back to my room? And in my bed?

I look down at my pajamas.

I grab my phone and look at the time—12:02 a.m.

I collect my unconscious thoughts, the ones that danced in my mind as I slept. It was Sonja, one of the survivors of October 1. I follow her Facebook page.

In my dream, I relived my version of what had happened on that day. What my unconscious mind threw together while she was center stage, and I grieved.

Envious of her family.

Rage.

Sadness.

She's still in the hospital. Her communication is limited. She uses a computer, a paper and pen, yet she's still here. Every time I see her picture come up in my feed, my loss is magnified, and my questions about God and his plan reorganize in my head.

Why didn't he save them? The victims.

I question how he could have let something this awful happen. How our situation turned out to be horrible and theirs survivable.

I question why all these particular people happened to be at the same place at the same time with so much more to give their lives, so much more to give the world.

What the fuck, God? That's what I want to say.

WHAT THE FUCK? I scream inside myself.

I rub my eyes and sit up, resting my head higher on the pillow.

Jasper Stone, 17
Bernice Carnes, 18
Jesus Eibel, 18
Xou Hong, 18
Amanda Alcaraz, 19
Treven Anspach, 20
Stephanie Moore, 44
Delma Dietz, 59
Lawrence Levine, 67

These people didn't survive on October 1, 2015. Why not?

My chest grows tight, the boulder growing by the minute.

I question why the young singer, Christina Grimmie, one of the contestants from *The Voice*, with so much life ahead of her was shot and killed at close range at a meet and greet after her concert. She was only twenty-two years old.

I question why Jessica Ghawi, who escaped a Toronto mass shooting at a shopping mall, was killed one month later in a mass shooting in Colorado. She was just twenty-four years old.

I question why Steven Stayner was abducted at seven years old, returned at fourteen years old, and died in a motorcycle accident on his way home from work at twenty-four years old.

Or Jessica de Lima Rohl, twenty-one, who organized an event for university students at the Kiss nightclub. Her boyfriend begged her not to go, so she didn't. Two hundred thirty-eight people were killed that night in a fire at KISS. She and her boyfriend died one week later in a head-on collision.

How about Hilda Yolanda Mayol, twenty-six? She was on the ground floor when the Twin Towers were hit on 9/11. She escaped. Only to die two months later in a plane crash on her way to the Dominican Republic. Flight 587 crashed into a New York Borough of Queens.

And how about David Furr? Due to an injury, he was the only member of the University of Evansville men's basketball team who wasn't on the Douglas C-53 chartered plane where all the players were killed. He and his sixteen-year-old brother were killed two weeks later by a drunk driver.

DJ Lawson was a nineteen-year-old Humboldt State University sophomore who moved up from Los Angeles, where he was raised, to go to college in a small town where it was safer, only to be stabbed to death at a party in the same small town. His murder still remains unsolved.

Or the five-year-old boy—his name was never released—who survived a massive tornado in Oklahoma, only to be killed by a bullmastiff dog days later.

Or Nicky Hayden, Formula 1 motorcycle racer, who died while riding a bicycle in Italy.

And let's not ever forget about Sandy Hook. Ever.

I question all of it.

The rock in my chest grows and pushes in ways my body doesn't allow. It hurts, and I'm not sure if it's the sadness or the anger.

Fate.

Destiny.

Devine will.

Providence.

Karma.

Kismet.

Maybe we don't remember, but maybe God gave us a number of days, and maybe he gave us a choice of how we'd vacate this world and move on to the next. Surely, if we knew the how and when of it, we wouldn't survive the wait. Instead, we'd fear the days until our days on Earth were up. If we knew our departure date, maybe we wouldn't enjoy the pure moments of joy that life provided. Maybe our souls have their own journey, and our bodies are just a costume we wear while our time is spent on Earth.

But this still doesn't explain Sandy Hook. I don't think any of us can explain that, and this is where I always end up: *God, if you exist, Sandy Hook never would have happened.*

I allow the awfulness of the world—the wrongdoings and the decisions people make, the unspeakable ones—to roll off my back and splatter onto the floor. But there they sit, waiting for me to collect them.

I can't cry, so I close my eyes and let the unjust world fall around me.

My phone vibrates, and it's an email.

TO: livie@gmail.com

FROM: Sonja Peet <peetfeet@yahoo.com>

SUBJECT: Jasper

Hi Livia,

I got your email from the FBI. I hope it's all right that I'm emailing you.

Anyhow, I know you're having a hard time right now. And I'm unsure of how to approach this, but I have, um, Jasper's last words if you want them.

I guess, if I were in your place, I'd want to know. I knew him for only an hour total, but he talked a lot about you. I'm emailing you against my parents' wishes. I just think it's the right thing to do.

Some people might think I'm crazy with PTSD right now. That I might not be well. That I shouldn't be approached. The truth is, I don't know what I am.

Your brother was special, Livia. In the sixty minutes I got to know him, he was special.

He did what I couldn't do.

He did what 99% of the world's population would not do.

He stood in his own truth.

Stood up for what he believed in.

I'm not sure how to close this email, so I'll stop here. Let me know if you want to...well, you know, know.

—Sonja

Immediately, I get out of bed and creep into the backyard and to the shed. I dig in the crate full of nails and find my relief—an airplane bottle of vodka. *This will do.*

I take it back to my bedroom.

I take enough to let my mind grow fuzzy.

I close my eyes and let the relief from hurt disappear into the night.

My head aches, and it can't be from the booze. It's got to be from the crying, the emotional hangover.

I'd rather stay home from school today, but Cao's counting on a ride.

I heave myself into the shower.

I wash.

Rinse.

Brush.

Apply.

And put a cold washcloth on my burning eyes for five minutes.

I leave.

And I try not to let Sonja's offer enter my head because the only thing the offer fills me with is awfulness. Jagged, rugged rocks stick into my heart, my spleen, gouging them from the inside first.

187

My heart contorts and moves, stretches. My head is full of scenarios that play like early morning infomercials, I can't stop it, and I know what will stop it. Give me the ease I need.

But I have to go to school. I sweep my thoughts, my feelings, under the rug, so no one can see them.

I'm half-tempted to delete the email. But something tells me not to.

Driving to Cao's, I look for Daniel. There's a need I can't explain deep down, a need that can only be met by him. Feel his leg pushing against mine with urgency. Maybe his wordless communication urging me to keep talking. His scent, the one that lulls me to say things and do things and think things I shouldn't.

Maybe I'll tell him about the email...or my thoughts on fucking fate or all the bad in the world. The conclusion I drew last night: Maybe there isn't a God.

Pulling up to Cao's, I see Beth following Cao out of the gate. Cao has some sort of odd figurine in her hand, and she's clearly annoyed.

She pulls open the car door, and she says, "Drive. Just drive, Liv," before she's seated in the car.

"That's all I need—attempted murder charges on me, Cao. With this pill thing at school, I'm sure the DA would have a heyday with that." *The old Liv.*

Sonja's email enters my head again.

I push it out.

Is she trying to ruin my life?

"What's that smell?" Cao asks. "It smells like mouthwash." Cao makes a disgusted face.

Panic.

"I used mouthwash this morning." I smirk like she's crazy. I think I need to tell Cao I can't take her to school anymore but decide to back-burner the conversation because Beth is approaching the car.

"Hey, Liv," she says as she leans in my car window. "What's that smell?"

I sit up straighter in my seat and pull my hair to one side, trying to mask the smell. "What smell?"

Beth takes a big whiff inside my car.

Cao shakes her head, and I look down to see some sort of monkey/cat-looking figurine in her hand.

"Would you just stop? Livia doesn't smoke cigarettes, Mom. Please. Just stop," she sighs. "Liv, can you just drive?"

Your mom is hanging out of my car window, I want to say. And, again, I want to mention attempted murder charges, but I think it's a moot point by now.

"Mom. Would you just stop? Please. Just go away." Cao's exhausted.

Beth pulls back from my window and nods, still looking at her daughter in the front seat. Slowly and rather uncomfortably, I roll up my window and pull away from their gate.

I don't dare breathe a word until we start down the Gulch. But she's still holding the monkey/cat thing in her hands.

"What's that?"

Cao is staring out the window. "It's another one of my mom's attempts at convincing me that I'm Chinese."

I think for a moment. "I'd say it's the offspring of a cat and a monkey if they were smashed together. It's a mon-cat."

Cao grins, still staring out the window. "It's feng shui supposedly. A Chinese thing. But the good-luck cat is a Japanese thing." She rolls her eyes.

"She's trying at least, Cao."

Her eyes make their way to my face. "I could say the same for your dad."

I frown. "Big difference, Cao. Your mom didn't leave you," I whisper through my thoughts. "I just think you put a lot of time and effort into hating what she does to make you feel accepted."

In a knee-jerk reaction, I turn down Daniel's road because my want to see him has now become a need.

"Where are you going?"

"To pick up Daniel," I say, as if it's been the plan since I left the house this morning.

"How'd it go with your dad last night anyway?" Cao gradually comes back into herself. The new Cao jumped out of the moving vehicle somewhere along Rockwell Lane. Thank God.

"This...this is...his house?" Cao leans forward to get a closer view.

On the outside, things are so well put together. A groundskeeper most likely keeps the estate. A housekeeper, or seven, keep the house. A cook, I assume. What this picturesque setting doesn't show is an absent father and a dying mother—two quintessential parts to making a family whole.

And maybe that's what Daniel meant by, *"It's just a house, Livia."*

"Do you think Daniel knows Ed Sheeran?" She's still staring at the grounds, the house.

"Why? Because they're both British? Doubt it."

I text him and tell him I decided to pick him up for school this morning. And then I go on to explain that it wasn't really planned and that it was an afterthought because I don't want him to think he's at the center of my universe. Right? No boy wants to think that because then it's like game over. I wait for his response, and as the seconds tick by, I rethink the whole text, wondering why I'm such an idiot.

I could have just simply said, *Hey, thought we'd pick you up on the way to school.*

I check the time—8:17 a.m.

8:18 a.m.

8:19 a.m.

8:20 a.m.

No response still.

"I'll be right back," I tell Cao. But, before I can get out of my seat, my phone chimes.

"Hey, would it be rude if I took a picture of his house?" Cao asks, preparing for a shot of the house with her phone.

"Yes!" I hiss as I open the text.

Daniel: Hey. Sorry, not going to make it to school this morning. Mum is in the hospital.

Me: Daniel, I'm so sorry. Is there anything I can do?

Daniel: Nope. Thx. I'll give you a ring later.

I want to text him back. But I shouldn't. *Don't look too desperate.*

When do we overcome caring about what others think about us in order to do the right thing? The one that's uncomfortable, that makes us vulnerable. Somehow, we allow it to get lost somewhere in the chaos.

Maybe, sometimes, we weigh opinions too much on what's acceptable, not what's right.

I put my phone down, and we make our way to school.

26

The funny looks, the smirks, but nobody says anything.

I know what they're thinking though:

Drug busts.

Drug cartel.

Prison time.

Suspension.

Expulsion.

I think about Sonja's email again. Great. Now, every time I check my email, I'll see it and start the whole heart-shake-stomach-drop despair process again. And this thought alone makes me feel as though I'm alone, surrounded by hundreds of students. I'll delete her email when I can.

And I know the only reason my peers don't say anything, not even Miranda, is because my brother just died. They'd be on me like heathens if he hadn't. Just like when Paul Pearce got arrested on campus for money laundering. Kids were relentless. He was a senior when Jasper and I were freshmen. Now, I hear he's in the construction business in southern Humboldt, probably working for Miranda's dad.

And, in the thought process of Paul, I find my mind wanting just a sip of booze and looking forward to my next drink so that it will take the edge off.

I just want a glow, I think to myself, *for my mind to take a break, a mini vacation, and for the worry, the grief, to fade.*

When I'm heading to my next class, Mr. Joe is heading straight for me, in the same path, the outside hallway, underneath the awning that connects building B to building C. An invisible orchestra plays a sinful line of notes as our free space comes to a close.

If I walked away now, it would look as if I was avoiding him—which I am, which isn't good, which is easier if I do, which I shouldn't do, but I want to.

But there's no running now because we're stopped, facing each other, staring.

I take my foot and push imaginary pebbles out of the walkway. This never works in the movies, but I try it anyway.

At any moment, I know he'll begin The Declaration of Livia Stone, The Bad—a lecture series.

He begins, "Has anyone told you that you're a runner?" His voice is light. A bit frothy, but he's not mad. His movements are quick, like his words.

"A runner? Like a competitive runner?" I ask, clearly confused.

"No. You run from problems you can't solve. Instead of solving them, you run from them."

I feel like a little girl being scolded by her mother for running down to the creek when she should have just stayed by the house. "No."

"Well, now, they have," Mr. Joe sighs. He pulls down on his plaid shirt. "Livia, you have so much potential, and you are throwing it all away. All away." He moves his hands in such a way. "I'm frustrated with you for not seeing that. I know how bad you hurt, Liv; trust me, I do. But this is your senior year—the deal-breaker year. And, if you don't get your stuff together now, it will take a long time to get there again. If ever."

"Why are you pushing me so hard, Mr. Joe?" comes out of my mouth.

Mr. Joe takes his hands and smooths his hair, as if he's not prepared to field this question. He sighs. "Forget it. You want to throw your future away? Then, so be it. But don't say I wasn't here to help." And he slides past me and keeps walking, his thin-laced fancy shoes tapping with each hasty step. "You're taking the easy road, Liv," he calls behind him. "Easy-roaders only make it to the curb."

Usually, when a situation I've been dreading is faced, I feel better but not this time. This time, I feel worse. I feel like Mr. Joe has it right. And I have it all wrong.

"Do you think I should text Daniel? See how he's doing?"

Cao and I are at lunch, sitting at the fifty-yard line on the football field, and I'm trying to distract myself from the email. The big, fat email that sits in my inbox, waiting for a response.

Cao, her humongous, round black sunglasses resting on the tip of her nose, leans back and absorbs the bright yellow circle shining in the sky. She pulls her head back and looks at me. "You haven't yet?"

I shake my head, looking at my phone.

Cao puts her face back toward the sun.

"I'm just going to text him."

"Who?"

"Daniel."

"Oh. Good."

I ask how he's doing and if he needs anything, how his mom is doing, and if his dad is there in three short, choppy sentences. I hit Send.

It says Delivered under the text, and impatiently, I wait for his reply.

"I met with Mr. Joe today. Well, *met* is a strong word. Ran into, I guess."

"Did he give you the speech that you'd expected?"

"Actually, no. I thought he'd give the slow, meaningful speech though emotionless. Unaffected. The normal one we're used to in class." And then I realize that we aren't in the same class anymore. A piece of my ego—the one that cares about college, my future—falls off the side of the planet.

"And he didn't?" Cao takes her eyes from the sun that's quickly being whisked away by the clouds.

"No. He was angry. Like really disappointed. Said that I had potential and that I was throwing it all away." I pick at the grass blades of the field that our community gathers on every Friday night from October to December.

"Wait. Mr. Joe was angry?"

I nod.

My phone chimes, and my heart jumps. It's a Blog Heiress update.

Cao looks down at her phone, too, with the update.

I swallow as I open up the post.

BLOG HEIRESS

Well, Belle's Bitches, it's been a long 24 hours. And busy. Between scandal and immoral behavior among Belle's Hollow's finest, I can't keep up. I've been a busy kitten unwinding this big ball of yarn, only to find the plot keeps on getting messier and messier.

First, as you know, Leah Moran was spotted at Belle's Hollow Women's Clinic not too long ago. I'm not sure if Leah has gained a few pounds or if her clothes are fitting a bit too tight, but it looks like she might be sporting a baby bump. Keep your eyes peeled and your mind open.

Second, Haunted House theme won for this year's prom. It has been scheduled for November 28. Get dressed in your scariest shit and bring a date. Tickets are on sale at the Associated Student

Body office, or you can buy them online when the link becomes available. Plus, I heard someone's bringing Jack and Daniel, so drink the punch. ;)

Third, the school carnival is next week.

Fourth, Mr. Lowery is off to rehab! But don't think we're getting away with NOT taking Chemistry. They are bringing in some wet-behind-the-ears teacher fresh out of college to fill his spot. Hope he's a hottie!

Fifth, see how it's getting juicier and juicier as we go along? Apparently, after Livia's drug bust, Principal Lundberg and Mr. Marty were working late on the Stone case when Livia swore she didn't take the pills.

Oh, please.

Caught red-handed and still won't confess.

Apparently, her dad—alcoholic, back to dad, back to lawyer—threw his card down like a bad mic drop. It's funny what you can get away with when you have a lawyer dad to protect you.

Fifth, and certainly not least, late, late into the evening, Principal

Lundberg—married—and   Mr. Marty—in his so dated *Hawaii Five-0* glasses with his pants hiked up to his crotch so far in fact that you can tell what side Princess Sophia sits on—grabbed dinner at Las Cazuela's.

I'd say there's more than meets the eye here.

BAE anyone?

P.S. PARTY at Mark Pattison's this Friday night!

TTFN!

BeLHo

I feel my heartbeat in my ears. The want to punch the writer of BeLHo in the face is prevalent and exists within my fists.

"Why does she have it out for me so bad?" It's more of a rhetorical question.

I check my text messages, trying to distract myself. Still no response from Daniel, which makes my stomach roll into knots as I try to forget about the blog post.

I need a drink.

"She's just trying to get under your skin, so you'll react."

I play back BeLHo's words. *It's funny what you can get away with when you have a lawyer dad to protect you.*

"And how about her outing Mr. Lowery for going to rehab? Totally messed up. It's like her heart is ice, and her lips are steel." Cao slips her sunglasses off.

I check my text messages. "Maybe I should call Daniel?"

"Won't hurt."

I pull up his number and hit Call.

Ring one.

Ring two.

Ring three.

Ring four.

Ring five.

And then I hear his voice mail. His voice is eloquent, as if I can hear when he licks his lips, when he pauses, and when he uses syllables. Like I can feel his accent over the phone. Hear the way he smells.

What if Rose died?

I hear the message beep.

Shit.

A message.

"Uh, hey, uh, Daniel. Just, uh, checking up—I mean, checking in on you." My face turns to fire. I shake my head. "I'm just calling to make sure you're all right. Call me when you get a minute. Gi-give Rose my best." The word *best* trails off with my stupidity because, now, I think of a million different ways I could have left the message, and none of them involve *checking up*. I hit End.

"Smooth," Cao says with a smile, putting her rice bowl that her mom packed her, again, untouched, back in her backpack.

I shake my head, tapping my phone to my lip.

We make our way back from the field, and my phone begins to ring.

It's Daniel.

Don't sound like you've just run a half-marathon. Jeez, Liv. Breathe. But answer!

"H-hello?"

"Hello, Livia?" The voice is familiar, but it's not Daniel's.

"This is Dr. Pearson, Daniel's dad."

199

Twenty-Nine Days After Jasper and Liv's Dad Left

"Liv, are you awake?"
"Yeah."
Footsteps to my bed.
"I got an email from Dad."
"I don't care."
"You care."
"I don't, so shut up."
"We need to give him a chance to explain."
"Get out of my room, Jasper."

I hang up the phone. "Rose died." I try to swallow, but I can't. I replay Dr. Pearson's words in my head. *"It's probably in his best interest if you give him space right now."* Like he asked me to tea, but really, he was telling me to stay away from his son, and he made it sound like a compliment.

Cao's hand slips into mine as I take steps I'm not sure I'm taking. "I say we make the party at Mark's tomorrow night. I think you need a break. And you need to chill." Her voice isn't more than a whisper.

I nod, thinking I might need a drink—or several—to tide me over before school is out. But I think of Cao and driving her home.

I can't do that to her. I wonder if she can find her own ride, like the other day.

"Listen, Cao, there's something I need to do after school. Can you find a ride?" Either I'll drink or go to the hospital to see Daniel. Either way, I give myself some alone time so I can do one or both.

Does Daniel really not want to see me?
I could go to the hospital. But what's the point?
Have they left the hospital?
Where's her body?
Is Daniel okay?
Do I really need to give him space?

"Please don't make me call my mom again. Last time, she showed up in my dad's VW bus, restored in cherry red. Liv, it backfired when she pulled up to the front of the school."

Cao's parents are older than most. In their sixties, they still like to live their glory days with some sort of piece from their past—whether it be the bus, the music, or the Kush they smoke on occasion that Cao and I used to smell late into the evening. I'm sure Cao threw that in Beth's face when she caught her smoking cigarettes.

"I just have something I need to do," I lie.

My gut tells me I need to go to the hospital, but my head tells me I need to stop at the liquor store. Like I'm old enough. Like they'll sell it to me—which, most likely, will be problematic until the age of twenty-one.

"Poppy," I say when I get in my car after school, "where are you? You've been MIA, and I'm pissed about it."

Still, no answer.

From the corner of my eye, I see Beth go by in the bright red VW bus, and guilt begins at my throat, but I swallow through it, just like I swallowed the pills. I'm probably saving Cao's life by not letting her ride with me.

You could have given her a ride and then went and drank.
Shut up, Conscience.

Booze.

Hospital.

Alcohol.

Hospital.

Relief.

Hospital.

From Belle's Hollow High to Redwood Memorial, it's a left, right, left, and a right again off Redwood Way. I turn left even though I really want to go home and dig through our shed in the back, but I don't.

I still have the power of choice. I can't be an alcoholic.

Questions start to filter through my head in the two-minute drive it takes to get to the hospital.

1. Why would Daniel not want to see me?

2. Why would Dr. Pearson tell me Daniel needs space unless it's true that he does need space, and he doesn't want me around?

3. What if I'm going to the wrong hospital?

I pull into the parking lot.

4. What if Dr. Pearson is here with Daniel? What will I say to him?

5. (Again) What if I'm at the wrong hospital? What if they are at St. Joseph's Hospital, twenty minutes north? It's a bigger facility.

I park.

6. What if Daniel flips out because I'm here?

Livia, seriously.

7. What am I doing here?

I get out of the car.

8. What if some things are worth fighting for?

Booze would have been the better option.

The sliding glass doors make a seamless whooshing sound, and the sterilized air wafts out in one big push. I check in with the elderly woman behind the volunteer desk.

Dear God, what do I say to her?

I approach the desk.

I'm looking for the late Rose Pearson.

Where's your morgue?

Please, direct me to the Pearson family who just lost a family member.

Where's the cafeteria? I'm starved.

"I'm looking for Rose Pearson." I swallow the tiny bit of fear that creeps in.

The volunteer at the desk scans a list.

Many things go through my head as I watch her well-groomed fingernail go down the list.

The Stones probably weren't on a list when Jasper died because there was no list. He didn't need a hospital. He didn't go to the hospital. Because, when he died, it was instant, the FBI said.

We had to wait several days before the FBI released his body back to us.

This is new territory for me, being on a list—or rather, pretending to be.

"Are you family to Mrs. Pearson?" Her voice is soft. The chain that attaches to her bifocals is bright gold, most likely a Walgreens purchase. Her eyes grow shifty. As if perhaps she doesn't know that I know that Rose Pearson is on the dead list.

"Yes, niece." If lying were a career, I'd be the CEO. I lick my lips and try to explain, "I know she's passed. Really, I'm just looking for my...cousin and uncle."

"Hmm. Let me make a phone call, dear."

Think quickly, Liv.

She's probably calling the authorities because she knows I'm lying. She's probably a grandmother. Grandmothers have an uncanny bullshit detector.

"Oh, you know what?" I point to my phone and pretend it's ringing. "This is my uncle now." I hold the receiver to my ear. "Hey, Uncle Rob." My words are cut short in my make-believe game because I don't remember what Daniel's dad's name is. "Yeah, all right. See you there," I finish. "That was my uncle, and they're at the cafeteria."

"Oh, good, dear." Her voice is wobbly from age. She nods and sits down behind the volunteer desk, waiting for the next liar.

Now what? I think to myself as I walk away. *I roam the hospital for Daniel?*

I pull my phone back out of my pocket and look for a text from him. Still, nothing. *Does he not have his phone yet?*

Hospital staff walk past me as if I'm supposed to be here. As if I were invited. As if I'm not sneaking around, looking for my *cousin.*

I know that asking for directions to a place I don't know is not productive. I sit down in the waiting room and stare at my phone.

Maybe these are all signs that I shouldn't be here and that this was all wrong, coming here.

The words, *Sit, wait, hold tight,* come to my head.

I lean back in my chair next to the gigantic fish tank. The fish are unaffected by the hustle of the hospital—the sick, the dying, the tests, the results, the people—unless, of course, you're a kid who taps on the tank until the fish are huddled in a corner.

Their wide eyes approach me. The tails move back and forth, curious yet cautious. I see a piece of my reflection in the glass, and I can't help but notice my gaunt face and the dark circles under my eyes from fake sleep.

"Paging Dr. Pearson. Dr. Pearson, please report to the Radiology department, please," comes over the intercom.

I stand, shove my phone in my back pocket, and quietly walk the wall that separates the waiting folks and the four-way stop for medical staff and/or visitors.

Looking to the other waiting room across the way, I see a woman and her two daughters staring at me. I give an awkward smile. The woman reaches over to her daughters, as if to say, *Don't stare.* The woman continues reading her magazine while her daughters plug away at their phones.

There's a sign with an arrow that says *Radiology Department, Patient Rooms 1-33* and *Cafeteria.* Pretending I'm not a creeper, I push my shoulders back and pretend to seep confidence.

As I'm following the hallway down to the Radiology department, Dr. Pearson passes me, and my heart stops. I can tell it's him by his stride—curt and quick, as if he uses it to communicate his importance—and his shoes.

Is he working?

Why else would he have his scrubs on?

But I thought he worked at St. Joseph's?

I'm sure though, surgeons can work at multiple locations. Right?

This pisses me off even more, knowing Daniel is probably by himself somewhere while his father can't get his feelings together enough to be there for his son.

I text Daniel again as I stalk behind Dr. Pearson.

Me: Where are you??

Dr. Pearson pulls a phone from his scrubs. It's Daniel's phone. I can tell by the cover on the back. It's black with silver wording on the back.

Shit.

Shit.

Shit.

Immediately, I stop, turn, and pretend to read a flyer on the wall. Thank God, there's something to read there, or this would look extremely awkward.

What if Dr. Pearson has Daniel captive somewhere against his will?

No, that can't be. Because I'm certain Daniel would contact me from a home computer, explaining the situation.

I stare at the Employee of the Month award like it's the Holy Grail.

With Dr. Pearson down the hallway and around the corner, I run/walk, knowing he's gained at least twenty seconds on me. When I turn one more left, the Radiology desk is right in front of me with Dr. Pearson standing front and center. His shoulders have taken a plunge; his demeanor has changed as he stands at the desk.

"I'm sorry, Dr. Pearson. But where would you like Rose's remains sent?"

Each finger—pinkie, ring, middle, index, and then thumb—tap on his green scrubs. He does the same thing again but the other way, beginning with his thumb. And back again.

"To 160 Lily Lane, Harpers Avenue, Hull, East Riding of Yorkshire, England, HU8 26P," he says, his voice unbroken. As if he's giving a food order at Happy Doughnuts or something. As if his wife didn't just pass, and he doesn't have his son to help. "Thank you, Eve."

Dr. Pearson bursts past me, just the way he did in the hallway, not noticing my presence. I'll ask Eve where Daniel is. Tell her I'm a friend. She'll ask why because of HIPAA guidelines that protect the privacy of others. Eve knows me. But I'll tell the truth this time.

Take your finger out of your mouth and stop chewing on your nails, Poppy would say.

I especially don't think she'd pay me a visit here, as she used to hate hospitals. Loathed them. In fact, just days before she died, when we knew it was time for hospice, we took her home to die. I think she appreciated it, though she never said anything about it.

I take my finger out of my mouth, tip my chin up, and allow it to lead me to the counter.

"Can I help you?" comes out of Eve's mouth, not looking up, almost too busy for my question.

I know they're overworked at Redwood and always understaffed.

At the last minute, she looks up and cocks her head to the right. "Oh, hey, Livie."

She's called me Livie since as far back as I can remember. *Jasie and Livie.* Used to drive Jasper crazy as we got older. Me? Not so much. She's a warm and fuzzy type, and for a nurse, that might be rare. But the only thing I have to compare her to is Tracy, and Tracy isn't the warm and fuzzy type. Eve ends almost everything with and *IE* when she can. I mean, I don't think she uses that type of language with patients. Well, maybe.

"Hey, Eve."

Eve is a Have. She came to Jasper's funeral. Made sure we had meals. Made sure Tracy and I ate. Made sure Tracy only came back to work when she was ready. Cleaned our house while we were down in LA. But I guess Tracy did the same for her when Eve gave birth to a stillborn named Lane. Jasper and I were only two at the time. But I remember the haunted look that followed her around for years. Still, I get a glimpse of it every once in a while, usually at Christmastime.

"Hang on a second. I'll page your mom and see if she's here yet."

"Actually, I was, uh, just"—I motion with my thumb in the direction I just came from—"wondering—"

Eve curves her back upward, like a string is pulling on her neck, her eyes passing mine. "Hello again, Dr. Pearson," Eve says. "What can I help you with?"

Uh-oh.

28

"Hello, Eve. One more question. Sorry to interrupt." His voice is cold.

I know he isn't talking to me, and I don't dare turn around.

Does he know it's me?

Would he even recognize me? I've only met him once.

Don't breathe, Liv.

"My son will be here about four thirty p.m. to pick up his phone. I told him I'd leave it here with you. He left the hospital right after Rose died."

Please, pick up eggs from the store after work, could you? Dr. Pearson, so frank. Matter of fact. No emotion.

"Yes, Dr. Pearson." Eve extends her hand and takes Daniel's phone. "You're sure you want to finish your rounds today, Dr. Pearson?"

He doesn't answer Eve's question because he's already halfway down the hallway.

Eve's known me since birth. She and Tracy went to high school together, and they've been close friends since.

Eve sets Daniel's lifeline on the desk behind the counter. "So, you were saying? You don't need your mom?"

I can't conjure up enough truth to validate a good, believable story, so here I go again. "Daniel and I are study partners." That could be the truth, the future truth. "I can take his phone to him. I'm heading to his house right now for a study group."

"Oh, could you?" Eve hands over Daniel's phone.

I grab it from her, praying she doesn't change her mind. "No problem." I grip the phone in my hand, trying to act casual.

"What was it you needed, Livie?"

I look up, still wondering how hijacking Daniel's phone became so easy. "Hmm?"

"What did you need?" Eve asks again.

"Oh." *Come on, lying comes natural to you now, Liv. You can't talk your way out of this one with the truth.* "I'll just ask my mom after her shift."

"You sure?" Eve picks up a big stack of files.

I rock back on my heels and question if running away would be suitable for this situation. Skipping? "Yes. Completely sure."

"Oh, how are college applications going?"

Ouch. They aren't. "Good." I pause. *Is that believable?* "Really good." *More enthusiasm. That's it.*

"And how are you?" Her eyes narrow.

I know she has my best interests at heart.

"Fine." *Fucked up. Insecure. Narcotic. Emotional. There, not lying now.*

I don't think Eve buys it either.

"Are you still seeing Dr. Elizabeth?"

You mean Holy Moly? "Yes."

Eve is the one who recommended Dr. Elizabeth to Tracy. How Eve and Dr. Elizabeth ever got along, I'll never know. Dr. Elizabeth is drab. Boring. A monotone voice that asks after every sentence, *How does that make you feel?* Just the thought of her voice makes me cringe.

"All right. I'll tell your mom you stopped in."

I freeze.

Why? Why tell her I stopped by? She'll have questions. Ones I don't want to answer.

I panic, pick up my phone, and pretend to call Tracy. "Calling her now. You don't have to do that."

Eve waves.

I wave.

I leave as quickly as possible and head up to Daniel's. On the way up there, I give myself questions.

What'll I say to him?

Will he even want to see me?

What will he need?

I'll hand him his phone.

The sun sets as I descend into the Gulch and turn into Rockwell Lane.

I text Tracy this time even though she won't be home.

> **Me: Be home by curfew. Have stuff to take care of.**

> **Tracy: Where are you going? What are you doing?**

Tracy never asks questions about my whereabouts. She's always trusted me to make the right decisions. And I guess that's why Beth allows Cao to ride with me to school, too. But, now, she's asking—probably because I've given her reason to.

> **Me: Don't worry, Mom. I'm fine. Just need some alone time.**

Simon texts me.

> **Simon: How are you? Can we talk?**

My stomach twists into knots.

> **Tracy: Your dad cooked dinner. I'm leaving for the hospital now. See you tomorrow afternoon. Be safe, please, Liv.**

I walk up to the well-lit castle. Dr. Pearson can't be home; he couldn't have beaten me here. He was doing rounds. I'll just be a few minutes. Check on Daniel and make sure he's all right. Give him his phone. Go.

I knock on the gigantic door made of solid wood.

My heart begins to pick up pace.

Silence.

I know I'm meeting grief in its early stages, at the door, where I'm not sure I want in.

I knock.

I wait.

Silence.

My heart is fluttering.

What if he doesn't want to see me? It'd be acceptable and perfectly normal.

Self-doubt consumes me.

With a deep breath, feeling as though my annoying factor is in full gear, I ring the doorbell that sounds more like a tower bell.

Dong.

Dong.

Dong.

I wait.

Still, nothing.

Don't go, stalker.

Don't go, stalker.

I check the door to see if it's unlocked, and it slowly eases open without a single sound.

"Hello?" I call out, not to be heard. Quietly and with effort, I close the heavy door behind me. "Daniel?" I say louder this time.

Looking through the entryway and to the living room, the lamps that are turned on by the sofas in the living room give the house an orange hue, calming. Not the melancholy someone-just-died LED lights. LED lights are the death lights. Like the overhead fluorescent lights, the ones in dated doctors' offices, like at Dr. McGoldrick's office, the only pediatrician in town. Those are death lights.

The house smells like suede and lilies. I try not to creep or tiptoe—because that's too stalkerish—into the kitchen.

"Daniel?"

On the vast dining room table, just off the living room, is a table full of lilies. Just lilies. *Rose's favorite type of flower?*

I turn around and go back toward the entryway and head up the staircase. Daniel's phone begins to vibrate in my hand, and the name Sienna flashes across the screen.

Sienna.

Sienna.

Sienna.

I try to place the name, one I know he hasn't mentioned because I would have remembered a Sienna. It looks like a mess of numbers, no hyphens—*+44793551212*.

A pod of nerves seep into my stomach as my heart speaks with fast, uneven beats.

I hit Ignore, and the phone stops vibrating. Only to vibrate once more to indicate a message left.

I want to check the message. Tell Sienna not to call back. Tell Sienna that Daniel is off-limits. But he's not. Nor is he taken. Nor are we dating. We aren't a *we* at all. We are Livia and Daniel. Two separate lives. Two separate people, only connected through a shared interest of each other.

When I'm standing in front of Daniel's closed bedroom door, the nerves reach up into my lungs.

I think twice about knocking, so instead, I slowly push open the heavy door and peek in.

His room, just like the house, is big and impeccably decorated with grays and dark blues, probably done by an interior designer, as I highly doubt Daniel is into decor, and it matches the motif of the house. The light in the room is the same light outside—dusk when the birds burrow down in their nests and finish their final tune. Where the outside becomes quiet, awaiting the coyotes that will call tonight for lost loves.

Daniel's room is a loft. Downstairs, there's a dark leather sofa, a simple banker's light with a green shade, and a desk. Framed pictures on the wall, but with the lack of light that fills the bedroom, they're hard to make out. I walk to the big bay window that opens up to the forest of trees, the same view Rose had.

I cover my elbows with the opposite hands as I cross my arms and stare into the beckoning night sky.

This is the perfect time of day. When the day welcomes night. When creatures begin to settle in their homes. When our side of the world begins to prepare for the next twelve hours. When loneliness is at its best. When life seems to take on its stride and prepares the drab of the sunrise, like a baker prepares bread.

The morning, the awful, dreaded morning, comes when fear floods back into the conscious mind like a bucket full of cold water. Like a set change, the stage hands move and brace for the change from light to dark. I imagine people tugging at a shade, pulling the tiny loop from the dark shade to the light shade. Arranging the birds and assembling them on trees, calling for morning wake-up. The roosters, the turkeys, the wild hogs take their places in the play among the meadow.

I imagine, *What if morning doesn't come?* Like for my brother. And Rose.

I release my elbows, my hands falling to my sides.

"Hey."

I hear the dents in his tone, the broken ones, the less broken ones, but I also hear satisfaction. And my heart rate picks up pace and slows at the same time. Just the sound of his voice makes me forgot about Sienna. About Jasper. Like I'm supposed to be here, in this exact moment, and I wonder when this feeling started with Daniel.

I don't turn around because I don't want him to see the ache in my eyes for his loss. For the things I've done that he doesn't know about yet.

Tears for his loss.

My loss.

Our separate brokenness.

My addiction to something I can't explain.

Daniel. The alcohol. Pills. Simon.

Our riddled future of defeat.

"Hey," I say, still staring out the window, hoping my gratitude is loud and clear, that there's no place I'd rather be. But I don't dare say that. Not yet.

I feel his fingers trickle down my arms and the firmness of his chest against my back. His breath is on my neck, and his next words are in my heart.

"You're here."

I turn around now because the need to see Daniel's face and read the lines that curve around his mouth when he frowns or smiles far outweigh any need I've needed to fulfill before. His eyes tell a million stories all at once—comedy, tragedy, love.

Crimson and pink, bloodshot, swollen from death, and plagued with mourning, regret, and pain, his eyes find mine. We share the same pain. A look I feel too well, tears that don't fall because it's too much effort and the body simply cannot produce the amount of water required when someone dies. A condition perhaps when death falls upon the living.

His hands slide to the small of my back, attach themselves, pulling our bodies together so that there's nothing between us but cells and organisms. I feel him—not in a sexual way, but in the way of commitment, obligation, and rightfulness. Beneath the plastic of his smile, his doting eyes, and a broken heart that only two people in grief would understand. My eyes meet his collarbone because I'm not sure I can face the death of his mother, his own path of mourning, and in turn, allow him to face the death of my brother.

Daniel's bare chest rises and falls. His breath is the sweet scent of mint. I want to tell him I'll most likely break his heart because of the alcohol. Just like my father did to my mother. My brother. And me.

I've seen what addiction can do. But, in this moment, I know he needs me, and I, him. I tell myself I'll allow our bodies to coil around each other in order to mask his sadness. Let him feel me the way he needs to—with his hands, his legs, his chest, the shell of a boy who won't ever be the same.

The poor, poor boy whose mother died too young, people will say.

I try to push my heart out of this, not let it connect with his, so I don't look into his eyes.

How did this happen so quickly?

My head resting on his bare chest, his arms tighten around my body, and I feel a drop of his sadness land on my cheek.

And I allow one of my own to fall, too.

Telling Daniel about his father asking me to stay away wouldn't be appropriate now. Neither would asking about Sienna.

So, we stand here as the sky welcomes the moon and the hour count to morning begins. The days of loss. Where the days turn into nights and the nights into days without so much of a blink of an eye. Where dates blend and months blur. And life seems to unravel.

Standing here with Daniel, I've never felt this way about Simon as he pushed inside me. Nor did I feel the tremble that went along with Simon's when he finished. I forced the bad feelings away through touch and allowed an unspoken need on both parts to be filled. An escape, a getaway, only to be met with the demoralization once I awoke from my momentary state of euphoria.

But this?

This is something so much more. Nothing like the feeling I got when Ben Novak, my first boyfriend, rammed his tongue down my throat. Or the time Lee Cunningham touched my boob on accident at Whitney's pool party during the summer of our freshman year. I didn't feel it between my legs, like I do now.

This isn't Simon.

Or Ben.

Or Lee.

Or any other boy for that matter.

This is Daniel.

"Promise me something, Daniel?"

His head rests on me, and it might as well be the weight of the world.

Daniel's bedroom door flies open, and there, in the doorway, is Dr. Pearson.

Daniel doesn't let go of me, but instead, he turns toward his father. "What do you want?" Daniel asks, pulling on the back of my top, his fingers brushing against the small of my back in a protective way. He grabs a T-shirt that's draped over the chair at his desk and slides it over his head.

"Miss Stone"—again, like ordering eggs at a restaurant—"perhaps I wasn't clear when I said Daniel needed space to process what happened today." Dr. Pearson pronounces *process* like *prow-cess*.

"What?" Daniel jerks his head back. "What did you tell her?" He drops my shirt and steps in front of me. Clearly bigger, broader than his father, Daniel points to his door. "I will never be the man you are. I will never be the father, the husband"—his voice cracks—"the cheater that you are. Mark my words," he spits with both poise and reason. "You put on a facade that you want others to believe. You run from any little thing that might cause a disruption in your life. What about Mum? I took care of her the last year of her life. AND YOU," he yells now, "were too busy banging your nurses to see that Mum needed you. Fucking bastard." Daniel runs his hands through his hair, staring down at the floor, his eyes wide with craze.

"You'd best hold your tongue, Daniel." His voice is barely a whisper. "I moved your mum here because that's where she wanted to die. I left my teaching, my hospital, everything for her."

Daniel laughs. His words are chosen and slow. "No, your fuck buddies just got too old. You needed new pieces of arse."

I've never heard Daniel talk like this. Gently, I touch his arm, and he's shaking. My fingers slowly slide around his wrist in the silence the conversation has offered the room.

"Daniel, walk me to my car. Come on." Barely recognizing my own hoarse whisper, I pull his wrist behind me as I step in front of him and approach Dr. Pearson, whose lack of emotion scares me more than someone who'd have any reaction at all.

My fingers slide into his hand, and I still feel his subtle shake. He hesitates as he walks past his father. As if a thought crosses his mind to throw a punch. I cling tighter and put myself between Daniel and his father as we pass him in the doorway.

We don't say a word as we slip out into the night air.

"Hang on." He pauses before he lets go of my hand.

"What?"

"Nothing," he says, running back inside and outside in less than thirty seconds. He comes back with a black sweatshirt with some sort of musical design on the back.

"Thank you." I pull it over my head, and his scent drifts into my nose. I want to linger in it, ravish in his sweet smell. If bright blue had a scent, it would smell just like Daniel.

We walk to my car in silence, an owl coos, and the frogs speak. It's a different world out here, different from town.

"I won't ask you if you're all right." My fingers dangle in his as I search for the right words to fix his father's mistakes. "Oh, I almost forgot." Sienna's number flashes in my mind. A mixture of emotions allows my mind to make excuses for her call. But I file those thoughts/excuses under miscellaneous because it doesn't matter right now. "Your phone."

He'll see the missed call.

"How'd you get this?"

"Long story." I give his shoulder a bump as we approach my car.

Without looking, he shoves his phone in his pocket. "Thank you." His hand tightens around mine.

He'll know that I saw the missed call. And, if he feels the need to explain, he will. And, if he doesn't, well, I guess I just have to trust he's made that decision for the right reasons.

But a tiny voice inside me pulls the reservation sign.

And I'm not sure if that's for Daniel's benefit or mine. I know I can't get too wrapped up in this with him. This unspoken pull we have together. Like somehow we were meant to meet.

I unlock my car door.

"You know, you probably don't have to lock your door out here." The calmness in his voice slowly returns. "I mean, you'd be taking your chances with the angry bear or the occasional rabid fox, but, for the most part, I'd say your belongings are likely safe out here," Daniel says as he pulls my door open, looking down at me with a get-in nod, trying to make light of what just happened.

It also makes me realize that I don't know Daniel, yet my hand in his feels like it's been there for a lifetime. As if he carved a spot for my hand that rests somewhere between his palm and fingertips. I also notice, this time, his fingertips are rough. Callous.

What's he done to rough up his hands?

Maybe he's a midnight boxer? Might be a bit farfetched. I can also conclude that he'd probably have the cauliflower ears to match if he were a midnight boxer. And he's got perfect ears, so scratch that guess.

A day laborer and nobody knows? Though I quickly reject this idea, as he's only seventeen.

Perhaps he's an avid fly fisherman? Plausible.

I decide I'll ask him later.

I sit down in my seat, and he shuts the door behind me, bending down to where we're at eye-level. A huge part of me wants to warn him that, tomorrow, when he wakes up, the ache will only be worse, and the pain in his heart will only increase. That the person he loves will come to him in his dreams, only if he's lucky. That surrounding himself with her things will make him want to die. And the thought of dying, his mind might tell him, seems like a viable option, the easier, softer way. I want to tell him that I'd like to hold his heart in my hands until he's ready to have it back, that I promise to nurture it and take care of it. Because there will be many days where he'll wish his heart would just stop. Disappear. Run. And, already, without knowing what Daniel's favorite color is, his favorite food, what he does between the hours of seven thirty p.m. and nine thirty p.m., where he sees himself in five years, I want to shelter his heart, says the sober me, the one without the alcohol, the one of sound mind and body.

But I know my urge to drink again, probably when I get home, will return because the hurt will far outweigh the life I've built in the last seventeen years. And Daniel will be here, and I will be there.

"You all right?" Daniel pushes a piece of hair behind my ear.

I say, "Yes," even though my answer is really no, and I say this only so he won't worry about me. "In my head, I'm trying to figure out what to say to you."

His callous hand reaches for mine.

Maybe a lead guitarist in a rock band?

"Also, what I've been contemplating is why your hands are so callous. I've thought of everything from a day laborer to fly fisherman."

Daniel smiles, though his eyes don't, like a plastic fixture on his face, ready and able to meet the Have-Nots in his life. Braver than me.

"I don't want this for you, Daniel," is all I think to say.

Daniel leans in my window. "Livia, I'd really like to kiss you right now."

30

Every tendon, every muscle in my body is on high alert. My heart screams, *PLEASE!*

"I'd like you to wait," says the sober me. The thinking one. The rational one. "I know that's what you think you want right now. A side thought, a feeling that can distract you, your mind from its current state, but I promise you, in the end, it will only leave you with regret."

He does the lip thing, the methodical lip thing, before he speaks, "Well, just for the record, in my opinion, Livia Stone and regret will never go hand in hand." Daniel says *record* like the *re* goes on forever and the *cord* is almost an afterthought. And the way he pronounces *hand* with an *O* rather than an *A* makes my lady parts want to get up and walk away.

Liv, keep his feelings first, I have to remind myself. Because the selfish me wants him to take his callous hands and put them on places on my body that we don't talk about while drinking coffee. Or eating breakfast. Or waiting for the bus.

So, I swallow instead, praying my mind will clear.

"Text me when you get home." And he stands, kisses my head, and backs away from my car, waiting for me to drive away.

I notice his jeans sitting loosely on his hips, and I imagine him without his shirt on again.

Before I pull away, I ask him if everything will be all right with him and Dr. Pearson.

He nods, more for my best interest than his own.

My dad is at the dining room table, going through a file when I walk in.

"Hey," I say.

"Hey yourself. Dinner's in the kitchen."

"Not hungry." I pull up a chair.

He closes the file and pushes it aside.

Not sure how to proceed because it's been so long since my dad and I talked. Cautious, I guess.

I tell him about Daniel's mom.

"The boy you like, right?"

"Yeah."

"Do you know what Daniel did?"

His question seems more loaded than the answer I'm unprepared to answer.

"What do you mean?"

My dad leans his cheek into his palm. "He called Principal Lundberg and told her he'd stolen the pills and left them in your car."

"Figured as much." I pause. "Did he also explain that Gabriel Struvio was selling oxycodone?" I want Gabriel to get what he deserves.

"Jill didn't elaborate, just said Daniel Pearson had confessed to stealing the pills. It's unclear how the school will handle this, but I did call Dr. Pearson and told him I'd represent his son—pro bono, of course."

Pro bono, before my dad got sober, was a cuss word. A word he never used in our home. He felt as though people should work hard for what they had, and if they couldn't afford a good attorney, then they got what they paid for.

And then it hits me. Why Dr. Pearson didn't want me around his son. Clearly, he thinks I'm a bad influence. That maybe I coerced his son into confessing something he hadn't done.

"It's the least I could do, Liv." Dad's eyes are more telling than what he's really saying.

I stare down at my phone and see Daniel's text.

Daniel: Are you home yet?

I look up at my dad, whose eyes are fixed on me. "Thank you for making the phone call." I don't say *Dad* yet because it's too soon. He was gone for too long.

Three missed birthdays.
Three missed Christmases.
Three missed years.
Not even a phone call.

"Good night," is all I say. "I have homework." Even though that, too, might be a half-lie. I do have homework, but I question whether or not I'll find the motivation from here to my bedroom to do it.

"Daniel's mom died today."

My dad leans back in his chair, takes a deep breath, places his hands behind his head, and doesn't say a word.

I turn and walk to the stairs.

"Liv?" he whispers.

"Yeah?" I turn just before I head up the stairs.

"I love you."

"I know."

When I walk past Jasper's room, I immediately shut the door between my room and the bathroom and attempt to push away the anguish that builds like a bad buzz.

I push myself on my bed and lie back on my pillow. I text Daniel.

Me: I'm home. In one piece. Safe.

The transparent bubbles appear almost instantly.
I wait.
And wait.
And wait.
The bubbles disappear, and I wait for the text message to appear, but it doesn't.
The bubbles appear again.
And disappear.
And reappear.
And, finally, the text comes through.

Daniel: I'd like to tell you about Sienna when you're ready.

When I'm ready? Why must I be ready? How do I respond to that? Besides, I'd rather he get some rest anyway than feel the need to explain why a girl with a weird number, a girl who's programmed into his phone, was calling him.

Me: Not tonight. Get some sleep. I'll pick you up for school tomorrow?

I wait for several minutes for a response, but it doesn't come in. I hope he's fallen asleep.

Facebook is the collector of fake facades, collector of smiles held for merely seconds while their lives are put on hold for a picture, lives that people want you to see, memories. I can't help myself as I pull up Facebook, thinking about the email Sonja sent earlier. It was shitty and pretty beautiful at the same time. The way she talked about Jasper, the reaching out to me—the beautiful—and Jasper's last words—the shitty. I do this every time, going to Sonja's page to see her progress. It's a sick, twisted thing I do, and it reminds me of my insides—warped, inflamed, and hurting, like I want to throw up.

There's a picture of her in a hospital bed, her once long beautiful, dark hair—the before photo—now short, bald in some places, as they had to surgically go in and remove pressure that had been building around her brain. Her face is swollen, in a neck collar, and it occurs to me, there are many unseen scars, the ones that hurt the most, that she'll battle for the rest of her life. The scars on the outside will heal with time. Maybe fade, maybe not. But the brain can't unsee things. Things that are so hellacious and awful, the mind just can't forget.

I scan through the page I've seen a million times. I read a post written just yesterday by her mom or a sibling, I assume.

Sonja is able to communicate now. Talk. We still have a long road ahead.

I need an escape. Can't rifle through the shed out back with my dad still awake. So, I try to wait, try to push a drink, the instant

224

relief, out of my head. I don't want to drink, but the lack of feelings that I feel when I do drink, that's what I want. Just momentary relief where I can shut myself off like a valve.

I read one of the comments. Why do I do this to myself? I set myself up. Self-sabotage.

You're here. You're healing. God performs miracles.

Immediately, the irritation starts just under my collarbone. The same as it always does when I look at Sonja's page. It's a prickle at first, and then it grows.

I can't help but think, *If God were so good, why didn't he save my brother? Why did he have to die? Why can't he still be here with us? Why did God choose Sonja to save and not my brother?*

Fuck off...Thelma Knight.

Under the post, I type.

My brother died in the incident on October 1. He didn't survive. Is God still that good, Thelma Knight?

I delete it.

I retype it.

I delete it.

I retype it and hit Enter.

I go back and delete my comment.

I also resist the urge to throw my phone across the room.

"Fuck you, God," I whisper. "If you were good, if you performed miracles like everyone says you do, why'd you choose not to save Jasper? SHIT!" I place my hands on my head. "Poppy, are you there? Why are you ignoring me? I need you!"

But, this time, I do throw my phone because I hate what's going on inside my body. It's agonizing and it hurts and I can't control any of it. I just want it to stop.

I need a drink.

Just need a quick fix.

I march downstairs, and my dad is nowhere in sight. In the shed, I search everywhere—behind canisters, through cobwebs, in

225

wheelbarrows, on shelves too high to reach without standing on an insufficient surface. But, in one of the drawers of the workbench, way in the back, I find a half-gallon, half-gone.

Jackpot.

I smuggle it up to my room undetected.

Grabbing my phone, I want to text Daniel again, but I refrain.

I tell myself he needs sleep.

I shouldn't drink this, I think as I go into the bathroom and empty out our toothbrush holder. I stare at Jasper's toothbrush. The one I haven't noticed since he died. The blue-and-green one.

I need a drink. I'm owed this. My insides begin to shrivel up, protecting themselves from my heart that's about to explode in my chest.

I shouldn't drink.

I should.

I shouldn't.

Daniel's going to need someone, and I have to be there.

Consciously, I screw off the cap, fill up my cup, and head back to my room.

I take a big gulp and allow the alcohol to burn all the way down my throat. It explodes in my stomach. I give it a few seconds for the euphoria to seep into my brain.

Yes.

This.

Is.

It.

I feel my inhibitions slip away. My not-caring factor flips on. My invincibility reach levels I've never felt. I finish the cup of alcohol.

Feeling braver, I throw *+44793551212* into Google. And it traces back to the United Kingdom. Sienna from the United Kingdom.

Does she have unfinished business with Daniel? Was she calling to express her condolences for the loss of Rose?

I should have gone back to look at Daniel's call log.

Livia, that's deceitful.

And then the most magical thing happens. My face grows warm and feels just like cotton candy. My mind begins to slow down. The tightness in my chest releases. My shoulders drop. And I can feel my lips begin to tingle. And the pressure of my recent unorthodox decision-making makes sense. The world falls into line, just as Dr. Elizabeth said it would.

"Everything has its place, Livia, and your new life will make sense again if you give yourself time."

Sex with Simon equals coping.

Dropping AP English, giving myself the gift of time.

Letting Mr. Joe down—that's his own issue, not mine.

The drinking. Well, if you lost your brother, wouldn't you want a way out, too?

Just. Like. That.

I can rationalize and justify any decision I've made because it's my truth. My life. And I'm the one who has to live with it.

As I look across the room to my bulletin board, I see the picture of Jasper and me on our fifteenth birthday. Our faces are happy in the yellow glow the thirty candles give off. While I'm smiling—a perfect image of what I did so perfectly in the past, which was following directions—he's making an awful face. Just like he always did in any of our pictures—not just with me, but everybody.

A scowl.

A look of disgust.

Wide-mouthed.

Tight-lipped.

Eyelids flipped up, exposing the red. That one always grossed me out.

If you look on his Instagram, you'll only find one picture of him without an antic face. It's the one we put in his obituary. It was one he'd posted with the caption, *See me.*

Now, my head is warm and fuzzy, and nothing matters. The place and space that I wish I could live in all the time. Take up residence. Pay rent here. I'd pay double. Because life on these terms is better than life on expected terms, that we're somehow supposed to cope without the stigma of that stupid quote by Robert Frost. What is it anyway? Oh, yes. "The only way out is through." Or something completely ridiculous like that. But it's only me who I want to exist in this small bubble of a world I've created, a safe, comfortable space where only I can breathe. Really breathe, the warm cotton candy air. Feel the clouds on my face.

In fact, this feels so good, I fill my cup up again.

The thoughts of Jasper, of Daniel leak into my mind. I want to fix everything, but the only way I see my hammer, my nails, is to down this entire cup, and then I'll find some sort of divine purpose to fix everything.

I drink the entire second cup in two swallows.

Two Days Ago

I throw myself on the couch,
My mom on the couch,
My dad in the chair.
"Our family is so fucked up."
Tracy: "Liv, mouth."
My dad: "She's right."

As expected, the hideous four horsemen return upon a flicker of light through my bedroom window.
      Terror: *Another day to live.*
Bewilderment: *How come I drank?*
Frustration: *Why did I do it again?*
Despair: *I want my brother back. I want Daniel to have Rose.*
    The bucket of feelings is dumped in my stomach as I try to again rectify the decisions that seemed so rational last night with today's clearer, though hurting, mind.
    No more drinking.
    It all started with the pills Dr. Elizabeth gave me.
    No more.

I find the bottle under my bed. *Good, at least I had some sense to hide it and not drink the entire thing. See? I'm not an alcoholic. If I were, I'd have drunk the whole thing, right?*

I take the bottle and go to our bathroom. Correction—*my* bathroom. Taking off the lid, anticipation and empowerment unite, and I feel a sense of life return back to me, ownership.

But I pause before I dump the alcohol down the toilet.

What if I need it?

What if I have a panic attack?

You've never had one before, my voice of reason returns.

Keep the alcohol.

I remember the Livia's I Can Only Be an Alcoholic If test. Drinking in the morning. That would be a qualifying factor of an alcoholic. I can't drink in the morning. My hands don't shake. It's not like I need it anyway.

And the idea of a drink was just a mere side effect of the peace and comfort surrounding me last night.

This isn't real, Liv.

That life isn't real, I try to explain to my other self, the one who can't seem to dump the alcohol down the toilet.

Okay, I'll save it, but I won't bring it to school. I need to get Cao and Daniel today.

With a pounding head and the metallic taste of metal in my mouth, I walk back into my bedroom and hide the bottle under my bed. Yes, this will make it better. I'll hide it, so I can't see it, and this will all blow over.

I pick up my phone to look at the time—6:42 a.m.—and see I have three missed texts from Simon.

Simon: Did you get my text?

R u OK?

Where R u???

Distract. Distract. Distract, I tell myself.

No text from Daniel.

I send him one.

Me: How are you this morning?

The seeping thoughts of euphoria from last night come into my brain.

Why won't Simon get the clue? We have to be done. It's done. We're done.

> Me: Simon, stop texting me. I'm fine.

> Simon: Meet me at Hawthorne Hill this morning before school.

> Me: No.

I don't need to explain myself to him. So, I ignore his text.

> Simon: Look, Liv…we were friends first. B4 we did what we did. Plz. Meet me. I have something I need to show u.

Ugh. I'll shower now, run up to Hawthorne Hill, and be back to get Cao by eight ten a.m. and Daniel, if he's home, if he's even going to school today, which he's probably not. The queasiness grows in my stomach from nerves.

In the shower, my tension grows and grows, and the feeling of inadequacy enters my bones.

Fear takes over my head.

I have a fear of school and my meagerness in my performance lately—or lack thereof.

Fear of being stuck at the local community college because I can't seem to get my work done.

Fear of failing high school. Will I graduate?

Fear for Daniel.

Fear of another day without Jasper.

And the fear that I don't think I can live without the alcohol and pills creates a noose around my neck, tightening slowly. I gasp for breath and lean into the wall, allowing the hot water to beat down on my head and neck. Shoulders. Thighs. And the hole in my chest grows bigger without my consent.

Slowly, the sobs begin, and I sink down to a puddle, gathering myself on the shower floor.

For several minutes, I lie here until the water against my body grows cold. The hole in my chest pulls at my ribs.

This, I cannot control.

Wrapping a towel around me, I walk into my bedroom and see my phone lighting up.

It's Cao.

Cao: Shit. Call me. I thought you ended things with Simon??

I did. Wait. What does Cao know that I don't?

Simon: WHERE R U??

Daniel: Hey. Not sure how I'm feeling. Numb, I guess. How about you? Not going to make it to school today, so come over after school?

I text Daniel back and tell him I'll be there after school and ask him if I can bring him anything.

Me to Simon: I'll be there in five.

Still unsure of what Cao means, I text her that I'll be to her house soon.

Numb, the leftovers of the booze still lingering in my head and my body, I put on a sweatshirt, my hair still wet, and try to throw on some mascara and lip balm, my head pounding.

Heading out of my bedroom, I think, *Maybe I can take one swig, just to get me through the day. One tiny swig, so I can deal with life.*

No.

No.

No.

I walk out of my room, shutting my door behind me, and walk downstairs. I feel the fear making its way up my stomach to my chest and shoulders; it's waiting to push me over the edge. The fear stops at my throat, and my heart begins to palpitate. My breaths become short, shallow, and my chest tightens once again.

I push myself to take one more step toward the light, but the darkness beckons me, tells me I cannot survive alone, and in one step backward, back up the stairs, my world becomes smaller. Less bright, dull. Dim. The satisfaction I felt earlier over the toilet, the empowerment, has left.

Opening my bedroom door, my hands shaky now, chaos in my head, I reach for the bottle underneath my bed.

A loud crash makes me smack my head against my bed frame, and I release the bottle from my hands.

A picture frame is lying in shards of glass on the floor.

Loud silence separates me from the bottle. This action makes me rethink the bottle. I reluctantly leave it under my bed.

Pacing, one hand in his thick, dark hair and the other holding his phone, Simon stares at the screen. He stops when he hears my footsteps. "Jesus Christ, Liv. Where have you been?"

"It's only been a half hour."

But the look on his face is concerning. Trepidation. Humiliation maybe?

Quickly, he walks to me and shoves his phone in my face.

I almost lose my footing as I stare at the photo in front of me. The page name is still trying to reach the making-sense part of my brain.

LivJam.

I've seen the term before.

Then, the longer title: *LivJam: Livia and Simon's Secret Garden.*
Skin.

Breasts.

Chest.

Simon.

Me.

Oh my God.

Someone was taking pictures.

"I've gotta go," is all I say.

"That's it?" Simon's hands are on his head. He's freaking out. "You've gotta go? Livia, someone took pictures of us having sex and created an Instagram account with it," he spits as he talks.

"What can we do about it?" My voice is higher, the stress becoming prevalent.

I'm going back to get the bottle.

"Take down the page for starters!" he yells.

"Who do we talk to about that?" I yell back.

Now, we're both yelling, and it isn't helping.

"You know what, Liv? Ever since this whole thing started, I've felt like the bad guy. Like I'm the one who coerced you into doing this. Like you're pissed off at me for our mistakes. You had sex with me. You agreed. We both did this. Fuck!" Simon picks up a rock and launches it down the hill.

There's a long silence between us, and all I want to do is run.

Head throbs.

Body aches.

I can't deal.

Simon places his hands on his hips. Taking a deep breath, he licks his lips. "Liv, trust me. I didn't want any of this to happen. I'm sorry it did. I'm sorry for all of it. The only thing I want back is Jasper. And he's not coming back. And I'm so fucking pissed. Motherfucker!" he screams so loudly, I jump, covering my elbows with my hands, staring down at the ground, trying to figure out where things got so messed up.

He rolls his eyes, watching his phone ring. "Yeah, great. It's Whitney." He hits Ignore. His phone chimes again, but it's a text. "The page has been taken down," he says, slipping his phone back in his pocket.

Slowly, he walks to me. My body is rigid. My hair still wet, my ears cold.

Simon is angry still, but his words are softer. "Every time I look at you, I see Jasper. It wasn't about the sex. It never was for me. It was about being as close as I could be with the person who loved him more than I did."

He pauses and reaches for my arm. I don't pull away, and I don't care if someone is taking pictures or not. I let him pull me to him.

His chin rests on my head. "I don't know, Liv, when this will get easier. I don't know if it will. I guess we will find out when we live a new normal—whatever that looks like. But, for now, we can miss him. We can miss his Vans. His stupid, disgusting toast he used to make. His laugh. And the stories he used to tell with his hands."

And I laugh. For the first time in a long time, I laugh. "Where did everything go wrong?"

"When Jasper died," he whispers.

"Did you know?"

There's an extremely long pause. A silent pause where I think the world has just fallen asleep. People. Animals. Aliens. The universe. A silent pause that is more telling than words.

Another moment passes.

"Know what?" Simon asks, his voice quivering.

"That he was gay."

And Simon's tears start to fall.

We make our way down the hill.

"So, who's the Daniel guy?" Simon looks at me as we reach the opening at the bottom.

But standing there, waiting for a rightful explanation, one that she might deserve is Whitney.

"I knew it," she says. "How could I not have known this? The lack of response to my texts. The disappearing in the middle of movies. All to meet poor Livia Stone, the heartbroken girl who can't seem to get her shit back together." Even when she tries to be mean, she can't. It's just not in her DNA.

But it's only been forty-seven days for the record. There should be some sort of time period that professionals give, a ballpark for the grieving process, so us planners know how long to plan for.

Loss of parent: 1,825 grieving days allowed
Loss of sibling: 1,095 grieving days allowed
Loss of friend: 730 grieving days allowed
Loss of cousin: 1,095 grieving days allowed
Loss of child: 3,650 grieving days allowed

But what happens if the day count is met, and I'm not done being messed up? I'm not done making wrong decisions. Tears still fall. My heart still aches. Maybe they'll put me in a home where they dope me up and do some sort of rapid eye treatment before sending me on my way with a nice little bow that says, *Cured.*

If it were only that easy, I'd have opted for that treatment right after Jasper died.

"Let's go, Simon. We have an image to uphold."

Simon's head cocks to the right, confused. "What?"

"I said, let's go." Her finger beckons him.

"But I—"

"People make stupidly heinous decisions when they're grieving, says my mother, Dr. Elizabeth Levine."

I look to Simon and wonder if he'll tell her. If he'll figure it out.

But Simon says instead, "How will it look to everyone if you're the one taking me back?"

Whitney laughs. "Who says I'm taking you back? I called you next to me to do this."

She slaps Simon across the face so hard, the clap against his cheek echoes in the trees just above us. It almost sounds like a tree branch snapping.

"I am taking you back, but you also deserved that."

And, with that, she grabs both sides of his face, hard, and kisses him to the point where it gets borderline awkward, and I feel like a voyeur. She stops. Simon's eyes are still open.

"Get in the car."

Simon does. He gets back in the car. It's easier than acknowledging who he is. What he stands for. As if ignoring a big, gaping hole of who he is. But, sometimes, maybe that is the easier way.

Whitney pulls down her sweater, her cheeks still flush. "As for you, Livia. You were the last person on earth I'd have ever thought would do this. You've lost yourself. You aren't the same girl you were two months ago, and you shouldn't be. But, if you don't find yourself soon, I don't know that you ever will. After all this, I can't help but like you. And it pisses me off that I like you." She stares long and hard. Whitney flicks her blonde hair as she spins on the ball of her foot and walks back toward her car.

Whitney just caught me cheating with her boyfriend.

She took her boyfriend back.

Offered advice.

And I'd accused her of being messed up when, clearly, the trouble exists on my end.

32

The Summer Before Our Senior Year

"Hey," I say.
Jasper jumps.
Simon leans.
The great divide exists between them. A whole world.
It's awkward when I sit down.
Faces red.
I shouldn't be here.
I leave them in the living room.

It's been a week since the Instagram page was put up and taken down.

Every day Cao and I showed up for school was like I was showing up for my daily punishment. Nobody said anything. But the uneasy snickers, lips moving behind hands, sarcastic smiles said it all.

I've been trying my best to limit my drinking. But it's only gotten worse. I managed to dupe my parents by telling them I had the flu when I missed school once last week because I was too hungover. I think my dad is catching on.

I keep my drinking to the evenings after work. And, when I don't work, I drink after homework or before. Or during. Something inside me tells me there's a problem. But the rational side of me tells me I'm too young. That I haven't lost anything of real consequence yet, so I can't be an alcoholic, right?

I'm reminded of my dad.

I think we go into denial. Trying to see something we so desperately want to see—the award-winning lawyer/father and the smart almost-valedictorian daughter. But the real truth is, the alcoholic father who's barely hanging on and the troublesome drinker of a daughter who's watching her life fall apart around her. As if I'm standing sideways, my view distorted, unreal, and no one can right me and I'm the only person who can save me.

Whitney hasn't said a word to me since. Nor has she played into others' games. She has kept her lips sealed. That makes it all the more difficult. I wish she'd lash out at me, so I'd have reason to hate her. But I can't.

It's Friday.

"Let's just go to the party and make an appearance. Then, we'll leave," Cao says, eating the rest of her egg roll at lunch, trying to drag me out of my state of mind.

I've been able to hide it from her, my best friend, the one who didn't leave my side while I was at home, sulking in my own mess. Who stayed with me, even when I wanted her to leave.

She purses her lips together when I don't answer, staring down at my phone. "He still hasn't called you?"

He meaning, Daniel.

I shake my head. I assume he received word because Blog Heiress put Simon and me on blast without a shred of evidence left behind. We haven't talked or texted in a week. Though I haven't let that stop me from texting or calling him nine hundred times.

"Maybe Daniel will be at the party," Cao says.

"Doubt it."

I remember Dr. Pearson telling Eve to send Rose's remains back to Hull. *What if he went back with his mom?*

I wonder how he's feeling.

How he's doing.

I want to throw up because the sober me can't deal with these feelings. And all I want to do is push them down. I've hurt Daniel. I'm sure he's seen all of this. The mess I've made of things.

I explained to Cao yesterday that I couldn't give her a ride because of new medication they had me on.

Side effects of the medication?

"Seizures," I told her.

Somewhere along the way, I've lost my moral compass but not enough to kill my best friend when I get into an accident for driving while intoxicated.

"Do you think he went back to England?" I'm desperate for an answer.

Cao tells me what I want to hear and maybe it's what she believes, "I don't think he could leave without saying good-bye."

I roll my eyes. "Did you see the photos on the Instagram page?"

Cao tries not to grimace. "Look, Daniel didn't know the before you. The one who was an impeccable student. Responsible. Caring." She shrugs. "The one whose heart wasn't broken."

"You aren't making me feel better, Cao."

"All I'm saying is that you need to win him back."

"How? He won't take any of my calls. I've called him. Texted him. Snapped him. And nothing."

"Have you gone to his house?"

Tempted? Yes. Sat at the end of his driveway?

"No."

"Let's go."

"No." I slowly shake my head. "Cao, I don't blame him one bit," I sigh. "I don't even want to be around me right now. How could I expect someone else to?"

"I want to." She looks hurt. "Does that matter for something?"

I wince. "I didn't mean that." I want to say, *Yes*, but I don't.

"I'm here for you." She's hurt.

It takes a lot more than a few words to bring her down. But I've managed to do it.

"You might not be able to see yourself right now, Liv, metaphorically speaking, but I do. I see the same seven-year-old girl who wouldn't give in to Liam Anderson because he wanted Lela."

Lela was Cao's stuffed animal sheep that she brought every day to kindergarten. Liam took Lela from Cao because he wanted it. Cao started to cry, so I ripped it from his hands and handed it back to her.

Then, Liam started to cry, pulling at Lela, so I pushed him back and said, "No."

I had to move my owl that day for pushing and stay in at recess.

"You're still the same girl who ran for student body president in eighth grade because you believed unisex bathrooms were important for our students to feel inclusive. The same girl who stood up for Marco Martinez, who barely spoke English, when he was called a wetback by our peers.

"I will always hang on to this girl. This brave, resilient girl who wouldn't give up and would stop at nothing to stand up for the underdog.

"You believed in me when I wanted to find my birth parents at a vulnerable moment in my life. And you were there for me when we found out they'd passed on. You were there for me when I questioned my own sexuality. You said it didn't matter. That I was still Cao Smith. And you promised that on my grave, it would say, *Cao Smith, an undecided woman who couldn't decide. Therefore, she died an old gypsy.*" She stops and starts again, "And just because you've lost your way doesn't mean I won't help you find it because you don't give up on others. It might be that you can't see the light right now, Liv, but I do. I'll be your eyes until you can see the same person I see sitting in front of me.

"Now, let's go to Daniel's. Make him hear your side of things. That this thing with Simon got started before you and Daniel became a thing. And let's go to that party tonight. And let's find the old Livia Stone."

Can I? Can I find the old Livia buried somewhere in the trenches of my new self? The one I loathe. The one that needs major fixing.

"Where do we start?"

"After school, you'll follow old protocol and give me a ride home, and on the ride home, we'll drive down Rockwell Lane. You'll confess to Daniel that what happened was before him. You'll tell him the truth."

I knock. Three times. Not like one, two, three knocks. Like knock-knock-knock three separate times.

Nothing.

I resort to the doorbell that sounds as though it's ringing in the dead.

It's against my better judgment, but, hell, these days I don't have better judgment, so who cares, right? I take a step down off the porch and peek in one of the windows to the left of the door.

God, what if he walks up and finds me snooping in his window?

My shock is met with tiny breaths that get lodged somewhere in my throat.

The house is empty.

At first, I try to rationalize why the house might be empty.

1. They're getting the carpets cleaned.

2. Redecorating.

Anything but the more plausible reason—they've moved. Upped and moved and left the United States, our country, which makes the move sound even farther away. The eight-hour time difference.

I step back up to the porch, and with my judgment now onboard, I try the door, but it's locked. I ring the doorbell once more because, as Cao said, Daniel wouldn't just up and leave without saying good-bye, right?

I look back at Cao, who's leaning against the car.

"He's not home?"

I shake my head. The tiny breaths are still stuck. "The house is empty."

"Empty?"

"Like no-furniture empty, *empty*," I say.

"Shut up."

Cao turns and gets into the passenger door as I get in. I stick the keys in the ignition, and we sit and stare only for a moment.

"You're sure the house is empty?" Cao's mouth is agape, too, more for empathetic reasons, I'm sure.

"Yeah." Numb, I am.

I try to text him once more, one last deliberate attempt to fix this.

Daniel, let me explain everything. Please.

My last-ditch effort to right the world of Livia and Daniel.

The feeling of uselessness returns, and right now, the party is an excellent idea tonight because I'll then have an excuse to drink. I won't have to cover it up. I can drink and not feel the feelings and not have to drink alone in hiding because maybe Livia Stone is a drinker.

But a quiet voice inside me says, *An escaper.*

And that might make me an alcoholic. But I don't dare say that out loud, for if I do, it would make it all too real.

Push down the feelings that are starting to creep inside your heart, Liv. Push them down and far, far away.

Emptiness consumes me as we pull away from the Pearsons'— or rather, the Pearsons' ex-house. I glance through my rearview mirror and look for a For Sale sign but don't see one.

And here my heart goes, holding on to hope: *Maybe they just made a quick trip back, took some furniture, but will be back soon.*

That's pathetic.

You're pathetic.

Daniel isn't coming back.

Cao talks me into my pink lace top that just barely shows my belly button. "Subtle yet a hint of your bod," she says. And black jeans.

Cao wears a red-and-hot-pink flannel with black jeans and a black tank underneath that barely covers the top of her jeans—and, of course, pink leg warmers. Unquestionable style, and Cao is the only one who can pull this look off.

The party is up two blocks on Nobb Hill. A house party, which we don't usually have because the chances of them being discovered in our sleepy little town is 99.9 percent.

I've wanted to drink since we got home from Daniel's, but Cao hasn't made it easy. She doesn't drink, and this is why I don't offer her any.

With my head a little soft and fuzzy, I didn't want her to know I'd been drinking, so I hid the evidence under my bed while she was in the shower.

"What'd you tell your mom?" I ask as our steps are in sync up to the party.

"I was studying at your house."

"On a Friday night?"

"With you, Liv, she'll let me do anything."

The party is filled with fifty-plus kids from Belle's Hollow. And even some from Eureka High, twenty minutes north.

As we arrive, I don't care what people think of me or the Instagram page because the alcohol has reached my mind. Also, like the news with Leah and Mark, the sex scandal of Simon and Livia has washed over because, now, the news is highlighting Leah's baby bump that she's rocking with a pink tight shirt that says, *Expecting*.

Cao turns to me, eyes wide. "I think I need a drink." She shoves me toward the kitchen with her shoulder.

"You do?" comes out more excited than expected.

"Kidding." But she turns to me and pauses, and then she lets out a sigh.

"What?" I eye a bottle of hard alcohol on the counter. Several actually.

"Why is it that, if a Chinese boy spots a Chinese girl in a predominately white community, the Chinese boy feels the need to approach the Chinese girl, fall in love, and have babies?"

I shrug. "Tell him you're dating Ed Sheeran."

Cao eyes me up and down. "Your jokes are not funny." She crosses her arms.

"If he were white, would it make a difference?"

"If he had red hair and sang with a guitar about love and castles and cigarettes, then yes, yes, it would."

The Chinese boy approaches us, and Cao slaps on a fake smile, one I see right through.

"Hey. I'm Chen. Do you know—"

Cao interprets him, "Let me finish the sentence for you. Chen, is it? You couldn't help but notice that I was the only other Chinese person in the room who happened to be a girl, and you thought we could connect via our upbringing. Laugh and joke about our homeland. Our culture. Arranged marriages. Amy Tan books and maybe, just maybe, find a little spark along the way. Have babies perhaps?"

He coughs an unprepared-for-this-sonnet cough. "Actually, I was wondering if you knew where I could get a water? Sober driver." Chen waves his keys at us.

"Oh, refrigerator. Garage," Cao says, completely embarrassed. "Nice to meet you," she finishes as he walks away.

"Maybe, next time, just start with your name. Not an entire explanation of what you think he's doing. Total buzzkill, Cao."

I look around the room, hoping to see Daniel. No, more than hope. *What's a word that means more than hope?* I think about texting him, knowing it won't make a difference. Knowing he's made his decision, and he's probably halfway across the globe already. Or wherever Hull, England, is. Yet I hope more than hope.

Cao moves her head to the techno music that's not quite blaring over the speakers.

We push through the crowd to find a spot on the deck that overlooks Belle's Hollow. The orange and yellow lights that twinkle below make me feel queasy. Like this quaint little town, the one we've grown up in, has somehow become so unfamiliar. The inside jokes; the streets traveled before and after school; Happy Doughnuts with Tracy, Dad, and my Jasper on Sundays; the Easter egg hunts downtown where Mayor Trent, who also owned her own hair salon, dressed up as the Easter bunny, passed out candy, and took pictures with kids. The town that cheered on my brother when he made the game-winning touchdown against Agatha Rice High School in the playoffs last year. The town that welcomed us back when we brought Jasper home after he was killed. Cooked meal after meal. Chicken after chicken. People gave because maybe they grieved with us. Yet everyone has continued to move about town—doing their business, eating, running errands, moving furniture, mailing letters, getting their hair cut, going to the movies, attending rotary meetings—while I begrudge the future and throw a thousand knives.

"Hey, I found the water. Grabbed you both one," Chen says as he approaches from behind.

Although I take his water, I won't drink it. Too much of a buzzkill. But I'll hang on to it, pretending to take sips.

"Can I reintroduce myself?" Chen asks, looking down at Cao, who is clearly two feet shorter than he is—not because she's short, but because he's tall.

I whisper in her ear, "I'm going to the bathroom, and then I'll go find a lost soul to shack up with while you go talk about prearranged marriages and plans for your wedding."

Cao doesn't whisper back because, now, she doesn't want to make a stupid comment and have to relive the previous experience of looking like a complete idiot.

I make my way back into the house and find an upstairs bedroom to make myself quiet in. It's some sort of aeronautical room with big airplane models suspended from the ceiling. All arranged by type and model. With a quilted bedspread in red, white, and blue, I comfortably push myself up against the pillow and welcome the silence. I pull out three small bottles from underneath my jacket. The thing is, I don't want to get drunk. All I want is a glow. Just a glow to make all my insecurities, all the sad feelings disappear so that I can be the person Cao still sees. The one I know Jasper is waiting for. And the one I want Daniel to meet.

"Poppy? Are you there?" I ask. This time though, I feel a bit weird, saying it out loud in a strange house.

I carefully twist the lid off the first bottle of Black Velvet, romancing how it will make me feel. I've had two of these before in the late hours of the night, trying to find the escape I found with the pills. But the good news is, the alcohol works much better than the pills.

I put the bottle to my lips, letting the brown magical elixir slide down my throat, holding my breath because the taste is horrid, and allowing it to explode in my stomach, making it fiery and hot. I oblige myself in another gulp. Almost instantly, as the sensation is felt in my stomach, it shoots up to my head, making my right eye twitch. The feeling of I *don't care* has reached the motherboard that makes me operate, and I'm powerless. Wanting to roll myself in this elusive feeling, I open and drink another, knowing it will bring far more promise than the first one did.

I drink all three in quick succession and rest my head on the pillow, staring up at the airplanes and the colors that are so beautiful and rich with history, I wonder where the airplanes came from.

What era?
What war?
My.
Mind.
Slowly.
Drifts.
Into.
Oblivion.
And.
I'm.
At.
Peace.
Finally.

My hands begin to tingle, feel numb. My legs are unmovable, and the smile I feel on my face is that of contentment.

Nothing matters. Absolutely everything is as it should be once again.

My lids slowly begin to close because the room is dark, and the only thing that gives off light is the tiny little thingy-besi-da-bed...

I jerk. Though my eyes don't open because I hear a noise, like a door opening and closing. I hear a voice that sounds just like Simon's. I want to say hey and tell him how good I feel, but the words somehow don't make it out of my mouth because my head is in full resistance.

I feel the bed move and then drift back into oblivion...

This time, my eyes jerk open when I hear a crash, like glass exploding against the floor.

But I see someone. A tall, dark figure in the doorway, and in order to make out who's in the doorway, I have to look past whatever is on my chest that weighs a thousand pounds.

Simon's head.

Shock reaches my face.

It registers.

My eyes adjust.

And I see who's standing in the doorway.

The look on Daniel's face is unforgettable. It's like watching his mom die all over again. I want the look he's giving me to sober me up, but it doesn't do the job. For once, I want to be sober. I want to tell him that I'm sorry. That this is not what it looks like. I want to tell him that I want to hear his heartbeat from the inside. I want to be the one who holds it. And all I keep managing to do is break it.

The only two words that come out of my mouth are, "You're back."

Daniel stands at the door, unable to speak.

Am I dreaming?

Is he really here?

I push Simon's head off my chest and do my best to stand, but my body weight is met by Jell-O, and I fall, my legs a mess on the floor. When I look back up at Daniel, I see he hasn't moved. I can tell by his face that he's more hurt than mad. But he doesn't help me up. So, here I sit, a pathetic puddle of what's left of a shallow shell, waiting for someone to save me.

In this moment, a moment of clarity, I realize I have become my father.

I see behind the hard look, the one where he bites his cheek, his eyes narrow, his heart hardened, as if he, too, has been here before. It's the same look Jasper and I gave our dad when he fell outside Las Cazuela's restaurant. Not once, not twice, but three times.

The same look when he went to rehab for the second time.

The same look when Jasper told him he hated him for what he'd done to us. Our family.

The same look that broke my heart over and over and over.

Now, I know how my father feels. I don't want to keep hurting people, yet I can't stop doing what I'm doing. I have the best of intentions when I drink. To soothe my soul. To help me unfeel. I don't set out trying to hurt anyone.

I try to choke out words because the silence alone, I know, will kill us both. He's still standing here, staring at me. Waiting for me to say something. Do something that will convince his mind that what he's witnessing is all just a bad dream.

"I'm going back to England," is all he says amid the confusion in his eyes. He quietly shuts the door behind him.

I close my eyes as silent sobs reach my throat, and I need to get out of here.

My eyes close again.

I wake up, only to see I'm being put in a truck. The driver, Cash, is a football player. I tutored him in English.

I close my eyes again, only to hear the squeal of the tires, and my eyes shoot open. The black asphalt that was once below us is now above us.

Now, below.

Above.

Now, below.

Above.

And then we take a hard thud against Cash's side and flip too many times to count.

Cash is gone. He's no longer in his seat.

Flying.

Quiet.

Tumbling.

Rolling.

Splattering.
And everything goes dark.

Black.

S omeone help me.

P*lease. I can't move.*

I'm alone.

38

I can't feel my legs.

I hear, "Lucky."

40

I listen. "Multiple breaks."

S ilence. *Am I dead?*

G od, *are you there? We need to talk.*
   I'm not ready to die.
   Is this what dying feels like?

Someone's crying. It's Tracy.

Please don't cry, Tracy. What happened? I'm right here.

"...in a coma...swelling of the brain."

Tracy's sobs are reaching places in me that make me want to cry.

I try to reach out my hand in the direction of the sobs, but I can't see if I'm moving or not because I can't see anything.

My dad says, "Will—" He coughs. "Will she wake up?" His voice quivers.

There's a long pause.

"That's our hope. But time is on our side."

"It's been two weeks," Tracy says. "And time is on our side, Dr. Miller? I've seen cases like this play out." I hear a hard steel line in her voice as she attempts to be strong. She's a nurse after all. She's used to seeing this. But not her daughter, the only child she has left.

A small part of me wants to die, the selfish side. But the other part of me wants to live.

"You think you're invisible, but you aren't, Livia Stone." Poppy's voice is curt, to the point.

"Poppy." I breathe in a sigh of relief. "You're back." I try to contain my joy and fear and trepidation.

"After all, God didn't put you on this planet to muck up your life with the way you're carrying on." *Muck* used to be her favorite word.

"Don't muck up the biscuits."
"Don't muck up the brand-new tablecloth."
"Don't muck up your Sunday school clothes."
"Oh, for mucking's sake!"

Poppy lights a match. Her bright pink housecoat glimmers in the small light the match provides. We're in the corner of the hospital room. My parents. Dr. Miller and Eve.

And me.

And me.

And me.

I see me.

With tubes connecting to places and no end in sight, my head wrapped, my eyes swollen, black, blue, purple, green. Unrecognizable. My hands and arms are scraped and bruised with dirt under my nails—dirt that wasn't there before the accident.

White surrounds us like it's infringing on my personal space, suffocating. Sterile. Untouchable.

"I was in an accident."

Poppy picks at her nails, not making eye contact. Her fingers shift and stroke in a hasty way. "I need to make this quick. There is only so much time you can coexist in both the living and the spirit realms." She sits up straighter and crosses her hands over herself. "Yes, you were in an accident. And, if you'd been in your right mind, you wouldn't have gotten into that truck with that drunk, irresponsible young man."

"Am I going to die, Poppy? Am I dead?"

She stops and looks at me matter-of-factly, and with such a look, I feel her irritation in my bones. "Yes. And no. Let me save you many years of heartache. You don't drink to have fun, do you?"

I hesitate at first. Not sure where she's going with this.

Can I lie to my dead grandma?

"No, you can't lie to me," she says. "I see everything." She goes back to her nails. "You drink because you can't handle life on life's terms. You drink because you want so badly to be fixed of your own feelings. Secretly, you want to fit in. Though you've never felt like you quite fit the mold like Jasper. You think drinking makes you everything *er*—prettier, wittier, smarter, funnier, nicer. You get the point."

Stop, I want to say.

"Look, Livia, I understand all those feelings because I was an alcoholic, too." She pauses. "Why do you think your mother is so closed off to you emotionally? Why do you think she only shows any type of emotion toward you when she's worried? Because of what I did to her when I drank," Poppy spits her words.

And, now, I realize she's not angry with me; she's angry with herself.

This is why she's hung on so long with me. She can't leave the living realm until she's resolved her need to say she's sorry to Tracy.

"This is why you call her Tracy. You've felt inadequate as her daughter. As if it's your fault. As if you have the power to fix something that isn't your fault. And, now, you have the disease. Alcoholism is a disease of perception. It's the only disease that tells us we don't have it." She pauses again, the anger righting itself in the outline of her existence. "Just because we aren't sitting under a bridge, drinking from a brown paper bag, doesn't mean we aren't alcoholics or drug addicts.

"When I hit bottom, I was sixty-two years old. The damage had been done. To your mother. To our relationship—or lack thereof. I had a beautiful home, went to church on Sundays, made casseroles for sick families and friends. But, when all my work was done, when the house was clean and quiet, I felt as though I deserved a drink; after all, I'd worked hard for it." Poppy purses her lips together just so and ponders her next words.

"And, when the drink went in, I would turn into a monster. When I put alcohol in my body, I had the best of intentions. I just wanted a glow. I didn't want to do what I'd done the night before—cause fights with your grandfather, be mean to your mother. I just wanted a glow, Livia. Happy, safe, content, like the good old days when alcohol seemed to work for me and not against me. But—when I took the first drink, I couldn't stop."

Poppy's eyes are on me like she's staring down the devil. My mouth hanging open, I'm grappling with the idea of insanity because it's my dead grandma pointing out my issue.

"Besides, it's not the tenth drink that gets me drunk; it's the first."

"I just wanted a glow," she said.

I've said this. She said this.

"But, somehow, I seemed to miss the mark every single time. Getting drunker and meaner. You are the only one who knows your own bottom. And you are the only one to decide when enough is enough.'"

I'm not sure what world I exist in right now, the living or the dead, but I've spoken those words before. I relate to every single piece of Poppy's story.

"Save yourself and your family years of heartache, baby. Your dad has the gene. I have the gene."

"How did this happen so quickly, Poppy?"

"Listen, it doesn't matter how you got the disease. The point is, you know you have it. And a more important question is, what are you going to do about it?"

"I'm too young to be an alcoholic."

She smiles and takes my hand in hers. "You're never too young to be an alcoholic. The truth of the matter is, it's just timing. When are you going to hit your bottom and say enough is enough before it's too late?" She looks around the room. "So, in your initial question, you asked if you were going to die. And I said, yes and no."

I nod.

"Yes, you will die a slow alcoholic death, and I can give you the details if you're ready. And, no, because, if you give yourself the gift of time and get sober while you're young, you'll have all the time in the world to live a happy, joyous life. Don't wait until you're an old mucky coot like me. And get that boy, Daniel, back. He's a keeper." Poppy shrugs in her pink floral housecoat that shines in the glow of the match that seems to be burning for an eternity.

"Is that why you came to me?"

"I can't speak for God or divine intervention, but there's a rhyme and reason for the world and how it flows. Death is inevitable. We live on borrowed days. It's my opinion that God doesn't create disease. Disasters are created out of human error, not God's error. People have free will. And they make choices. God also doesn't interfere with life plans. And bad people do bad things, as was with the case of Jasper. Jasper was in the classroom when the gunman opened fire that day. Why Jasper was there at that exact time and in that exact moment when everything turned into chaos, we will never know." Poppy brushes her hand against my cheek. "Truth is hard. He stood up for what he believed in, who he was, Liv. You've got to understand that he lived, really lived, in those final moments, Liv. Know that." Poppy's eyes begin to water.

"Some are willing to live in denial, in anger, and never stand up for what they believe in. His death was a statement, a testimony in faith. He knew where he was going, and he was at peace with it." She pauses. "Forgiveness can be hard if we aren't willing to see the situation with grace. But, if we don't have forgiveness in our heart, the pain will take front seat, and it will eat us alive from the inside out. We will harbor it, nurture it, keep it alive, and then we will allow the anger to manifest into our lives by treating others badly, depending on alcohol, drugs."

I look back at Tracy—*my mom* and my dad, who surround my frail, badly beaten body—in more ways than one. "I can't hurt them anymore." A sob chokes my throat. "They have been through too much."

Losing two children. Watching my father battle his own demons, hiding behind a well-known mask. Knowing I have a disease that will likely kill me if I allow it.

I look back to Poppy, who has vanished but I hear her in my ear. "Then, live."

"What if I can't?"

"Are you tired of getting what you're getting? Are you happy with your life and where you're at?"

"No. Wait! Poppy! Why did you leave me? Why did you disappear for a while?"

Poppy reappears. "Oh, honey, I didn't disappear. You just couldn't hear me."

And, like a gravitational force, I'm sucked from the corner of the room and into the shell of a body that lies on the sterile white bed. I wait for the hurt to hit me like a cold blast.

"Did you...did you see that?" I hear my mom's voice hide behind her guarded excitement. "Her eyes just fluttered."

"Mimi"—I feel my dad's words in my heart and against my forehead—"if you can hear me, squeeze my hand."

I feel fingers in my hand, and I will them to move.

Did they move?

A gasp comes. "Oh my God."

Someone curls up beside me—my mom, I bet.

And, all of a sudden, I'm conscious of my body—every ache, every hurt, every muscle, every organ, every bone—as I settle in the shell of my existence, the only shell that keeps me human, connected to the living world, and I wait to wake up.

I hear Dr. Miller talking to my mom and dad while I lie awake, eyes closed, pretending to be asleep. They're discussing my discharge from the hospital. The rehabilitation I'll need to get my muscles and my body back to where it was before the accident.

The physical bruises have begun to heal.

Fade.

Though I haven't looked in a mirror yet, my mom doesn't look at me anymore like she's going to cry every time her eyes fall upon my face.

I hear my mom say, "Hey."

But I don't open my eyes because I'm not quite ready to accept a situation with talking. I'd just like to lie here and listen.

But then *he* speaks, "How's she doing today?"

44

He pronounces *how's she doing today* with the accent. I know it's him, and my heart begins to flutter. The machine that detects my heartbeat begins to freak out. Through my squinty eyes, I see my dad, Tracy, Dr. Miller, and Daniel staring at me. Dr. Miller walks to me and takes out his stethoscope.

I slowly open my eyes. "I'm all right." I look at Daniel. "Hey," I say mushier than I want it to sound. Weaker and incredibly lame.

Dr. Miller and my mom figure out why the machine changed temperaments.

My mom touches Daniel's arm and gives him a look. She walks to me, kisses my forehead, and whispers, "We will be out in the hall." But, before she leaves, she takes the lip balm and puts some on my lips. "Dad says you like him. We like him."

Daniel keeps his distance, standing across the room. He shoves his hands in his pockets. "Hey," he says.

"Hi." The heart machine starts to flutter again.

Daniel walks to my bedside and reaches across my bed, so my chest is almost flush with his. He hits a button, and the machine stops.

"How'd you know how to do that?"

"I've learned a few tricks along the way during your mini vacation." He smiles, only partly, as he pulls back. He slides a chair over and sits down. Guarded.

I look down at my once dirty nails, trying to figure out what I want to say next. And it isn't because I have nothing to say; it's because I have everything to say to him.

"Daniel, I'm really sorry."

He starts to talk, but I reach for his hand and give it a squeeze.

"Please, let me finish."

"I never in a million years thought I'd fall in love at seventeen years old. I also never thought that the two of us would have to grapple with losing two of the most important people in our lives right around the same time." I ponder my next statement.

"I've been a jerk. An asshole. But I deserve you. Here's why." I reach to the bedside table and read him a list I wrote two days prior. This is an old-me move. A move I would have done before Jasper passed. A move that tells me that girl is still inside me.

"I deserve you because, the moment I saw you, you saw me for who I was, not for the girl who'd just lost her brother. I really enjoy your English accent and your red hair. I deserve you because, when I talk to you, my mouth won't shut up, and it feels the need to keep babbling; I deserve you because I really like your bacon sarnie. I deserve you because, when I thought you went back to Hull, I died. I deserve you because I don't think my heart can ever feel the same way with someone else. Nobody's ever had that effect on me. Not even Twenty One Pilots when Cao and I saw them in concert. Though, if we are comparing, I think Cao might have loved Twenty One Pilots more than Ed Sheeran that night. But don't tell her I said that." I give a half-smile. "I deserve you because, when your mom passed away, I saw your heartbreak from the inside, and I wanted nothing more than to mend it. I deserve you because I love you, and nothing will ever change that. But, most of all, I deserve you, but you deserve more. In order to be the person you deserve, I need help."

I contemplate these last words in a selfish way, praying I don't screw things up with Daniel, but knowing, in my heart, it's the right decision for him and for me. This isn't written down in the notes, and I begin to panic, but I feel a warm presence on my shoulder, perhaps Spirit, Poppy, reassurance that I'm not alone.

"Daniel…I'm an alcoholic, maybe a drug addict. Before I can love you the way you deserve to be loved, I need to fix me. Love me first. What you saw me as a puddle on the floor, that was me making poor decisions with my life. I don't want to make those anymore. I want to be happy. I want to be free to love you and treat you the way you deserve to be treated. But I can't until I get the help I know I need." I pause, looking up at him.

This was so not on the sheet of paper I prepared earlier. Too much, too soon.

I roll my eyes at my completely idiotic candidness. "I don't know how to grieve the right way. I sought the easiest solution, and I couldn't stop, Daniel. I can't stop." I'm being honest for the first time in a long time. And the metaphorical noose around my neck loosens. I can breathe a little more easily. I'm becoming free.

"Please say something. Or I'll keep talking and really screw things up, and I don't want to do that right now. Or ever," I say, toying with my fingers. And I'm not sure if it's the medication they've given me or my rapid heartbeat that feels as though I'm on the last leg of a marathon and making me talk like a crazy person. "Just say something."

Daniel tries not to smile. "You finished?" He scoots the chair closer to the hospital bed.

"Yes." I try to cross my fingers and lay my hands across my lap, but I pull my hospital gown to reassure myself I don't have a stray anything hanging out instead.

"My turn." He takes his hand and runs it across the length of my collarbone, and then he puts my hand in his. "That is one of the best parts of you."

"My collarbone?"

"*Clavicle* is the correct term. Do you know it's the shape of a Roman key? And it's one of the only bones in our bodies that's only protected by skin, not muscle." Daniel pauses because that's how he works. Slow, methodical. "Do you also know, it's the most commonly broken bone in the body for people under the age of twenty-five?"

"I didn't."

"It reminds me of your heart. I see your heart. Exposed, though many people can't see it because you keep it hidden behind a layer of skin—or a brick wall—whereas I see a key. It's fragile right now. But deserving of the world and everything in it. Do you know that heartbreak is more common in those under the age of twenty-five, just like the clavicle?"

I shake my head.

"I can't tell you what to do, Liv. The only thing I can tell you is, my heart will never be the same after meeting you."

Daniel takes my hand, pulls it up to his lips, and gently kisses it.

Through my chills, I whisper, half-hoping he doesn't hear my question, "Why aren't you fighting this?"

He smirks. "Isn't that what love is? Letting go of what you want, so the other one can live?"

I allow his words to sink into my heart, to break through the barrier made up of years of protection from my father, my mother, her lack of emotion, the walls I put up to protect my sanity. My love. "Yeah, something like that."

I take his cheek in my hand, and he pushes it to his shoulder, allowing no room for escape.

"Where are you going?" I ask.

"Where are you going?" he asks.

"I-I don't know. I still haven't told my parents."

"Do you want me to be here when you do?"

"No. 'Letting go of what you want, so the other one can live.' Isn't that what you just told me?" I smile through the sadness. "Let's plan a date," I say. "Let's say, in one year from now, we meet at Bob's…or maybe somewhere in England?" In my head, I start to contemplate the money for an airline ticket halfway around the world. I stumble over the next sentence because just thinking that he might be in a different time zone makes my stomach drop. "Will…will you be leaving Belle's Hollow?"

"I don't know yet."

"But your house? It's totally empty."

"Yes. My father had the movers move everything back to Hull. I was planning on flying back with him until this"—he looks down at my body—"happened."

"So, you've been here the whole time?" I whisper, my heart sinking lower into my chest, embedding itself in my stomach. "But where have you been staying?"

His face turns red. "With your parents." A coy smile. "Your father insisted."

I think about my room and in what condition I left it in. *Has he seen Jasper's room? Does he think we're crazy for not cleaning it out yet?*

"I'm really sorry I didn't tell you about Simon."

Daniel shakes his head. "Don't."

"No, I owe you an explanation. What I did with him was before you—mostly. I'm sorry I didn't tell you."

"Listen, Livia, we weren't together, *together*. I've had some time to think about this. A lot of time actually." He pronounces *actually* like *act-chully*.

"But you didn't deserve to find out that way. Nothing happened with Simon that night you saw me on the bed with him either, Daniel. I swear. My recollection is vague, but I do remember the door opening and closing and then a head coming to rest on my chest. And that's it."

"There's no need to explain, Livia. Did it hurt? Yes. But we didn't write anything in stone. We didn't make anything official."

He pulls his left shoulder back, more like a twitch, uncomfortable, and his face changes. "But I do need to tell you about Sienna."

45

Exactly One Year Later

My hands clammy, I trace a heart on my black slacks and look down at my watch. The applause starts, and I use my cane to take the stage but not without the winging of the butterflies that explode in my stomach. I'm back at Belle's Hollow High.

I trace the word *Hope* on my slacks before I begin.

"My name is Livia Stone, and I'm a recovering alcoholic."

"I'm not the girl I thought I'd be. When I was eight, I dreamed of going to a prestigious university. Getting advanced degrees. Meeting the boy of my dreams at a fraternity party and wearing Harvey College T-shirts on the weekends while in my dorm room. I never thought I'd be an alcoholic at seventeen. I never thought my alcoholism would rob me of my dignity, my self-worth, and my self-love.

"On October 1, 2015, when my twin brother, Jasper, was killed in the Kellogg Community College shooting, I wasn't sure I wanted to live anymore. He'd been there to check it out on a visit. Never in a million years did I dream I'd recover from that. Plus, I never thought that that would be the beginning of my bottom. But I believe, if it wasn't for the awfulness of my brother's death, it would have been only a matter of time before my alcoholism took away so much more.

"My grandmother once said, 'You are the only one who knows your own bottom. And you are the only one to decide when enough is enough.'

"The day of my last drink, I was in a bad car accident that I believe I was supposed to die in. Not because of fate, but because sometimes we make decisions by mistake. The report said we flipped over nine times. Hit several trees down an embankment. When the emergency personnel arrived, they assumed there were no survivors because the truck was wedged between two redwood trees.

"Cash Livingston was killed when he was ejected from the truck.

"But I lived.

"I spent four weeks in the hospital with a shattered leg and bruises and cuts that eventually healed. While I don't want to bore you with my past, I do want to point out the warning signs.

"I was drinking every day. I was hiding it.

"I wasn't making the right decisions anymore.

"I just knew, when I took a drink, I could not control how much I drank.

"And, toward the bitter end, every time I drank, I would pass out. Black out. Alcohol controlled me. Owned me.

"Here's the deal. I had a good home—for the most part. I was headed to a prestigious university, had a bed to sleep in, had a job. Saved money like I should. I wasn't living under a bridge, drinking out of a brown paper bag, like how most people assume alcoholics live.

"And, every time I looked in the mirror, I realized that I was fading, losing sight of who I was. With every drink I took, I couldn't see the person I was losing.

"After the hospital stint and after I talked to my parents about it, I went into a treatment facility for six months; it also included grief counseling. So much for the prestigious university, right? But, by making that decision, it saved my life.

"Today, I attend Skagit Community College. I've written a novel, which I submitted to Harvey College under the name of Professor Livingston, who nominated it for the Lelia Cruz award. It's titled *Standing Sideways*. I did not know though that, when students are given this accolade, they are also awarded a full scholarship.

"I found out last night that I'd not only won the Lelia Cruz scholarship, but more importantly, this book might also help others. It might help them to see that the disease of alcoholism knows no barriers, no age requirement. It doesn't care about where you work or how much college education you have. It doesn't matter where you sleep or if you get up for work or school in the morning. The thing is, if you think you have a problem with alcohol, you probably do, and it's only going to get worse as you get older. Trust me, the only reason I tell you this is because I would not be here, standing before you, telling you about my disease and the depths it took, if it wasn't for the fact that I got help. The toll it has played on my family and on me."

I go on about the heartbreak, the havoc I caused my family.

"I still grieve for my brother, but I don't wallow in it. I miss him with everything that I have. I wish I could take back just a few minutes of his time. Have him yank my hair again. Tell me how I am overreacting about an A-minus versus an A.

"But, today, I have everything in me that I need. Not what I want, but what I need. What I didn't mention earlier is that my mother and I had a very tough relationship, but a lot of it was me being bitter at her for how she treated my brother and me; it was just different. I was resentful toward her. There's healing today. We have a great relationship now. We talk about things that I was so scared to talk about before, for fear of what she'd think about me."

I look to my mom, who's wiping tears from her eyes—in a good way.

"I was angry with my father for being the alcoholic."

My dad's sitting next to my mom, but he's beaming. He no longer lives with as much regret than he used to. I'd say, from here, he looks pretty proud.

"Today, my father and I have the relationship we have because of where we've been. And I'm so grateful to be on this journey with him. You see, even though my dad saw my life spiraling out of control, he never told me I was an alcoholic. He led by example.

"I'd like to close with this. A few months after Jasper's passing, I received an email from one of the survivors of the Kellogg Community College shooting. Sonja Peet. She asked if I wanted to know what Jasper's last words were before he was shot seven times in the chest. It took me six months to respond to her email. The truth was, I was terrified.

"You see, my brother was gay. And he lived his life trying to deny the fact that he was. As his twin, I didn't know this." I casually cough because I feel the tears gathering in my throat. "The shooter asked questions of his victims. Whether they believed in God, Allah, Jehovah. He asked if they were Republican, Democrat, Gay, or straight. What nationality. Pro-life. Pro-choice. Presbyterian, Christian, Catholic, Muslim, nonbeliever. That day, the gunman asked my brother the gamut of questions. When asked if he was gay, this was his response:

"'I stand up for those whose beliefs don't match social norms.

"'I stand up for God, Allah, Jehovah. I stand up for freedom of choice.

"'I stand up for those who are gay and straight.

"'I'm a gay man, and I believe in God. I will never back down from defending that anymore.

"'I stand up for those who suffer in silence.

"'And I stand up to you.'"

I pause for a minute, trying to collect my words, tears silently falling down my cheeks. Because I don't say what happened next; it's assumed.

I try to speak.

I stop.

I try to speak again.

I stop.

"When you're put to the ultimate test, when your life is on the line, stand up. Speak loudly. Stand in your own truth. And, when you go to the I AM wall this year, make sure you put your mark on the world. Be bold. Be brave."

Silence.

Silence.

Silence.

Silence.

Maybe it was too much? I think to myself.

My eyes scan the gymnasium with the sea of people. Stunned silence.

One person claps, and then the whole gymnasium erupts, explodes, in applause.

I know I have exactly seventeen minutes to get to Bob's. Once the group of high schoolers is released, they rush me with questions. And I answer them as best as I can while trying to be as honest as possible.

"How did you know you were an alcoholic?"

"I think my mom is an alcoholic. How do I get her to get sober?"

"What rehab did you go to?"

"Can I have your autograph, Livia?"

"How did you overcome drinking?"

Once the crowd disperses, I glance at my watch. Six more minutes. Then, I look to my best friend standing in the doorway, silently clapping.

She strolls over to me with open arms. "Still, every time I hear that story, I get all freaking teary-eyed," Cao says, sliding an arm around my neck.

Cao had a lot of guilt after the accident. She said it was her fault and that she shouldn't have allowed me to get in the car with Cash. But I know that's her own stuff she has to work through. I can tell her until I'm blue in the face that it wasn't her fault, but I guess she needs to come into her own healing.

"Six minutes." I follow Cao out of the gym and to her car.

Beth finally decided to allow Cao, who goes to Caltech now, to get her license the summer after her senior year with all the commuting she'd be doing.

My mom and dad meet us at her car.

"You're headed to Bob's, right?" My mom pushes my hair behind my shoulders, tears in her eyes. "I'm so proud of your strength and for telling that story over and over again."

My mom went to Betty Ford Clinic, a place that helps families of alcoholics. She regularly attends Al-Anon meetings. She also did grief counseling and still does. I don't think the loss of a child, the pain that goes with it, ever goes away. It changes. But I think, through me, my brother still lives.

My dad kisses me on the forehead, "Mimi, I love you." Water starts to converge at his eyelids.

"You aren't supposed to cry!" I say. "You promised me."

"No, they're just leaking. I'm good," he says, taking his hand and wiping the leak.

My parents make their way back to their car and Cao and I jump in her car. She drops me off at Bob's. "Call me when you get back to school. Love you."

I kiss her on the cheek.

She came back home just for my talk at Belle's Hollow High. But what I've learned is that friends do things like that for friends. We're here. We're present. Because, as much as I told her it wasn't a big deal, when she showed up at my house to drive me to the speaking commitment, my heart exploded. The truth is, I did need her.

I take a deep breath, trace the words *true love* on my slacks, and step inside the orange-and-cream-colored eatery—also known as Bob's.

My heart begins to pound.

I look from left to right. The place is nearly empty.

Behind me, I hear, "I hear the cheese fries are deadly."

I whip around.

All the heaviness of what I just told, the story, disappears. And everything in the world falls into its rightful spots. Stars explode. The sun expands. The man on the moon is singing.

I breathe.

His hair is shorter, and his glasses are different, but when our eyes meet, nothing has changed. Absolutely nothing.

Daniel takes my hand and pulls me into him. I feel his heart pound against my chest, and he leads me to the spot where the only space between us is molecules and dust bunnies. I can feel the burn of my fingertips as they dig into his back. My heart begins to pound in rhythm with his, making perfect sense in this crazy world we live in—this complicated, sad, exciting, beautiful world. If a heartbeat had a louder sound, it would sound like two sparrows conversing about the sun and the warmth that it brings. It would sound in tune and keyed up. And sweet.

"I'm glad you came."

It's the first time I've seen Daniel, and we both held true to our promise that, no matter what happened in a year, we would meet at Bob's on December 21.

Daniel stares down at me. "I have a feeling, Liv, that when we are old, cheese fries will be our choice of death."

I laugh. I laugh so hard, I feel it in all the places that matter.

We slide into a booth, a new one, one that we can make new memories in—him on one side and me on the other.

He takes my hands in his. "There's this weird thing in your eyes."

I take a hand from his and touch my right eye. "Where?"

He laughs a deep, throaty laugh, and his Adam's apple bobs. "Right here." He gently touches the corner of my eye. "I think it's called happiness."

A smile spreads across his face and mine, too.

"I've decided something."

"Yeah? What's that?" he asks *that* like it's got an *O* in it.

"I'm in love with you."

Daniel reaches across the table again, this time taking the sides of my face into his hands. "You are worth fighting for, Livia, today and all the tomorrows. I'm the man who is supposed to be your person until the rest of the tomorrows run out."

We eat cheese fries.

And kiss.

And drink Cherry Coke.

And kiss some more.

I know it's a question that needs answering—if not for me, but for us. I finally ask, "How did it go with Sienna?"

Daniel lets out a huge, exhausted sigh. Maybe of relief or fear. I'm not sure because I can't read the look he's giving.

"She's good. Heath is over a year old now."

Good. That's good.

I nod, trying to talk myself out of the doubt that's creeping in.

It's good. Tell yourself that, Liv. It's good.

46

Daniel stares down at the simplicity of how our bodies can intertwine with such ease—or at least that's what I'm thinking he's thinking. I try to push away the distance that we've spent apart by scooting closer.

He lets out a breath he was holding, and I can't help but breathe in his minty smell.

"After we parted that day, I flew back to Hull and tried to help Sienna with her pregnancy and getting ready to take on the role of a father. But you know what, Liv? I kept thinking about you and your quest for truth about who you are, the mistakes you've made. Walking through what you had to walk through to get to the other side." He stops and chews on his lip. "I asked Sienna to get a paternity test after Heath was born. Because, if Heath was mine, I wanted to do right by my child."

I swallow.

I wait.

I pray relief comes soon, but I also have faith that everything is as it should be. But my wants are overriding logic in this situation right now. And then I trace the words *not yours* against my pants, under the table, and let the feeling go.

"Did she comply with your request?" I try to sound convincing. Rightful. Supportive. Though part of me wants him to run for the hills. But the good side of me, the unselfish side, wants him to stay. Get the test done. Do what's right for Heath and Daniel. Not for Livia Stone.

"Yes, but only after I pestered her."

"And?" I'm louder because the suspense alone is making me want to barf all over this table.

"Heath isn't mine." Daniel's hands tighten around mine.

I want to jump across this table and straddle his lap, but I won't, for the sake of public displays of affection. It's gross. I mean, the making-out part at least or the lap sitting. But then, too, public displays of affection don't seem so bad with Daniel. Maybe I just didn't find the right guy, and that's why I didn't care for it.

I contain my excitement and offer a compassionate tone. "How are you doing with all that?"

"It's good. I'm glad. I mean, I wasn't ready to have a baby at eighteen. And I didn't want you to have to deal with all that."

"What did your father say?"

"Doesn't know. He pretty much checked out and gave me my trust fund. But it turns out, there's this little college down the road called Harvey and a community college nearby." His eye twitches.

I crawl across the table and straddle his lap, putting myself directly on top of him, and then I pull his lips to mine.

When two people are supposed to fit exactly together, it's said that they fit like a glove—mind, body and spirit. Rightfulness of the world.

Although I know we're only eighteen, I also trust my heart. I trust that things will work out the way they are supposed to. I know that I've never felt this way about someone—the way I feel about Daniel. I also feel there's a reason Daniel, Rose, and Dr. Pearson moved here, to our tiny little town of Belle's Hollow.

After Daniel and I catch up for an hour, I see the couple I'm waiting for. Since I've already told Daniel my plan, he stands.

"I'll meet you in the car?" he says to me.

He kisses me half on the lips and half on the cheek, the kind of kiss that brings my body alive. An ache begins to form, an ache that can only be fulfilled by Daniel. His lips linger on mine, and I sigh.

"Meet you at the car," I say but not without one last kiss on the mouth.

Daniel walks to the car, and I walk to the couple sitting near the back at a window seat.

"Thanks for coming," I say to Mr. Joe and his wife, who's in a wheelchair. Not one you sit in for a week or two to mend a broken leg or hips. One you sit in indefinitely.

I slide into their booth—them on one side and me on the other.

"Livia, this is my wife, Morgan," Mr. Joe introduces his wife, pretending like her accident, their tragedy, didn't bleed all over the local newspaper headlines—probably out of respect for her feelings.

She smiles. Even though she doesn't say a word, I feel her words in her smile. They're kind. Gentle even.

"Quite a talk you gave in the gymnasium, Liv." He's proud. I see it in the crow's-feet lining the corners of his eyes.

"Nice to meet you, Morgan."

But, in her smile, I see her regret. I remember her accident.

Morgan was returning from a work conference. She looked down at her phone—so the newspaper said. The drunk driver had come out of nowhere and swerved into her lane, hitting her head-on on Highway 101, just south of Belle's Hollow. The accident left her unable to speak or walk.

I remember Mr. Joe's words.

"I know what you're going through. I know what loss feels like."

In my bag, I reach in, grab a copy of *Standing Sideways*, and slide it across the table. "You believed in me when I didn't believe in myself. You knew I could do things I didn't know I was capable of. I might not have done them in the timing we both wanted, but I did it. This book is for you."

Never in my life have I seen Mr. Joe with a lack of words. Carefully, he pulls the book toward them, and his long fingers brush over the cover, the title. He opens the book and sees the dedication page. Immediately, he searches the table—for what, I'm not sure. Morgan looks down at the page and then to her husband. A tear falls from her eye. Then, two. Then, three.

Mr. Joe locks eyes with me. His eyes fill with tears, ones he doesn't allow to fall. "*Life is an adventure in forgiveness.*" His voice breaks, and truth spills between his whispered words.

"Norman Cousins," I reply, allowing a tear to fall. This time, I don't push it away. I don't push it down.

And it hits me all at one time.

In this moment, Mr. Joe forgives himself. Forgives the drunk driver who hit his wife. It is this act alone that makes me realize that I need to forgive, too. I need to forgive the shooter who killed my brother. I am not a victim of circumstance. I will not allow bitterness and anger to eat away at the future plans I have for myself. But, first, I must forgive myself.

I do. I let go of all of it.

If he can forgive, so can I.

Before this becomes a scene, I leave Mr. Joe and Morgan. There are no hugs exchanged, but a knowing of forgiveness is left in the little space of time we shared.

"Liv?" Mr. Joe tries to clear his throat as he calls after me.

"Yeah?" I turn back to them.

"Thank you."

I shake my head. "No, thank you." My fingers touch the air and fall in unison.

"Where do you want these?" Daniel opens Jasper's closet.

"Hang on." I brush past Daniel, give him a half-grin, and shut the closet door in his face.

Jasper, if you want me to keep your entire shoe collection, I will, or if you want me to give it to someone else, just give me a sign.

I hesitate before opening the door, and when I do, Daniel is still standing in the same position I left him, arms crossed, not surprised.

"I will never question why you do things the way you do them. I like you a bit strange."

Still, I love his accent.

I brush against him to where my chest pushes against his, and he quietly sighs against me, pulling me to him.

I want to be touched by his hands only. And in places unspeakable and by his hand that slides down to the small of my back, sending an electric current up my spine. I rest my head on his chest to regain any composure I might have left in me.

My phone chimes, and the only reason I know it has chimed is because Daniel says so.

"What?"

"Your phone."

"Oh."

I gently push off the lower part of his stomach, wanting to savor my hand in that area, and Daniel does something between a half-laugh and groan.

"You do that again, Miss Stone, and you might not get away with your fingers next time," he says, taking my hand and sliding his fingers through.

I look down at my phone, and it's a text from Simon.

Simon: Ready 4 the shoes when you r.

Thanks, Jas.

"The shoes go to Simon." I text Simon back and tell him to come get them.

Daniel stops but not for the reason I think he does.

"Don't worry; there's nothing there between him and me." I don't tell him that Simon came out to me while I was in rehab, only because it's not my story to tell.

It's not your job to right the world, Livia. It will right itself.

Daniel takes my waist in his hands. "I never worry about that, Liv." He looks past me, into Jasper's closet, at the box of shoes. "I'm just wondering how in the hell one chap owned this many pairs of shoes."

"Yo! Anyone here?" Simon's familiar knock sounds on Jasper's open bedroom door. "Oh, hey. Didn't mean to interrupt."

That was quick.

"I'm Daniel by the way." He pushes the box to Simon and doesn't reach for his hand.

"Simon." He reaches for Daniel's hand.

There's an awkward exchange between the two, like a sort of changing of the guards. An unspoken agreement that Daniel is now to watch over me as Jasper used to. Daniel is three inches taller than Simon. He's four inches taller than most boys our age. Then, there's a slight nod between the two. An agreement reached. Settled.

Simon looks around Jasper's room. "Wow. Bare," he says. "Thanks for this."

"Jasper wants you to have them."

Simon meets my eyes. "When are you leaving for school?"

"Tomorrow."

"All right then. Daniel, take care of her. She's special," he says as if he's reciting the preamble to the Constitution.

Daniel doesn't answer. He just reaches for me instead, proving that actions speak louder than words ever will.

Simon leaves, and Daniel and I finish Jasper's room.

"What about this rucksack?"

I turn to Daniel, who is standing next to Jasper's dresser. "What?" I laugh. "What is a rucksack?"

"This." He holds it in the air.

"A backpack?"

"Right. A rucksack. Americans." He playfully rolls his eyes.

"I'm going to keep it. Use it at Harvey."

I pause because a memory comes to the front of my mind, and I need to share it because this is one of those moments when I struggle to breathe. "When Jasper was killed, I was terrified to ask the FBI for anything that Jasper had on his body that day. Because of"—I swallow the big knot in my throat—"the way in which he was killed." I stop. "The blood, I guess." I feel my face contort, just like my thoughts. I hate that I have to talk about my brother in ways that most people shouldn't.

"One morning"—I cough to push down the tears—"I woke up, and there was this nagging voice in my head that said, *Get my backpack.* This was two weeks after Jasper died. The words stayed in my head all day long. So, I called Gina, our FBI victim's specialist, the one who represented our family, and I asked if we could get Jasper's belongings back. And, the next day, they were hand-delivered in a sterile clear bag." I pause. "You know the weird thing?"

Daniel shakes his head as he takes a few steps toward me.

"There wasn't a drop of blood on the backpack." I smile because, today, I know that wasn't my conscience telling me to get the backpack back; it was Jasper.

"My mum used to say that those who pass only give us messages when we're ready for them."

This time, I wrap my arms around his waist. "How's your grief?"

"Fine."

"No, it's not. You're lying." I pull back and look into his eyes. "Has anyone told you what *fine* stands for?"

"I'm positive you'll enlighten me."

"Fucked up. Insecure. Neurotic. Emotional."

"Well then, I guess I'm fine today. Fits about right."

I feel his slow, confident, deep laugh against my ear as he takes his hands and runs his fingertips against my bare arms.

"Come on. Let's take the bags to the donation drop-off."

We load the stuff in back of my dad's old Ford that he uses for yard clippings and dump runs. I stare out the window as Daniel drives to Miranda's Rescue. Jasper would have wanted us to donate his clothes. Everything, except for his Vans. Those were always meant for Simon.

A feeling of calm comes over me as the realization hits. I think Jasper didn't survive that day because he would have seen things that were too much to live with. That his soft, kind heart wouldn't have been able to handle it, and his time here on Earth wouldn't have been good because of what he'd seen. And maybe God needed him more than I did. Though what happened that day won't always be clear, I have peace in my heart, knowing that I don't have to drink or use to cover up my feelings today and that my sweet Jasper is at peace.

As for Daniel and me, who knows if our relationship will stand the test of life? Though I have high hopes for us. The point is that there's no permanence in life. Nothing stays the same forever. Though there are moments I wish it would, like this one right here, with the cool winter air breathing down our necks, his hand in mine. And, if we don't make it through the ups and downs, the twists and turns that life has to offer, it will be all right. I will be okay.

For I have found Livia Stone, standing sideways but nevertheless found.

EPILOGUE

Seven Years Later

Belle's Hollow

"Mommy, who's this?"

We unpack the last box with Jasper's picture.

"That was your uncle." I take the picture, remembering all the ways he'd change a picture by the faces he made.

"You mean, the one who stands in the corner of my room at night?"

Goose bumps imprint on my skin, over my entire body. I look to Daniel and then back to our daughter. "What did you say, baby?"

"Yeah, him and Grandma Rose. They watch me at night."

I can't breathe. "Does-does it scare you, Rose?" I feel my heart surge and my mouth go dry. I believe fear and faith can be experienced at the exact same time because this moment, right now, consists of both.

She smiles. "No, Mama. Grandma Rose sings to me, and Jas—" Rose looks to me.

"Jasper," I clarify.

"Japper says I'm tough like Mimi."

The hair on my neck stands at attention. I look to my husband standing above me. "I've never told her that nickname before."

"Sorry we're late!" Cao and her husband, Ed, come dashing through the front door. "Since when did we get another traffic light in Belle's?" She kisses Rose and me on the cheeks. Cao stops and looks around the room. "Wait, did we interrupt something?"

Daniel speaks because he knows I can't, "Rose was just telling us that Jasper and Grandma Rose come visit her in her room at night."

Cao kneels down next to Rose. "You know what I think?"

"What, Aunt Choo-Choo?" Rose looks up with her big blue eyes.

"I believe, when people go to heaven, it takes a special person with a big heart to see them and feel things that others can't. Just like your mama."

I'm not blown away by Cao's response, coming from a science- and math-based person who graduated from Caltech, who is now a talented engineer, because she believes more in love than in science. Just like she believed more in me than what I was doing with my life eight short years ago. And, although she didn't end up marrying Ed Sheeran, Ed Wattenberg is a close second. He's Jewish, and he celebrates Hanukkah, Christmas, and Lent. And he writes music and plays the guitar. They met at Caltech during Cao's senior year. While they don't have kids, it's not because they don't want them. Cao says she's not ready until they can agree upon a name.

Rose's name was easy for us.

Rose Jasper Pearson.

I walk into my normal Tuesday night meeting of Alcoholics Anonymous, my father beside me.

The odd thing is, we got sober on the same date, just eighteen months apart. Happenstance? I think not. We've mended bridges, my dad and me. And all we can ask for is one day at a time.

I get the coffee while he gets the seats.

Looking back, I'm not sure if Poppy was a figment of my imagination or if what I saw and heard was real. Grief makes us do funny things. But, whatever she was or whatever I thought she was, she came at a time I needed her most. She has yet to come back since that day at the hospital. I believe that, when people pass on, they give us signs that they're still with us.

Jasper comes to me through different avenues. Music. My daughter. And not only that, but a day has yet to pass where I don't notice a pair of Vans. Whether it's in a store window, someone has them on, or I'm tripping over a pair.

When we brought Rose home from the hospital, there was a package on the porch. It was a pink pair of Vans, just her tiny little size. And, every year, on her birthday, the box appears again, though the pink Vans are a size bigger. My sneaking suspicion is it's Simon.

The door to the meeting opens, and a frail girl with dark circles under her eyes and bleached hair, uncombed with different lengths, enters. She's all but swallowed by the big, bulky sweatshirt she's wearing. The untold stories, the ones I used to hide behind, are buried deep within the confines of the pain I see in her eyes. I see the shame that she bears, like she wants to run, especially because we know each other.

It's a small, small town after all.

I hand my coffee to my dad. "Hold this, would you?"

And I walk to the front door, take her by her shaking hand, and say, "Come on, Whitney. I have a spot just for you, next to me."

It's in the quiet moments in time, when the world is silent, that we know we're right where we're meant to be.

My phone buzzes in my back pocket. I keep it on hand for Daniel, just in case there's an emergency with Rose. It's a text from my agent, Hattie Mathers. We've been waiting on some news. I tell Whitney I'm going to get her some tea, and as I make it to the pot of hot water, I open the text.

**Call me. Now. World Pictures wants to sign
a major motion picture deal for the book.**

But some things can wait.
I'm right where I'm supposed to be.

I close the text and do the next right thing. I take the tea to Whitney, and the meeting begins.

THE END

ACKNOWLEDGMENTS

Writing this book was the hardest one yet, the most personal one to date.

On October 1, 2015, nine people were killed in the Umpqua Community College shooting. My cousin, Jason Johnson, was one of them. This book is a personal journey through my own grief, although, a lot of it is fiction, there's a lot that isn't fiction.

Many times, I wanted to walk away from *Standing Sideways*, too hard to feel through all the emotions all over again. It broke my husband's heart to watch his wife feel through the process, sometimes, in the dark. It brought out the ugliness in me, the sadness, the suffering, the hurt, but in the end, it brought the healing.

Before I give my thanks to people who made this book possible, I want to talk about the dried roses.

At Jason's funeral, after we followed his casket out, and right before they loaded his body and took it away to the place of cremation, Jennifer, an employee from the funeral home, took a rose from his casket and handed to me and said with tears in her eyes: *I'm so, so sorry for your loss*. I know *that* particular funeral home had to do many funerals that week due to the tragedy. To this day, the dried rose Jennifer gave me sits on the dashboard of my car. It's to remind me of the many, many lives lost to mass shootings—

there are still traces of their beauty—we just need to be open to see it.

Standing Sideways would not be possible if it weren't for the following people:

> Hang Le, your book covers amaze me. When I saw the cover for the first time, it made me cry. Thank you for bringing this book to life.

> Jovana Shirley, you are a master at what you do. Your passion, your attention to detail, your support, your dedication is unparalleled. Thank you for making *Standing Sideways* shine.

> Julie Deaton, your eagle eye goes far beyond the words of this book. Your final touches (and your sweet comments) made my heart soar.

> Cassie Graham, thank you for our candid conversation that night about the book. Wink. Wink. It was you who was supposed to tell me the words I needed to hear.

> Devney Perry, my dear friend and fellow author, without your guidance, and sharing your wealth of knowledge in the self-publishing world, I'd be lost. I adore you.

> My beta readers: Julie Hagemann, Dana Barrote, Karyn Clark, Abbey Pearson, Chandra Moomey, and Heidi Payne. Thank you for your candidness, your tears, and honest feedback. Your time is important and I appreciate you giving up that time with your family, your hobbies, your life, to read Standing Sideways.

> Fisher Van Duzen, you, my dear, will always be a treasure. I'm eternally grateful for you and your feedback in more ways than one.

Poorhouse Publishing, thank you for your donation of the ISBN numbers, knowing all proceeds of this book will be going towards Jason's scholarship.

Dawn Newton, Jason's girlfriend, you gave me encouragement even when you may not have known it. You said, "Jason was so proud of you for the book thing and he loved you so much." It gave me the push I needed to finish writing the book.

Trina Pockett, Julie Hagemann, Kim Emmons, Faith Hansen, Kelly Losey, and Heather Barkdull, you picked me up off the floor after Jason died. You listened. You brought food for my family. You were present. These actions I will never forget.

To my community, the small, small town of 'Belle's Hollow', you've always supported my writing endeavors since they came to fruition, thank you.

Teyler and Kate, my beautiful children, you remind me how precious life is. I love you both more than you will ever know.

Last and most importantly, my husband Brandon, you are my rock, my voice of reason. I cannot be who I am without you. You are my Daniel. For the last twenty plus years together, you still make me laugh. Still give me the butterflies. And love me warts and all. You've had my heart since I was seventeen and always will. Thanks for putting up with me for all these years!

To the families of the survivors and victims of the Umpqua community College shooting:

May we all have the grace, faith, and trust that our loved ones did on that awful day, to stand in our own truths, to be brave.

A NOTE TO THE READER

Thank you for reading Standing Sideways.

If you enjoyed this book, please leave an honest review on Amazon and Goodreads. By leaving a review, it makes *Standing Sideways* more visible to more readers. The more reviews, the better promotional opportunities for the author.

Keep in touch. Subscribe to my newsletter at www.jlynnbaileybooks.com. Subscribers get first dibs on top-secret book information, giveaways, and more.

ALL the profits from *Standing Sideways* will go toward the Jason Dale Triumphant Return Scholarship at College of the Redwoods. This means I don't make a dime off this book. So, please, if you loved the book, share it. For more information on Jason's scholarship, visit http://www.times-standard.com/article/NJ/20151211/NEWS/151219973.

Want to be notified when I release a new book? Visit https://goo.gl/forms/Cyst1xxEKftp5Bmr2.

Alcoholism doesn't care how old you are. What color. Ethnicity. Faith. Occupation. It will rob you of your dignity, self-respect, and your life.

While Livia got sober and into recovery, it's not that easy for many, many people. Everyone has their own path and in order to recover, they have to find their own bottom. Many die chasing it. That's the devastating truth.

If you, or someone you know has a drinking problem, there are two programs that can help:

Al-Anon is a program that helps families who have someone in their lives struggling with addiction. https://al-anon.org/

Alcoholics Anonymous is a 12-Step program recovery program: https://www.aa.org/

ALSO WRITTEN BY J. LYNN BAILEY

BLACK FIVE (THE BLACK BLOOD CHRONICLES)

Seventeen-year-old Penelope Jackson has a seemingly ordinary life until she learns of the bizarre and magical world surrounding her, a world that is nearing extinction because of one man, Vacavious…the same man who wants to destroy her. Penn's adventure begins after a stranger's death puts her on a collision course with the very person she has been sheltered from her entire life. No one is who they seem to be, including those closest to her. As powerful forces await the fall of her protective veil on her eighteenth birthday, Penn prepares to fight against unseen evils before it's too late. The world of Nighmeriantotte and its people depend on her survival, for she is Sanguine.

COMING SOON

Crimson Lace (The Black Blood Chronicles)

ABOUT THE AUTHOR

J. Lynn Bailey has loved to write since she learned to read around the second grade. When she isn't running after her children, watching *COPS*, or on the hunt for her next Laffy Taffy joke, you can probably find her holed up in her writing room, feverishly working on her next book. She lives in Northern California with her family.

68010905R00195

Made in the USA
San Bernardino, CA
30 January 2018